The Watsons Reunited

LK Wilde

ISBN 978-1-0685491-3-7

Cover design by Jarmila Takač

Author's Note

If you would like to receive a FREE eBook of the *Watson Family Saga* prequel, *The Island Girls*, sign up to the LK Wilde Readers' Club monthly newsletter at lkwilde.com.

Two women, one island. Is it big enough for both of them?

Islander Rose McGuire dreams of a future filled with romance. But when tragedy strikes, her world is turned upside down. Propelled into the arms of local scoundrel Alex Watson, her dreams soon become a nightmare...

Mainlander Anna Allinson lives a life of luxury but is trapped within a gilded cage. When a chance encounter with an island fisherman ignites a spark within her, Anna decides to leave behind all she knows and risk everything for love.

But island life proves far from idyllic as Anna struggles to adapt, and not everyone welcomes her arrival, least of all Rose.

As Rose and Anna navigate their tumultuous lives, events bring them together, forging an unlikely friendship and forming bonds that will pass down through generations...

Chapter 1

2008

Annie screwed up the letter she had been writing and buried her head in her hands, trying to stem her threatening tears. She took a deep breath, picked up her pen, and tried again.

Dear Grace,

I'm sorry to say this will be the last letter I write to you...

No, she couldn't do it. Annie bashed the heel of her palm against her forehead, willing the thoughts to form a coherent sentence. She had to get the truth down on paper before it was too late, before... But did Grace really need to know now? Wouldn't it be better to wait until... until after?

Annie looked around the room, once so carefully furnished, and now full of cardboard boxes and bin bags. Her last night in her home. The last night of sharing a space with Sam, Frank, Marnie, and all the other ghosts who comforted her at night as they slipped into her dreams. Could she really leave them? What would happen to her once the ties that had anchored her all these years were severed?

Dear Grace...

Annie slipped the letter in an envelope and in as clear handwriting as she could muster wrote on the envelope *to be given to Grace Trevorn in the event of my death*. There, it was done. Annie picked up a glass of water with a shaking hand and took a sip. The cool liquid steadied her. She took a fresh sheet of paper from the desk and picked up her pen once more. The best thing was to pretend everything was normal. When the letters stopped, Grace might be worried, or hurt, but it would be the best thing in the long run. And wasn't it better for Grace to remember her like this? After all these years, she wanted to be remembered as the Annie she was now, not the one she would soon become.

Dear Grace,

How are you? How is Elle getting on with her fancy new job down in Bristol? You must be so proud of her!

Life here continues at pace. Last week, my grandson Luke received his exam results and did far better than we had all been expecting. Sophie was so relieved she cried. We had fish and chips to celebrate and, as ever, the smell of salt and vinegar transported me back over many years. Many memories, many meals shared.

I sometimes wonder whether I should have shared more of my past with my family. But would they be interested? The young are so flighty these days with their computer games and this blasted new 'world wide web'. I don't suppose they'd want to hear about my days at the factory, or the fishing industry, or the village below the cliffs, now buried beneath a sea of concrete.

I've enclosed a new pair of mittens for you, and I hope they fit. My fingers are not so nimble these days, but I still like to get the needles out from time to time...

Annie finished her letter, sealed it in an envelope and addressed it to the same cottage in Padstow to which she had posted off letters for the last sixty plus years. Grace would reply, but she would no longer be in this house to receive it. Perhaps the new owners would forward the letter, but it was probably best if they didn't.

With the letter held between trembling hands, Annie planted a kiss against the paper, closed her eyes and thought of the little girl with the red curls. What a history they had shared.

Chapter 2

February, 2018

The colours had faded with time, but the blanket held as much intrigue as ever. Elle's finger traced the patchwork fabric covering her legs; indigo, azure, navy, midnight, slate and the many shades of green which made up the changing colour of the sea beyond her window. She pulled the blanket up to her chin, wondering about the blood, sweat and tears that had gone into crafting it. All the questions of its creator lay unanswered in its threads, an unspoken buried history.

Elle sighed and a cloud of breath rolled from her mouth like a sea mist. The toughened skin on her feet met bare wood as she swung her legs from the bed and readied herself to face the day. Every bone in her back clicked as she stretched towards the ceiling, her fingertips skimming flaky plaster, reminding her of yet another job that needed doing.

Elle flung wide the curtains. If she only looked out, not in, her resolve to cling on to the cottage would remain. Turn her eyes inward though, and the mould, spongy wood, temperamental heating and intermittent hot water made her reconsider. Elle walked to the bedside drawer and pulled out a stack of papers. Each piece of paper held an offer higher than the last, slipped through her letterbox by holidaymakers and investors desperate for a slice of the Padstow pie. There were other demands too; an overdue electricity bill, the same from the water company, and a pile of increasingly bad-tempered correspondence from the owners of the shop below complaining about the condition of the building.

The sound of a loud snore through the floorboards reminded her she couldn't leave. Not yet. Elle flung on a dressing gown and shoved her feet into thick walking socks. On the way to the door, she ran a hand through her hair and sighed. A halo of messy red stuck out from her head, and she knew her skin shone a variety of purples and greys beneath a mass of freckles. She spat on her hand and attempted to calm the unruly mass of curls. Failing to tame her hair, Elle grabbed a beanie from the back of the door and shoved it on her head. Grace would tell her to let the curls fly free, but Elle felt they mirrored the mess of her life and wished her straighteners still worked.

Downstairs in the bathroom, Elle tried to ignore the green and black colouring the contours of the shower tray, or the crack in the sink that deepened and darkened with each passing month. The toilet groaned like a hungry beast as she pulled the long chain, watching as wet toilet paper swirled round and round without leaving the pan. Elle kicked the toilet bowl, pain shooting through her toes. Another call to the plumber was needed, but he would only manage a temporary fix. She wondered how many times he'd accept her calls, given on each visit he insisted she needed a new bathroom suite, and on each visit she ignored him.

Elle lifted the rusty kettle onto a chipped gas stove and lit the hob with a match. She spooned loose tea into the pot and took out the glass bottle of milk Grace had delivered each day from the local farm. For all their money worries, a small part of Elle loved the way they lived. *Waste not want not*, was Grace's motto, making her unwittingly the most eco-conscious resident in town. Not that there were many residents these days.

"Elle?" The cracked voice reached her from the sitting room. Elle ran upstairs, opened the door and smiled at the sight of Grace, white hair bouncing against a sun-weathered face.

"Kettle's on."

"Thank you. Cold in here, is it?" asked Grace, pointing to Elle's hat.

"How you don't feel the cold is a mystery to me," said Elle, shaking her head.

"Must have inherited it from my parents," said Grace, smiling wryly.

"We could try to find out about them again if you wanted? The internet has moved on since we last looked."

"Nah, they didn't want me, did they? I'm not going to waste any of the time I've got left on them."

Elle shook her head and sighed. Grace might have a dodgy knee, but there was plenty of life in the old girl yet.

"Do you need a hand getting to the bathroom?"

"Just pass me my stick, will you? Bloody NHS. The other knee will have gone by the time they get round to fixing this one. When my ship comes in, I'm going to forget my principles and go private."

When my ship comes in. If only, thought Elle, grabbing the wooden stick and handing it to Grace. She helped Grace to her feet and watched her painful progress as she shuffled down each step on her way to the bathroom. If she thought it would do any good, Elle would write to the council again to complain about NHS waiting times, the amount of second homes in the area, the lack of well-paid jobs. The list was endless. But the politicians had heard it all before and nothing changed with the letters she sent.

"What time are you off?" asked Grace, emerging from the bathroom and easing herself into a dining chair.

"My shift starts at twelve. Do you need me to do anything this morning? I was going to attack the windows with some of that mould remover spray I bought."

"You're fighting a losing battle there, love."

"I know," sighed Elle, pulling out a chair to join Grace at the table. She'd done the right thing moving home, but at forty, most of her contemporaries were preparing themselves for a second youth once their children flew the nest. They owned sensible houses, drove sensible cars, went on holiday to places like Italy and Greece, and spent their weekends at dinner parties or watching their teenagers play rugby. She, on the other hand, was single, childless, and had found no work locally that could replicate the generous salary offered by her previous employer in Bristol. There wasn't much call for a PR executive in a small seaside town, so the choice was bar work or waitressing, and Elle had opted for the former.

"Do you have any plans today?" Elle asked.

"I thought I might try to get as far as the harbour."

"You don't want to put unnecessary pressure on that knee."

"I'm sure I can manage the hundred steps it will take to get there."

Elle wasn't sure Grace could. "Why don't you reconsider the council's offer of an electric wheelchair? It would only be a temporary solution until your knee is fixed."

"Ha! If I take the wheelchair on offer, they'll only put me further down the list for an op."

Elle wasn't sure that was how these things worked, but decided it was best not to argue. "Alright then, I'll come with you. I've got ages till my shift starts."

"You're a good girl," said Grace, smiling across the table.

After breakfast, the two women put on their coats and headed out into the early spring sunshine. Grace's progress was painfully slow, despite the help of her walking stick and Elle's arm. A few shopkeepers were out and about, setting up chalk boards and opening shutters. They called a friendly hello to the women, enjoying the relative calm before the summer saw the town bulging well beyond its capacity for visitors.

"Let's stop here, love," said Grace, waving her walking stick towards a bench by the water's edge.

They settled themselves down. A comfortable silence descended, interrupted only by inquisitive seagulls on the hunt for discarded chips and pasty crusts. Boats bobbed on the harbour's calm water, the few working boats a reminder that once the town had been a very different place.

"Do you remember what it was like before?" asked Elle.

"Before what?" said Grace, keeping her eyes fixed on the water.

"Before Padstow became overrun with tourists, when it was still a working harbour."

"It still is a working harbour," said Grace. "You'd better not let any fishermen hear you talking like that."

"Do you though? Remember what it was like, I mean?"

"I do, though I'm not old enough to remember the days before steam power, if that's what you're suggesting. I remember Aunt Helen knitting furiously when we'd been hit by a storm, and her brother Jack was out on his boat. Her forehead would crease up with worry, and knitting was the only thing keeping her still. She'd be standing by the harbour for hours in squalling wind and rain, watching for any sign of Jack's boat on the horizon. It drove Uncle Richard mad, all that waiting, all that worrying. He told her many a time that Jack would be fine, but it didn't stop her fretting over her little brother. I can tell you no man ever received such a welcome home as Jack did on those occasions. It was like Aunt Helen had prepared a feast for royalty."

"When did you find out Aunt Helen and Uncle Richard weren't your birth parents?"

"Oh, I always knew. I never called them Mother and Father. It was always Uncle and Aunt. They made no secret of the fact I was adopted."

"Then why not tell you about your birth parents?"

"That's a question I asked many times. By the time I was in my teens, it was a question I shouted and screamed, but they claimed not to know. Claimed it was best for me not to search for answers. The only thing they told me was I was sent down here during the war from London and that my mother died in the Blitz. How much of that is true, I'm not sure." Grace stared out to the horizon, not seeing the sand banks or far-off shore, lost instead to her memories. Eventually, she tutted to herself and turned to Elle. "Have you ever resented the fact I made you call me Grace?"

"No," Elle answered truthfully. "It always felt normal to me. I think my friends thought you were cool not letting me call you Mum."

"Hmm," said Grace. "I've sometimes regretted that decision, but in truth, the name Mum never sat right on my tongue and to hear it spoken in the house would only remind me of what I had never had. I suppose it was selfish of me."

"Well, I've certainly never held it against you."

"I know," said Grace, reaching across and squeezing Elle's hand. "We need to talk about the cottage."

"Not now," said Elle.

"Love, it's falling down around our ears. We have to do something. They've built some nice bungalows up on the hill. They'd be warmer, and a lot better for my knee."

"We're not leaving. I'll find a way for us to manage. That cottage is part of you. I won't see you forced to leave it just because we're hard up."

"Hard up's an understatement."

"I've got things under control. I'm looking for better paid work."

"I know you are. Speaking of work, before you head to the pub, I don't suppose you'd go up to the attic for me, would you? There's not much I can do at the moment, but I could easily sit on my bum and sort through some boxes from up there."

"What's in the boxes?"

"All Uncle Richard and Aunt Helen's possessions. You probably don't remember much about Helen, and Richard died long before you arrived, but they were wonderful people. I couldn't bear to see their things around the place once they'd gone, but enough time has passed for it not to hurt."

"Of course I'll get the boxes down for you, but I don't want you lifting anything heavy while I'm out."

"Deal. I'll just set myself up in a chair and take my time going through them. I doubt there's anything of any value, but you never know."

Elle thought the chance of finding anything of value in their loft cupboards was slim to none, but if it kept Grace occupied and out of trouble while she was at work, it would be worth getting those dusty boxes down.

"Come on," said Grace. "Let's get back so I can make a start. There's no time like the present."

Chapter 3

February, 2018

Sophie chained her bike against a railing and stared at the sprawling, squat old folks' home. *Seawinds* was an optimistic name for a place huddled half-a-mile inland, any hint of the sea absorbed by the yellow brick boxes of the surrounding estate. Guilt tugged at her, and Sophie shook her head. *Remember what Cassie said*, Sophie told herself, *the guilt you carry will only drag you down. You are not responsible for the happiness of a parent.*

Sophie wasn't sure the therapy was actually helping, but if nothing else, it gave her a chance to escape the demands of her family for an hour or two every Wednesday. She always assumed by her fifties she would be child free, her and Will spending evenings eating out, their weekends spent on mini breaks in posh hotels. Instead, one man-child still lived with her rent free, the other calling round for food and use of the washing machine multiple times a week, and the man she had dreamed of spending romantic evenings with had left her for a younger woman just as menopause hit.

The buzzer rang, and a smiling nurse appeared at the door.

"Hi, Sophie. Come on in. I'm afraid Mum's not doing too well today. Might be best to keep your visit short if that's OK?"

That's music to my ears, thought Sophie, who had been dreading a prolonged visit to the cabbage-smelling room. "That's a shame," said Sophie. "Is she in pain?"

"No, just not really with it. She seems lost in the past this morning. Like I said, best keep the visit short if you can."

"No problem," said Sophie, smiling at the underpaid nurse before making her way along the corridor.

At the sight of Room 18, Sophie paused and took a deep breath. She knocked lightly against the wood before clicking the door open and poking her head round.

"Mum?" she said, stepping inside and closing the door. "Mum, it's me, Sophie."

A nest of white curly hair tickled the top of an armchair, but the woman's head did not turn. Sophie walked to the chair and placed herself in front of her mother, who had her back to the room, eyes fixed on the horizon.

"Mum, I said it's me, Sophie." She took hold of her mother's hand, stroking the crepe paper skin beneath her thumb.

"I'm Annie."

"Yes, Mum, I know. And I'm Sophie, your daughter."

"Which one?"

"What do you mean, Mum? You only have one daughter, me, Sophie."

"There were two."

"No, Mum." Sophie reached in her pocket for the selection of photos she always brought with her to jog her mother's memory. "See, here you are in the hospital. That baby in your arms is me, Sophie."

"Ah yes," said her mother, taking the photograph in her shaking hand. "And where's the other one? Mummy had two babies, but she didn't want me to know. But I found out. I knew. Where's the other one? Where is she?" Annie's rheumy eyes cleared and she fixed Sophie with a piercing look. "Where's the other one?"

"Mum, I don't know what..."

"Where's the other one?" Annie's reedy voice raised a notch, her eyes darting across Sophie's face.

"It's OK, Mum," said Sophie, clasping her mother's hands to calm her. But Annie would not be calmed. She repeated her question over and over, her voice turning from whine to shout, tears flowing in frustration and desperation.

The friendly nurse poked her head around the door and, on seeing Annie's distress, rushed over and wrapped her arms around her bony shoulders.

"Perhaps wait outside for a moment," the nurse told Sophie. "I'll get Annie calm, then we can have a chat."

"Sure," said Sophie, picking up the photograph which had dropped to the floor.

In the bland nursing home garden, Sophie pulled a packet of cigarettes from her bag and turned her back on the wind to light one. Will hated her smoking, which was partly why she'd resumed the habit after a thirty-year break; that and the stress of putting Mum into a home. A seagull squawked overhead, the only sign they were near the seaside. Hadn't she heard on the radio that gulls were just as likely to be found in cities as by the sea?

"Sophie?"

"Hi," said Sophie, crushing the cigarette beneath her shoe as the nurse approached. "Is Mum OK now?"

"Yes, she's much better. I wanted to talk to you about some things she's been saying."

"About having two babies? I can tell you for a fact that isn't true. My birth was difficult, and Mum was told she couldn't have more children. A second child would have been impossible. And before you ask, there were no older siblings. My dad never stopped telling me how hard they tried to have me, what a miracle I was in their eyes. No, I'm telling you, I'm an only child, more's the pity."

"What if she's not talking about herself?"

"What do you mean?"

"Well, sometimes she talks like she had two babies, other times it's like she's talking about her own mother. Do you know if your mother had a sister?"

"Not that I know of. I don't know much about her family, to be honest. My grandparents died when I was very young, and Mum didn't really speak about them. I always had a feeling there was something Mum didn't want to tell me, but I assumed she'd had a difficult relationship with her own mother and didn't want to revisit old wounds."

"Do you have any photos or documents at home that might shed some light on what she's talking about? It may help to bring her some peace."

"I sorted through most of her belongings when she moved in here, but I'll look again when I get home."

"Thanks. See you tomorrow?"

"Yes, I'll swing by on my way home from work if I don't finish too late."

"Great, see you then. Bye."

"Bye."

Chapter 4

February, 2018

"What's that?" asked Jago, putting his hand to Elle's hair. She stood still while his fingers felt between her curls.

"You know this is what gorillas do to each other?" she said.

"Quiet," he said. "I've nearly got it."

Jago pulled his hand away, his fingers folded. "What is it?" asked Elle.

Jago uncurled his hand, and an enormous spider scuttled up onto his bare forearm. "Want me to squish him for you?"

"No," said Elle, horrified at the thought. "Give him here." She cupped her hands around the spindly legs and removed the spider safely into the yard.

"What are you doing with spiders in your hair, anyway? Have things got that bad in the cottage?"

"We share the cottage with plenty of eight-legged friends, but that one probably came from the attic cupboards. Grace had me searching around for boxes before I left for work. She fancied a trip down memory lane, and if it keeps her out of trouble, I'm happy to indulge her."

"How is the lovely Grace? Knee still playing up?"

"Yeah, going from bad to worse. It's criminal she can't get it sorted. It's turned her into a helpless old lady, and you know she's never been like that."

"She is pushing eighty."

"Yeah, but would you describe Grace as old?"

"Nah, she's one of the youngest people I know, in spirit, at least."

"It's horrible seeing her so frail. The lack of independence makes her pretty grumpy too."

Jago moved beside Elle and began rubbing her back. "Don't," said Elle, stepping away from him. "Just don't."

"Fine," said Jago, more than a hint of frustration in his voice.

Elle moved out from behind the bar and grabbed a piece of chalk to write the specials on the board. She avoided looking at Jago, knowing his face would scream disappointment. It was becoming harder and harder to work beside him without giving in.

When Elle had finally moved back to her hometown, she had convinced herself that any feelings for her childhood sweetheart had been left in the past. If it weren't for the staff Christmas party, they would have been. One moment of madness when they were alone in the cellar was all it had taken to throw their tentative friendship into uncertainty and confusion. It had felt so right to be held in his arms that night, but Elle had felt nothing but regret since.

Now she was trapped between her head and heart. Of course she wanted him to touch her, who wouldn't? But she was back home for Grace. The last thing she needed was a flighty free spirit leaving her broken-hearted for a second time as soon as wanderlust gripped him, as it inevitably would. She had spent the past twenty years protecting herself from another heartbreak. She wasn't about to let her guard down now.

Within half an hour, the pub was three quarters full thanks to a sunnier than usual February half term. Elle's legs ached even at the thought of summer and the crowds it would bring. Everyone thought she'd moved to Bristol for its buzz, but in truth, Elle had found the steady rhythms of city life far more peaceful than the volatile lurches between deathly quiet and rammed that Padstow experienced.

In the city, Elle knew what to expect. She could keep her head down, moving through life with a consistent busyness that left her occupied without being stressed, not quite lonely, and not quite overwhelmed. In Padstow, she was alone with her thoughts on deserted streets, or squashed among crowds whose presence left her exhausted.

"I'm going down to the cellar to change a barrel," said Jago, breaking into Elle's thoughts.

"Sure," said Elle, breathing a sigh of relief as he disappeared down the stairs.

The hours passed in a blur of pulling pints and grabbing expensive bottles of wine from the fridge. As she totted up each bill on the till, Elle calculated what each amount would pay for. She could have fixed up the whole cottage just from the lunchtime takings.

By three, the pub had calmed down enough for her to take a break. She took a glass of lemonade and a plate of crab sandwiches to a picnic bench outside and revelled in the joy of taking the weight off her legs. She was eating the last bites of sandwich when a familiar clicking caused her to look up.

"What are you doing here?" she asked in exasperation. "You should be resting."

"No rest for the wicked," said Grace, the tapping of her stick growing louder as she crossed the stone-flagged courtyard towards her daughter. "Ah, Jago, get me a dry white wine, would you, love? I don't think my legs can make it to the bar."

Elle turned to see Jago watching them from the doorway. How long had he been standing there? By the time Grace had maneuvered herself onto the bench, he had reappeared with a large glass of Sauvignon.

"Come and sit with us, love. I've made an exciting discovery and could do with an audience."

Chapter 5

February, 2018

Sophie turned her head from the entrance to the nursing home as her car sped past its gates. *It's too late anyway*, she told herself. *Mum will probably be asleep by now.* The clock on the dashboard showed six o'clock. Sophie stifled a yawn and opened the window to wake herself up. Zayn had a unique ability to wear her down in a way no child had managed over her thirty-year career. The lowest point in her day had been chasing a stinking Zayn around the classroom with a packet of wet-wipes after he'd not made it to the toilet but refused to get changed. Perhaps she was getting too old to do the job? But what was the alternative? Teaching was one of the few jobs in town that could earn her a decent salary, and with no Will to help pay the mortgage, she needed all the cash she could get.

Sophie's thoughts turned to her sons. Grown men still reliant on their mother. More guilt, more regrets. It seemed she was incapable of being a good daughter or mother. She must have failed as a parent to have both sons still living within a mile radius of their childhood home. *Go travelling*, she'd encouraged, *go to university, take a gap year*, but as usual no one listened.

There had been a glimmer of hope when Ben got a place at college to study sound engineering. It might have led to something good if he'd left Lowestoft, but he could never quite cut the apron strings, and

Sophie's was a lone voice. Will saw no reason the boys should see more of the world. *Think how great it will be when we're grandparents and our grandchildren live close*, he'd said. But now he was up in Scotland with his stick insect of a new wife, about to start a second family, and it was Sophie who'd been left with two unambitious twenty-somethings still demanding she cook their tea each night.

Sophie pulled the car up outside the house and switched off the engine. She willed her body to move, but it resisted, her limbs leaden against the tatty fabric of her car. Her head fell back against the head-rest, and Sophie closed her eyes. Five minutes, then she'd go inside. Her mind drifted on the cusp of sleep, fluttering with thoughts sliding like oil on water.

Lids forced open, Sophie heaved her body out of the car. In her half-asleep state, a blast of air refreshed her, salt sitting on her tongue and filling her nostrils. She threw her many bags onto the backseat, turned her back on her house, and crossed the road. The air held a hint of warmth she'd not felt for many months.

Sophie stepped out of the path of a bike and crossed the promenade. Ahead of her lay a sweep of pale sand, a grey sea tinged with a faint wash of blue, the sound of waves lapping away at the stress of the day. In rare moments like this, she felt some sympathy for her boys' choice to stay. There were times, like on a summer's day when families spilled out of beach huts, and the sun burned bright, when the town felt hopeful.

In the day-to-day throes of life, the fact she lived opposite a living painting often went ignored. The sweeping beauty of sea meeting land became ordinary, so ordinary it was no longer seen, taken for granted. With her blonde curls flying around her head, Sophie took a deep breath of sea air, rolled her shoulders and let the day's stress seep from her body. She turned back to face the house, ignoring all the cheap bed and breakfasts that now surrounded it.

Any sense of failure at returning to her hometown after university had been outweighed by the house. How many twenty-one-year-olds could say they owned a three-storey house with sea views? Twelve miles further south, the same house in Southwold would have cost twenty times what they had paid for their piece of Lowestoft real estate.

Sophie remembered the plans she had made with Will that first night in their new home. By then her belly was already expanding with the baby, and decorating a nursery had been top of the to-do list. Looking at the house almost thirty years on, the years had taken their toll. The sash windows needed repainting, red peeling from the front door to reveal the green chosen by previous owners. Sophie resolved to write a list for Ben. Until he found more than part-time work, the least he could do was earn his keep by doing some jobs around the house.

It was only as Sophie turned the key in the lock that she remembered her promise to search out more of her mum's belongings. With no expectation of finding anything to answer Annie's questions, Sophie called hello to her son and trudged up the stairs towards the attic.

Chapter 6

February, 2018

Jago threw a confused look to Elle, who shrugged her shoulders and tried to ignore the warmth of his leg as he settled down beside her.

"Is this to do with the stuff from the attic?" Elle asked.

"Yes," said Grace, eyes gleaming. "I think I've found something that could be important." She reached into her deep coat pocket and pulled out a black-and-white photograph and a stack of what looked like letters, tied up with a piece of string. She slid them across the bench, and Elle and Jago's heads met as they bent over to get a good look.

In the photograph, a group of people were standing beside the harbour. A middle-aged couple stood close together, the woman holding a baby in her arms. To their right stood a tall, broad man dressed in a fisherman's attire. To their left, a beautiful woman held the hand of a child, a suitcase resting beside their feet. The second photograph showed the same woman, this time lying in bed. She looked as though she was sleeping, a baby nestled in the crook of her arm. Elle wondered if she'd even known someone had photographed her.

"Who are these people?" asked Elle, pushing Jago's hand away.

"This is my Aunt Helen and Uncle Richard. The man beside them is Helen's brother Jack. As for this woman, she was called Marnie. She and her daughter Annie were from Lowestoft and lived with us during the war. These," said Grace, sliding the letters across the table, "are letters from Annie. Marnie left midway through the war, so I never knew her, but her daughter Annie kept in touch. We wrote to each other for years, then about ten years ago the letters suddenly stopped."

"I've never heard you mention these people before."

"No, well, I rather enjoyed having Annie as a secret pen-pal. We were so close during those war years, and when things were difficult with your father, it was nice having something just for me."

"Dad didn't know about the letters?"

"No. Annie and I were pen-pals for decades and I never told a soul. Anyway, the reason I'm telling you now is they were here, Marnie and Annie, when I arrived. So, they might have known something about my birth parents."

Elle glanced at Jago, who reached beneath the table and squeezed her knee. Elle coughed and moved her leg away. Jago turned his attention to Grace. "I know you'd love that to be the case, but it sounds like a long shot. Wouldn't Annie have said something over the years if she knew where you'd come from?"

"I don't know," said Grace. "I always had the feeling Annie was holding something back from me. In the early days of us writing to each other, I'd regularly suggest meeting in person, but Annie always had some excuse or other about why she couldn't. In the end I gave up and accepted that our relationship would be confined to pen and paper, but I always wondered why she was so reluctant to see me." Grace stared into Jago's eyes. "I can't be sure, of course I can't, but I just have this feeling... I know you probably think I'm a mad old woman, but I'm telling you, something about this photo hit deep in my soul. What if it's her?"

"What do you mean, Grace?" asked Elle.

Grace let out a long sigh and shook her head. "I was wondering whether Marnie might have been my mother. Oh, ignore me, I'm just a mad old lady grasping at straws."

"I'd never dare describe you as mad or old," said Jago, laughing. He picked up the photograph and squinted closely at it. "This might be a stupid idea, but how about I take a copy of this and put it up in the pub? Some of the old boys may recognise Marnie and know about her time in Padstow."

"It's worth a try," said Elle. "Would you be happy to make this public?"

"I don't see why not," said Grace. "Seeing these photos has piqued my curiosity. I'd given up on ever knowing where I came from, but perhaps it's about time I found out. Better late than never, as they say. And besides, the only person in that photo I know for certain is still alive is me. No one can object from beyond the grave, can they?"

"You know, if this is your mother," said Elle, "It would make Annie your sister."

"Yes," said Grace, "the thought had crossed my mind. But if everything was as straightforward as that, I can't see why they wouldn't have told me the truth. Besides, given how abruptly Annie's letters stopped, she's probably dead by now."

"Ever the optimist, Grace," laughed Jago.

"Did you try to contact Annie after the letters stopped?" asked Elle.

"Of course I did, but they all came back marked *return to sender*. Annie mentioned a daughter, but never told me her last name once she was married, so that was another dead end."

"Let's start by making a copy of the photo and see if anyone remembers Marnie. Then we can take it from there."

"You're a good boy, Jago," smiled Grace, giving Elle a pointed look.

"I'd better get back to work," said Elle, finishing the dregs of her lemonade.

"It's pretty quiet in there," said Jago. "Why don't you stay here with Grace for a bit? I'll cover for you."

"Fine," said Elle, wishing Jago was not her boss. It was a power imbalance she could do without, however fair and generous he was.

Grace waited for Jago to head back into the pub before she launched into an inquisition so familiar that Elle was tempted to yawn with boredom.

"Why don't you give him another chance? He's clearly smitten with you."

"Have you forgotten what happened last time?"

"That was twenty years ago. Surely you've forgiven him by now? Besides, people change. Twenty years is a long time."

"I'm here for you, not him. I can't risk getting my heart pummelled again."

"But you've just turned forty. Don't you want children?"

"If that happened, it would be great, but I'm not desperate to have kids."

"Your clock is ticking..."

"Remind me again how old you were when you had me?"

"Hmph, that's beside the point."

Elle laughed. "I'd say it's an excellent point."

"Anyway, you could do a lot worse than Jago. I should know."

Elle winced as she pictured the mild-mannered man who'd turned out to be a snake. Rather than being heartbroken, she had felt nothing but relief when her father moved up country and left them in peace. These days she was grateful to him. He'd taught her a valuable lesson:

that men were not to be trusted, especially the nice ones. They were even better at pretending.

"Have you heard from your father recently?" asked Grace, reading her daughter's mind.

"Just a card at Christmas. He seems to be living it up in London. The twins are hotshots working in the city last I heard. They've paid for both his hip replacements."

Elle had only met her half-siblings a handful of times, none of the occasions endearing them to her. In her view, they were spoiled brats, and she was glad they lived hundreds of miles away.

"Well," continued Grace, "don't let nature decide for you. Take control of your own destiny. I wouldn't mind meeting a grandchild or two before I cark it."

"You're not going anywhere, anytime soon, so enough talking like that. Anyway, I really should get going," said Elle, cocking her head to a group of tourists who were walking into the pub.

"Yes, love. You get on. I'll take the photo up to the library and get a copy made."

"You'll do no such thing. Leave it to me, I'll sort it out at the end of my shift. I think there's a copier in the office. If you leave the photos here, I'll make sure I bring them home with me later."

Grace seemed unwilling to let the photograph out of her sight, but eventually relented. She insisted on pulling herself up from the table without assistance, despite the obvious pain it caused her.

"What about the letters?" asked Elle.

Grace hesitated, her hand hovering over the pile of envelopes. "I'd like to read them again. It's been so long since I last went through them. If there's nothing too shocking, I'll pass them to you to read."

"Alright, but if you consider them too private, I won't be offended."

Grace picked up the letters and slipped them in her bag. "I'll see you at home later," she said, waving with her free hand as she hobbled back towards her cottage.

Elle sighed, gathered up the empty glasses, and headed back into the pub to finish her shift. She prayed the photos would prove more than a wild goose chase. If nothing else, it would take Grace's mind off the constant pain that dogged her days.

Chapter 7

1955

Dear Grace,

What a lot of news I have to share with you! But I'll begin with an apology. I'm sorry you weren't able to join us for the wedding, but after the rocky road Sam and I had to get here, we wanted a small ceremony where we could express our vows without a big audience looking on. Mum and Kitty were our witnesses, and we were joined by our immediate family afterwards in the Rising Sun for a toast.

Our honeymoon was wonderful. Once upon a time I would have gone to the island for our honeymoon, but given all that happened there, we decided to go somewhere new to both of us, without pre-existing memories, good or bad. Mind you, it would have been far easier to get to the island, as the new causeway is now complete. It's hard to imagine a road stretching from the mainland to the island, but Uncle Jimmy sent photographs, so it must be real.

Sam wouldn't tell me where we were going on our honeymoon, so you can imagine how surprised I was when we took a train to Liverpool and boarded a ferry to the Isle of Man. Thank goodness I've inherited good sea legs, for the crossing was rather rough, and I was one of the few passengers (along with Sam) not to be ill. Even those not actually sick turned a funny shade of green, but I suppose that's the Irish Sea for you!

We only spent three nights on the island, but made the most of the time we had. There was so much to see and explore, but on our first day we were rather tired from all the travelling and spent the day in Peel, where we were staying in a lovely guest house with views over the bay. On our second day, we took a bus to Douglas, which is a very quaint town, or possibly a city, I'm not sure. Sam bought me a new dress, and we ate crab sandwiches while watching the ferry come into port.

On our last day, we signed up for a bus tour, which took a day to drive right around the island. Unfortunately, the weather was not on our side, but despite the wind and rain, we thoroughly enjoyed ourselves, and lowered the average age of the tour by about forty years! My favourite stop was Port Erin, a coastal village that reminded me of Cornwall. The sun briefly poked out from behind a cloud and lit up the bay as we strolled across the beach.

Apart from seeing the sights, it was lovely to spend time with Sam, just the two of us. He organised romantic picnics on the two days we had good weather, and treated me like a princess the entire time we were away. I know we're lucky to be surrounded by so many family and friends in Lowestoft, but it means we have little time when it's just the two of us, so we savoured our time alone while we were away.

On our return, we moved straight into our new home. It's only a small two-up, two-down terrace, but it has a pretty little garden, and I've enjoyed making it our own in the few weeks we've been living there. It is on the outskirts of Oulton Broad, so near Mum and Frank, but not too far to walk into town for work. The broad itself is lovely. Sam suggested we get a small dinghy to explore the waterways, but I've told him one boat in the family is more than enough.

In sadder news, there was an article in the Lowestoft journal this week announcing the 'First Stage of Slum Clearance Programme' on the Grit.

I'm not sure how much I've told you about The Grit, or Beach Village, but it's the fishing community below the cliff, and has always been considered separate from the main town. My dad's family and Sam's dad's family all came from there, and my Uncle Jimmy also lived there briefly during his fishing days. Since the war and the flood, the living conditions down there have been awful, but even so, I worry this so called 'slum clearance' will be something people live to regret. There's so much history in the place, and some beautiful old flint cottages. It's an entire way of life that's disappearing, and I'm not sure we'll see the likes of it again.

On the topic of fishing, Sam is in his element aboard the Sally Ann. Bobby says he'll retire in the next five years, so is busy training Sam up to take charge. Sam already knows the boat and the local fishing grounds like the back of his hand, but although he comes home complaining about his dad 'teaching grandma to suck eggs', he indulges Bobby's explanations, as he knows what a big step it will be for him to retire and wants him to feel the boat is in safe hands.

How are you, Grace? I know it must be a difficult time trying to decide whether to stay at school or leave to find work. By the sounds of things, you are clever enough to warrant staying on beyond O levels, but I remember the allure of leaving to earn your own money. It sounds like you've made a lot of friends at the grammar school, and I'm sure you're a popular member of the group. How is Aunt Helen? Mum and Frank asked me to send their love to both of you. I'm sorry I've taken up so much of this letter with my news. Write to me and tell me all about what you have been up to. It's always a joy to hear from you,

All my love,

Your friend,

Annie

Chapter 8

February, 2018

Sophie pulled cobwebs from her hair and breathed a deep lungful of fresh air. Perched on the ladder, she waited for her heart to stop pounding in her chest. She had never been fond of small spaces. The attic was a dark, precarious, musty place to be, and Sophie had spent far longer up there than she would have liked. It was hard to get at anything since she'd filled the space with Will's belongings, flung into bin bags ready for a time he decided to collect them.

After climbing over mountains of rubbish, Sophie reached the small pile of suitcases belonging to her mum. Annie never believed in throwing things away, and the cases were so battered Sophie feared they would crumble to dust as she threw each one to the bottom of the ladder.

The suitcases had been in the attic for a good ten years, ever since Annie moved in with them, right until Sophie could no longer cope on her own and decided to put her into a home. The image of pulling up to the nursing home that first day was one Sophie would never forget. Annie's face had been filled with concern and confusion. Her scaly palm gripped Sophie's shirt as, deep in her subconscious, she finally made the connections to understand what was happening.

Forty-six years earlier, it had been the other way round. It was Sophie's first memory, clinging to her mum's long skirt, begging her not to go. The tears, clawing and tantrums became a daily routine which lasted the full year Sophie attended the playgroup, only stopping once she moved up to the local primary school and finally found her feet.

That was how it should be, a child clinging to their mother, not the other way round. It had taken three care workers to manhandle Annie into the care home that first day, her heels scraping a line in the gravel as her legs locked in place and she refused to move. Sophie had given permission for the manhandling, she had signed her name on the appropriate form, promising not to lodge a complaint, or worse, sue. Yet seeing her mother dragged kicking and screaming into her new home had been the straw that broke the camel's back. She remembered crawling into bed once she was home and sobbing for eight hours straight at the cruel choice she had been forced to make.

As she stared at the pile of suitcases below her feet, tears pricked Sophie's eyes. How did it come to this? That one moment in a car park over a year ago had broken the fragile threads that joined mother and daughter. Annie had never forgiven the final betrayal, and if Sophie were honest, she couldn't blame her. As much as her therapist Cassie insisted Sophie could not have done more, a small part of her wondered if she could have held out a little longer and kept her mother in the safety of her daughter's care rather than handing her over to strangers.

"Put the kettle on," Sophie shouted in the direction of Ben's room.

"I'm busy," yelled the deep voice behind the door.

It was almost a decade since Ben's voice had broken, yet Sophie still expected to hear the high-pitched tones of a boy. She climbed down the ladder and crossed the landing.

"Hey, knock, will you?" moaned Ben, as she threw open his door.

"I thought you said you were busy?" asked Sophie, climbing over piles of clothes to open the window.

Ben lifted his eyes from his Xbox for a second. "Don't open that. It's cold enough already."

"It stinks in here, Ben. No wonder, given the amount of dirty clothes on the floor. You know the deal. You can stay here, but I'm not cleaning up after you."

"Yeah, you've said a million times."

"Could you tear yourself away from that screen and help me?"

"What do you need?" asked Ben, taking off his headphones and laying them on his desk. He swung round in his gaming chair and gave Sophie the smile that always melted her heart. For a moment the years slipped away, and he was back to her cheeky little boy, doling out cuddles and laughter freely.

"I've got Gran's suitcases down from the attic, but some of them are quite heavy. Could you give me a hand lugging them downstairs?"

"Yeah, sure."

"Really?" Ben's answer surprised her. Sophie thought he'd put up more of a fight.

"I said yes, didn't I? Where are they?"

"Bottom of the ladder."

Ben downed the dregs of a can of coke and wandered through to the landing. "What are you doing with these, anyway? Did Gran ask for them? She didn't mention them when I went to see her earlier."

"You went to visit her?"

"I've been three times this week."

Sophie wondered why the nursing home hadn't mentioned Ben's visits. Then again, he was always closer to Annie than she'd ever been, so it shouldn't come as a surprise. "She's been rambling a bit about her past. The staff suggested I take in some photos to help calm her.

I thought I'd been through all her belongings, then I remembered the cases we put up in the attic when she first arrived."

"Yeah, she's been going on about stuff to me, too. Something about another child. You don't have a sister, do you?"

"No, I'm certain I don't. I was thinking maybe she did, though. She never spoke much about her childhood, and I was so young when my grandparents died. I never knew them."

"Cool, let's have a look then." Ben grabbed a suitcase in each hand and carried them effortlessly down the stairs. Sophie, with only one in her arms, struggled behind him.

"Where do you want them?" Ben asked as they reached the ground floor.

"How about the living room? More space to spread out in there. I'll just make a cuppa before we start," said Sophie, throwing her suitcase down beside Ben's. "Can you open a window? All the dust is making me sneeze."

"Yes, boss," said Ben. There was that smile again. Sophie wondered if she was too hard on her sons. They were good boys really.

Chapter 9

February, 2018

"Elle, come here."

Elle frowned at Jago who was leaning over the bar, talking to Nosey Ned, a local gossip and drunk she usually tried to avoid. "I was just on my way home."

"This is important. Ned thinks he may know something about this photo." Jago waved the photograph Grace had found in the air, leaving Elle with no choice but to take the bait.

"You knew this lady?" Elle asked Ned, climbing up onto a barstool and taking the glass of wine Jago had poured her.

"No."

Elle felt a rush of disappointment and jumped down from the chair. "Not to worry."

"Hold your horses," said Ned. "I didn't know the lady, but I knew old Jack Tristan well."

"Grace's uncle?"

Ned sniggered into his pint. "Uncle?"

"What's so funny?"

"Come on, Ned, now isn't the time for playing games," said Jago.

"What do you know about old Jacky boy?" asked Ned.

"Not much. I was only ten when he died. I remember him taking me out on his boat, and he was always kind to me and Mum, especially after Dad left."

"Hmm, I suppose he was a decent enough chap. A bit of a weirdo, though."

Elle swallowed down the words that Nosey Ned was a fine one to talk. "Weird in what way?"

"He was a loner."

Touché.

"Is that all?"

"Yeah, but there was never a sniff of any woman that I heard about. Usually, these types of fellows have a few skeletons in their closet. Anyway, Jack Tristan could also be a grumpy bastard, and we got into a bit of a scrap one Christmas after I spilled my beer over him by mistake. I was angry. So, when I went round Mum's for lunch the next day, I asked if she had any dirt on him. You know, gossip?"

Elle knew all about Ned's penchant for gossip, and now she also knew where he must have got his passion from. "So, your mum knew something about Jack?"

"She may have heard a rumour..." Ned looked pointedly at his empty pint glass. Jago sighed, poured him another, slid it across the bar and waited for the man to continue his story.

"You were saying?" asked Elle.

"Right," said Ned, taking a sip and wiping away his frothy moustache with the back of his hand. "Mum reckoned there were rumours about him during the war."

"He served in the war?"

"Nah, he stayed here to fish. He'd have been too old to be called up, is my guess. So, he was here at the same time as this lovely-looking lady," said Ned, pointing a grubby finger at Marnie's photograph.

"And that is relevant how?"

"According to Mum, this lady had come down here with her little girl to meet her husband, but something happened to him before he arrived. Anyway, the war came, and everyone thought the lady and her child would stay here for the duration, only that's not what happened."

"What happened, Ned?"

Ned shrugged. "She left, all of a sudden, like. But before she properly left, she disappeared." He looked at the confusion on Jago's and Elle's faces and grinned. "Not disappeared in a magic way, just stopped going out. Before that, she used to help Richard in the shop, but one day she wasn't there behind the counter and when folk asked, Richard told them she was unwell. Anyway, a little while after that, two things happened. One, Richard and Helen are suddenly lumbered with a baby, and two, this young lady is hotfooting it back to wherever she came from but leaving her young daughter behind."

"OK," said Jago. "But what makes you think it's all connected?"

Ned rolled his eyes and let out a dramatic sigh. "Come on, man, use your brain. A pretty young lady confines herself to her bedroom, then a baby magically appears, and the woman runs away. Got to be more than coincidence."

"But there's no proof?"

"Nah, according to Mum, Helen and Richard always claimed the baby was an evacuee and would hear no more about it. But then the baby grew up, and anyone with eyes in their head could see what had gone on. She was the spit of old Jack Tristan."

Elle looked at Jago, her head spinning. Marnie and Jack? Surely not. "But if that was the case, surely Marnie would have stayed here and married Jack. They were both single. I don't understand what the problem would have been if they'd married?"

"Like I said, Jack was a weirdo. Maybe the woman fell for his charms and realised too late what he was really like. Who can say?"

"It's an interesting theory," said Jago.

"True," said Elle. "But that's all it is. There's no evidence that any of it is true. It's all hearsay and gossip."

Ned made a disgruntled sound from his nose and took a sip of his pint. "Wish I'd stayed quiet now."

"No," said Jago, "we're grateful for your information, Ned. We just need to look into these rumours more, that's all."

"No skin off my nose what you do with the information," said Ned. He downed the rest of his pint and held out his glass. "Same again please, barman."

Once Jago had poured another pint, Elle said her goodbyes, but he insisted on walking her to the door. "Are you going to tell Grace?" he asked under his breath.

Elle shook her head. "I don't think so, not yet. Let's do a bit more digging. At the moment, all we have are rumours, and I don't want to disrupt Grace's life over some gossip."

"I think you're right," said Jago. "Ned's story is pretty convincing, but I wouldn't trust the bloke as far as I could throw him. He could be making it all up for the sake of a few free pints. Leave it to me and I'll see what I can find out."

"Thank you," said Elle. As she walked away from the pub, she made a mental note not to get too comfortable sharing secrets with Jago. He might be helping now, but there was no saying how long her family situation would hold his interest. As soon as he got bored, he'd scarper, true to form.

Chapter 10

1960

Dear Grace,

Thank you for your suggestion of meeting in person next summer, but I don't think we'll be able to manage it. Things are very busy between Sam's work on the boat and my work at the Birds Eye factory and we only have a few days' holiday left. You're right, it has been a very long time since we last saw each other. I'm sure we will see each other again one day.

The evening classes I've been attending for the past two years have paid off and I've left the production line at Birds Eye and now work in the office on mainly secretarial duties. It's a lot calmer and quieter in the office, and I still get to have lunch with my friends in the canteen, so it's the best of both worlds. Also, I now come home with ink on my fingers rather than red-raw skin from the cold, so that's another positive.

How are you getting on at secretarial college? It's a shame you weren't able to follow your dream of going to university, but it sounds very romantic that you've stayed in Padstow for love. I'm sure Aunt Helen is glad to have you closer to home, and your new fellow John sounds like a nice chap. Will there be wedding bells in the air soon? I don't think it matters that he is a few years older than you, as long as he treats you well. What does Aunt Helen make of him?

I know it must be frustrating that Jack hasn't warmed to John, but Jack has always been a little gruff, and I'm sure he just has your best interests at heart. I couldn't help but laugh when you told me about your trip out on Jack's boat. Poor John, it's easy to forget how badly the sea affects some people. It must have been humiliating for him being so ill, especially if Jack was being less than welcoming. But surely the fact Jack invited you both onto the boat in the first place is a good thing? He wouldn't have done that if he weren't taking your romance seriously and wasn't interested in getting to know John better. Perhaps suggest you stick to dry land the next time you all meet?

We had something very exciting happen last week, Prince Philip visited the factory! I wasn't one of those lucky enough to meet him, but I watched as he was shown around the factory. He came across as a lovely man and seem to take great interest in our work. He was shown kipper filleting and sprout cleaning, so goodness knows what he made of that!

There are well over a thousand locals employed at the factory now, and this has gone a long way to ease the pressure of a declining fishing industry. It seems like there are always new factory buildings under construction, and Birds Eye will have taken over the whole of the Grit if they keep going at this rate!

Fishing here is really in dire straits. Gone are the days when crews and herring girls would descend on the town from all over the country. Even when I was a girl and the herring was long past its glory days, my nanny hosted a group of herring girls each year. Between the war and overfishing, it's truly the end of an era. I may have already told you that a couple of years ago, just one curer came down for the season and never handled a single herring while he was in town. There are now only three coopers working and making barrels on Hamilton Road.

That grim assessment of the fishing industry leads me on to our next piece of big news. The Sally Ann is no more, or at least the name lives on, but not the vessel. Sam and Bobby's new Sally Ann is a motor trawler, far better equipped to catch cod, plaice and hake. It's taken a combination of all our savings, and it will be years before the boat is fully paid off, but we have to move with the times. Given we've had no luck starting a family yet, we've decided to delay future attempts until our finances are in a less precarious position. Not the most romantic decision, but a sensible one I hope, as it means I can continue working and my wage is more crucial than ever these days.

Mum and Frank are well and asked me to pass on my regards to you and Aunt Helen. Frank retires next month and is trying to persuade Mum to give up her work on the nets. She's always prided herself on her work ethic, so I don't suppose he'll convince her, but she's started to get arthritis in her fingers so nature may intervene and leave her with little choice.

I'd better end my letter here, but I hope you are well. I'll look forward to hearing all your latest news, and send my love to Aunt Helen, and of course to Jack,

All my love,

Your friend,

Annie.

Chapter 11

February, 2018

With tea made and cooling on the coffee table, Sophie and Ben opened the first suitcase. In it were a set of clothes, musty and crumpled. They systematically worked their way through, folding the skirts and blouses into piles as they went.

"These are pretty old-fashioned. Do you reckon these are Gran's from when she was younger?"

"I wonder if they belonged to Gran's mum, my grandmother Marnie. Look, most of them don't have labels and the fabric is cotton or wool. I never remember Mum wearing anything like this, even when she was younger."

"Why would she have kept a case full of Marnie's clothes?" asked Ben.

"Because she wanted a reminder of her?"

"Maybe."

They moved on to the second suitcase. "No wonder this was the heaviest," said Sophie, blowing dust from the covers of hardback books.

The third suitcase contained photographs. "Wow, is this what Lowestoft used to look like?" asked Ben, flicking through scenes of the beach and fishing boats in the harbour.

"Yes, it's changed quite a bit over the years."

"For the worse," said Ben, squinting at the black-and-white shots.

"Not necessarily. The beach hasn't changed much."

"Hmm," said Ben, "at least there was plenty of work in those days."

"Fancy yourself as a fisherman, do you?" teased Sophie. "There is work here, but it's a different kind. There are plenty of apprenticeships and jobs in the offshore energy sector. But, if that's not your thing, you could leave Lowestoft? You could move elsewhere."

"Why should I have to? I should be able to live in the town I was born and earn a decent wage."

"If only that was how the world worked," said Sophie, pulling photographs from the case.

Near the bottom of the pile, Sophie pulled out a photograph of a woman and a child. Their smiling faces stared at the camera. Behind them fishing boats, creels and squat cottages lined a harbour. "This doesn't look like Lowestoft," said Sophie, turning the frame in her hands. On the back, in a faded scrawl, someone had written something. "Can you read this for me? Even with my reading glasses on, I can't make it out."

"God, Mum. You're getting so old."

"Shut up," said Sophie, whacking her son with a cushion. "Can you read it? What does it say?"

"It's not very clear..."

"Ah ha, so it's not just me then. Perhaps you need to get your eyes checked, too?"

"It's not that. It's so old and faded. Hang on, I think that's a P... Padstow, that's it. Padstow, 1939. Is that little girl Gran?"

Ben passed the photo to Sophie, and she looked at the small girl, curls framing her face, her mouth turned up in a smile. "Yes, it must be. Gran was born in 1935, so she'd be four years old in that photo. That must be her mum, Marnie, standing beside her."

Both Sophie and Ben silently gazed at the faces before them. The woman was beautiful, curls flying freely around her shoulders, her skirt blowing in the wind. Sophie felt a pang of sadness as she stared at her grandmother. She was smiling, but it was a tight smile which didn't reach her eyes.

"Hang on, look at this." Sophie pointed to a corner of the frame where the photograph had slipped. "I think there are more photographs behind this one. Can you get me a knife from the kitchen? The back's taped and stapled on, and I don't want to break the frame."

Ben sliced a neat line along the faded brown tape of the frame, then inched the staples out with a care that surprised Sophie. She leaned over him, waiting to see if her hunch was right and there were further photos hidden behind the first. Both were prepared for the possibility they were more harbour shots, but each hoped for something more.

"Go on, Mum, you do the honours," said Ben, holding out the frame.

Sophie inched the back off the frame and pulled out the photos behind it. "Oh wow. Look at this."

Ben took the photograph and squinted at the image. Four adults and a child stood beside a harbour. One woman held a baby in her arms. "Isn't that....?" said Ben, handing the photograph back to his mother.

"Yes, that's my granny, but the men..." said Sophie, pointing to the image before her. "Neither of those men is my grandfather."

"That's so strange. Surely if they'd gone to Padstow, it would have been together?"

"You'd have thought so. I can't think why they would have gone to Padstow unless it was for a holiday, perhaps? My grandad Bobby was a fisherman, but I don't think Frank ever was."

"A proper mystery then. Let's see what else is there," said Ben, taking the pile from Sophie. "Hang on, what's this?" Ben's fingers scrabbled around in the back of the frame and emerged holding a piece of jewellery.

As she leaned over Ben's shoulder, Sophie's eyes widened. "My God, it's a locket. Open it but be careful. It looks old."

Ben passed the locket to Sophie, who perched her reading glasses on the end of her nose, and carefully opened it, revealing two locks of hair. "This is so strange," she said. "Look, this one must belong to Mum as it's so blonde, but this one..." Her fingertip stroked a red curl, held together by a thin piece of ribbon.

"I knew there was some truth in what Gran was saying. She's doolally, but not so much she'd make up a sister. Why would Marnie have a locket with two locks of hair if she hadn't had another child? You are going to show Gran this, right?"

"I'll show it to the nurses first. Seeing this might really upset her. After all, we don't know whose hair this is, or if it belongs to the baby in that photograph. I'd say the most likely explanation is that the baby died, and no one ever spoke about it. It's how things were done in those days."

"Maybe Gran could tell us?"

"Maybe," said Sophie. She thought of the shell of her mother, sitting in a soulless room, unable to catch the thoughts flying around her head. "Maybe. Let's not get our hopes up, though."

Chapter 12

March, 2018

Elle stretched her arms up above her and felt the release of muscles that had been pulling long and hard all day. *Damn these staff shortages*, she thought, yawning widely and rubbing her eyes. It was gone midnight, the sky an inky blue peppered with stars. With the noise of punters fading as they staggered their way home, the night was quiet enough to hear the plopping of water as it nudged against the harbour's walls.

"See you tomorrow," Elle called behind herself, to where Jago was folding up umbrellas and stacking chairs.

"Bright and early."

"Don't remind me."

Elle wandered the short distance to the cottage, uninterested in the lights reflecting on the water, or the gentle chiming of a boat's metal chains. All she was interested in was her bed, and the moment her head hit the pillow could not come soon enough.

As she approached the cottage, Elle noticed a light was still on. Her pulse quickened. Grace always switched everything off before she went to bed. And she never, ever, stayed up after ten. Elle forgot her tiredness and broke into a run. At the back door, she fumbled with her keys, dropping them twice before finally slipping them into the keyhole.

On opening the door, Elle's worst fears were confirmed. The lightbulb flickered above the prone form of Grace. Her face had drained of colour, her right leg lay awkwardly beneath her.

"Grace," said Elle, dropping to the floor beside her mother. "Grace? Can you hear me?"

Tears of relief flowed as Grace let out a soft murmur.

"Oh, thank God," said Elle, bending her head so it was level with Grace's. "Can you tell me what happened?"

"Fell... on my way... to the bathroom."

"Oh God, I should never have left you alone. Can you sit up?"

Grace tried to lift herself, but her face screwed up in pain with the effort. Elle drew her phone from her pocket and dialled one of only two numbers she knew by heart. Jago answered on the second ring.

"What have you forgotten this time?" he asked, laughter in his voice.

"It's Grace. She's had a fall."

"Oh no. OK, don't worry, I'll be right there."

Elle wondered if Jago had even bothered locking up, for within two minutes of putting the phone down, he was crouched beside her on the kitchen floor.

"Have you phoned for an ambulance?" he asked.

"Yes. Just after I called you."

"Did they say how long it would take?"

"No. They just said the service was very busy, and they'd get to us as soon as they could."

Jago jumped up and filled a glass from the kitchen tap. Elle gently lifted Grace's head so she could take small sips. After laying her back on the floor, she ran upstairs and grabbed her patchwork quilt. She laid it over Grace, just as Grace had done every night when Elle was a child.

After half an hour on the floor, cramps and pins and needles forced Jago and Elle to their feet. "Shall I put the kettle on?" asked Jago, checking his watch.

"May as well," sighed Elle, looking at the clock on the wall.

"I could do with a cuppa if you're making one," croaked Grace.

Elle smiled down at her mother. "I'm sure that can be arranged. How are you feeling?"

"Sore. Very sore."

"And your head?"

"There's nothing wrong with my head, don't worry. I put my hands out to break my fall. Saved my head, but my wrists hurt like hell."

"Her head and neck seem fine," said Jago, having run gentle hands across Grace's body while they waited. "I think she's fine to have a pillow if you can fetch one? She may as well be comfortable if we're in for a long wait."

"Sure," said Elle, running up the stairs once more, and grabbing a pillow from Grace's room. "How did you know to check her over like that?" she asked, once Grace's head rested on the pillow.

"Did my lifeguard training while I was in Sydney. Comes in handy at times like these."

Elle felt a pang of sadness, and a sharp stab of anger. While she had been stuck at home nursing a broken heart, Jago had been off halfway around the world pretending he was in an episode of *Baywatch*.

"Here," said Jago, breaking into Elle's thoughts and placing a steaming cup of tea in her hands.

After helping Grace take a few sips, Elle and Jago leaned against the kitchen wall, legs pulled up, tea in their hands. Grace's breathing slowed and she let out a snore.

"Shouldn't we keep her awake?" asked Elle.

"Nah, she'll be fine. It's probably better if she rests. Her head is fine, so I can't see any harm in letting her sleep."

"I'm going to call and find out where that ambulance is. It's been an hour already."

After a call with a very apologetic woman, and no assurances that the ambulance would be on its way anytime soon, Jago suggested they take Grace to the hospital themselves.

"What if we hurt her more by moving her?"

"On balance, I think the risk to her health from lying on a cold kitchen floor all night is worse than the risk of moving her."

"If you're sure?"

"I'll get my van."

When Jago returned with his van, he pulled it as close to the cottage as he could and left the engine running. Crouching beside Grace, he scooped her into his arms. She woke, crying out in pain, and Elle rushed to her side to reassure her everything would be alright.

"Are you OK with her?"

"Yes, it's not as though she weighs much. Can you open the van doors? You can sit in the back with Grace and try to keep her as still as you can."

Elle ran outside and opened the doors to Jago's van. Despite his many invitations, she had never been inside. Even with the gravity of the situation they faced, she couldn't fail to notice the care that had gone into making the van habitable. She climbed into the back and waited for Jago to lay a sobbing Grace out on the bed.

"Let's get these cushions all around her. It will stop her from moving around too much."

With Grace secured by cushions, and Elle holding her hand, Jago jumped up into the driver's seat and began weaving the van through the narrow Padstow streets.

"Don't drive too fast," called Elle from the back. "It's pretty bumpy back here."

"I'll go as smoothly as I can," said Jago, slowing his speed.

After her initial discomfort, the rocking of the van soothed Grace and, like a small child, she soon fell asleep. Elle sat beside her, stroking her hair, repositioning cushions and watching for any signs her mother was in distress.

At two in the morning, the roads were empty, and they made it to the hospital in under an hour. Jago pulled the van up outside the entrance to Accident and Emergency, and left Elle with Grace while he went to find a doctor. Moments later, two men appeared with a stretcher, and maneuvered Grace onto it with the ease of experience.

Jago and Elle followed the nurses into a large waiting room. It surprised Elle how busy it was in the middle of the night. There were men passed out, old folk with cuts and bruises, and anxious-looking mothers clutching pale-faced children.

"I hope they don't keep her waiting in some corridor," whispered Elle.

"No, she's a priority, so I'm sure she will be seen quickly."

"Let's hope so," said Elle, yawning loudly.

"You'll be no good to anyone if you don't get some sleep," said Jago. "Why don't you have a lie-down in the van?"

"No, I want to stay here till I know how she is."

"Fine," said Jago. He removed his jumper, rolled it up, and placed it on his shoulder. "If you won't make use of my van, at least make use of my shoulder," he said.

Elle hesitated, then relented, leaning into the warmth of his neck and letting her eyes close.

At four, Elle woke to Jago shaking her shoulder. She rubbed her bleary eyes and saw a doctor standing over them.

"How is she?"

"Your mother is sleeping. We've taken some X-rays, and other than a broken wrist, she is fine. We'll keep her in for observation, but all being well, she should be able to go home tomorrow."

"Thank you. I'll wait here till she's able to come home."

"I would suggest you go home and get some rest. We'll do some more tests on her tomorrow, and these things can take some time. Go home, and we'll call you when she's ready to be collected. Do you have transport? We can arrange some for you if needed."

"I can collect her," said Jago.

"Are you sure?" Elle looked at him, too tired to refuse his offer.

"Of course I am. If I need to close the pub early, so be it. Some things are more important than profit."

"Thank you."

"We'll keep you updated. Here's the name of the ward your mother is on, and a telephone number should you need it."

"Thank you, doctor."

The doctor smiled and rushed off to deal with his long list of patients.

*

When Elle woke up, she saw they were outside her cottage.

"Do you want me to come in with you?" asked Jago.

"No, you've done enough already. Are you sure about going to pick Grace up from the hospital?"

"I wouldn't have made the offer if I didn't mean it. I need to get a couple of hours' kip in first. You sure you'll be OK by yourself?"

"Certain. You go home and get some rest." Elle opened the door of the van and jumped down. She waved to Jago as he switched the engine on and set off in the direction of his house.

Dawn had arrived, the birds filling the air with their chorus. Seagulls perched on masts, summoning the energy needed for their fight for visitors' scraps. With a weary sigh, Elle walked to the cottage and let herself in. The light was still on, still flickering, another thing to fix. Without Grace in it, the cottage felt strangely lifeless. Elle walked from room to room, wondering what they'd look like filled with another family's belongings.

Was holding on to the cottage the right decision? Elle imagined Grace leaving hospital and returning to one of the warm, modern bungalows she had mentioned. Wouldn't that make life so much easier? There'd be no curious tourists trying to see inside, no flickering light bulbs, God, even the toilet would be guaranteed to flush each time.

Elle pondered what was stopping them moving. Was her own stubborn refusal to sell up really for Grace's sake? Or was it a way of proving she could cope, not giving in to the easy option? Elle tried to imagine living in the cottage without Grace. It was impossible. The cottage was part of Grace, and Grace was part of the cottage. One without the other felt half-formed. No, whatever offer came through that door, whatever financial peril it drove them to, Elle would hang on to their home for as long as Grace was still around to live in it.

Chapter 13

March, 2018

Sophie opened the door to the sound of men laughing. She dumped her bags where she stood and opened the door to the kitchen-diner. Her two sons were sitting at the dining table, each with a beer in hand.

"Are we celebrating something?" Sophie asked, bending down to kiss each in turn before heading to the fridge to pour herself a glass of wine.

"No, just catching up," said Luke. He smiled at her, and she felt the familiar mix of love and pain. Unlike Ben, Luke was the spitting image of his father. The old familiar longing for her ex-husband returned, and she smothered it with the anger and hurt that had invaded her heart since the day he left.

"Any exciting news to share?" Sophie asked, joining her sons at the table.

"Luke's thinking of moving to Edinburgh."

"Really?" Sophie placed her glass down and stared at her eldest son. "What are you planning to do up there?"

"Dad called me the other day. Says he can get me a job with Rosie's firm."

Rosie. Sophie couldn't think of Will's new partner without conjuring the image of a Rosie she had taught the previous academic year.

The little girl had looked like an angel, flowing blonde hair, jade green eyes. All the boys wanted to kiss her, and all the girls wanted to be her best friend. The trouble with little Rosie was that inside, she was ugly. A spiteful child who tormented the children who so willingly flocked around her. Somewhere along the line, Sophie had assigned little Rosie's character to that of Will's partner. She'd never met Will's Rosie, but somehow, thinking of her as a prize class cow made Sophie feel a little better about things.

"What is it you'd do at Rosie's company?" Sophie couldn't keep the scorn from her voice as she mentioned the *other woman's* name.

"Dunno. Something office based. Dad reckons I could work my way up to decent money within a few years."

"Does he now?"

"Mum..." Ben's tone was a warning. He was reminding her of the promise she had made, to never slag Will off in front of the kids, to never stand in the way of a relationship with their father. Ben had little interest in staying in touch with Will, but she knew Luke missed his dad and was the only one of the three who still spoke to him regularly.

"It's you who's always banging on about us leaving Lowestoft," said Luke.

"No, I don't. I'd love you to stay here, I just worry there's not much excitement for young people anymore. Or jobs, for that matter."

"Exactly. I thought you'd be pleased for me."

"I am. I just don't want to see you get hurt."

"I'll be fine, Mum. I'm a grown man who can take care of himself."

Sophie spluttered into her wine. "You'd better learn to use a washing machine before you go. I can't see *Rosie* wanting to touch your dirty boxers."

Luke sighed and took a swig of his beer. Ben looked between Sophie and Luke. She caught his eye and shrugged an apology. Her youngest son had never liked tension and could sense an argument brewing long before an angry word was spoken.

"Hey, Mum," said Ben, "tell Luke about the photos."

"Photos?"

Sophie smiled at Ben, understanding his distraction technique and silently thanking him for his rescue. "We found some old photos of Gran's up in the loft. It seems her past may have been more interesting than we thought."

"Looks like she might have had a sister."

"A sister? So, we could have some long-lost aunt out there?"

"Possibly. Though if she's the same age as Gran, there's a strong chance she could be dead by now."

"Ever the optimist," muttered Ben.

Sophie grinned at him. "Why don't you grab the photos and show your brother?"

"You want to see them?"

"Sure," said Luke. "You never know, this long-lost aunt might be a rich old spinster who wants to leave everything to us in her will." Sophie tutted and Ben threw his brother a disapproving look. "Oh, come on, you can't say you haven't thought it. Imagine what we could do with a bit of cash. We could do this place up, for starters."

"There's nothing wrong with this house."

Luke laughed. "You should see Dad's new place. It's well posh, all glass and steel."

Before Sophie could think of a cutting retort, Ben appeared with the photos, and the moment passed. Luke wasn't as interested in the photographs as his brother was, but he attempted to appear so for Ben's sake.

"I've been searching up links to Padstow today. Did you know loads of Lowestoft fishermen used to go down there each year? Some took their families, which is probably how Gran came to be there with her mum and dad."

"So, it wasn't a family holiday, then?"

"No, I don't think so. Working people were mostly too poor for holidays in those days. From what I read, it seems like the fishing season ended here around December. The fishermen would follow the fish down to Cornwall. There were also tons of Scottish fishermen who came down here, too. For a while, Lowestoft was the place to be. It's pretty cool when you think about it."

"Yeah, if you're into fish," said Luke.

"Well, I think it's fascinating," said Sophie. "I have a vague memory of Gran telling me her mum was from up north somewhere. Do you think she could've come down with one of the fishermen? I thought Frank did something office based, but I could be wrong."

"There were plenty of women who moved around with the fishing industry too. Herring girls, they were called. I'd like to know more about it all, especially the connections to Cornwall."

"Maybe we should go down to Cornwall in the holidays and see what we can find out?"

"Yeah, that would be cool," said Ben. "I could try my hand at surfing while we're there."

"Remember when you tried skateboarding?" said Luke. "That didn't exactly end well."

Ben instinctively rubbed the wrist he had broken as a child. "Yeah, well, falling off a surfboard into water can't be as bad as falling off a skateboard onto concrete."

"Except you could drown," said Luke, his mouth curled in a teasing smile.

"That's enough, Luke. I'm sure Ben would be great at surfing. Let's have a look for places to stay later and keep going with the research you've been doing."

"Thanks, Mum."

"Anyway," said Sophie, turning back to Luke. "When are you planning on leaving us?"

"Dad says I can go any time. He's going to send me money for my train tickets, then I'll be off. I might go as soon as next week."

"Next week? But that's so soon."

"No time like the present. Anyway, I'd better get going. I'm meeting Becky for a drink tonight."

"And what does Becky think of your plans to move to Edinburgh?" Sophie couldn't imagine Luke's girlfriend would be thrilled at the thought.

"She's cool with it. She's decided to go to uni this year, anyway. Dad says Becky can come and stay anytime."

*

After Luke had gone, and Ben had retreated on his Xbox, Sophie poured herself another glass of wine and curled up under a blanket on an armchair by the window. Luke's news had shocked her. For all the times she'd wanted her boys to spread their wings, the reality felt very different. How long would it be before Ben was tempted by the generous offers of his father and abandoned her, too? Tears sprang from her eyes and Sophie wiped them on a corner of the blanket. What would be left for her once the boys moved on? She'd have to sell the house. It was too big for just her. And then what? The relentlessness of her job meant she had no time for friends. She had no hobbies, and no time to find a new relationship, even if she wanted one.

Sophie allowed herself a moment to wallow in self-pity. What a mess she'd made of things. Her eyes fell on the pile of photographs. Perhaps, if she had another family out there somewhere, it would help fill the void opening in her heart? In the meantime, looking into the Lowestoft-Padstow connection would be a project that could bring her and Ben closer.

She whispered her thanks to the group of people in the photograph, tracing her grandmother's features with her thumb. *What happened to you?* Sophie wondered. *What happened to the child?* Sophie couldn't shake the feeling that the story could not possibly end well. The most likely outcome was that the baby had died. But what of the baby's father? Was Grandad Frank the father, or had Marnie met someone else in Padstow? What had happened all those years ago that burdened Annie and continued to torment her long after other memories had faded?

Sophie wished she could talk to her mum. She wished she had asked more questions when her mind was still sharp. What a wasted opportunity. All those years they had bickered over nothing, when they could have been talking, really talking.

Sophie climbed out of the armchair and retrieved one of her school bags. In it, she found an empty exercise book. She turned to the first page and wrote QUESTIONS. It wasn't much of a plan, but perhaps if she wrote all the questions in her mind, she would find enough moments when Annie was lucid enough to answer them.

Chapter 14

1964

Dear Grace,

Enormous congratulations on your engagement! And please, never apologise for voicing your concerns to me, it's what I'm here for. I've moaned and groaned to you plenty over the years. I understand your worries about John, but it is normal for people to be a little tense in the run-up to a wedding. And as for the jealousy, you could take it as a sign of how much he loves you. Of course, I've never met the man, and you should listen to your instincts, just don't confuse doubts over John for fears over becoming a wife.

If a woman as flighty and foolish as me can find peace and happiness in a loving marriage, anyone can. All those years I spent searching for belonging and excitement and I've found both things with my Sam. Our marriage isn't perfect, (whose is?), but he's my home, my security, and in the ten years we've been together he's never stopped making me feel loved and telling me I'm the most beautiful woman in the world.

It may help to talk to John about your concerns. Often, a frank conversation is all that is needed to put both of your minds at rest. Or if you don't want to worry John, could you talk to Helen? I'm sure she'll know something isn't quite right and could offer a fresh perspective on things, especially as she must know John well by now.

My own rather dramatic news is that last week I was caught up in a fire at Tuttles department store. I was shopping for curtain fabric when a fire broke out in the furniture department. All us shoppers were evacuated along with eighty staff (I read that number in the newspaper). It took the fire brigade over an hour to get the blaze under control, while we watched on from across the road as a Lowestoft institution burned. Thankfully, no one was hurt, but goodness knows how long it will take to repair my favourite shop (not that I'd admit it's my favourite to Mum, as she worked in its rival Chadds when she was a girl!). There was a report about the fire in this week's paper, and apparently a pigeon sat on her nest of eggs throughout the debacle, only a few feet from the flames. She was black and scorched by the time the fire was put out, but alive. It's remarkable, particularly as I've met human mothers who don't care so greatly for their offspring!

Lowestoft, and in particular the Grit, continues to change rapidly. Recently, the 100-foot chimney of the gas works was demolished, and it's very peculiar to see a gap in the sky where the chimney once watched over us all. There was an article in this week's newspaper which described the Grit as 'a relic of less prosperous days' and this made me feel very sad, but I suppose life moves on.

One recent phenomenon I think is unique to Lowestoft is the latest fashion of the fisher boys. These young chaps arrive home from a trip with money in their pockets and head straight to the nearest tailor to get measured up for a new bespoke suit. So far, so ordinary, I hear you say. The funny thing about it all is that they try to outdo one another. No grey or brown suits for these fisher boys, they opt for the most outrageously loud colours and patterns they can find.

I saw one the other day when I was out doing my shopping. He couldn't have been older than eighteen and was prancing around in a bright purple suit with a wide black lapel. As he walked past, I noticed the back was pleated with contrasting insets and piping. Can you imagine! These lads will get a shock when they find themselves with a wife and kiddies to care for. Their pay packets won't stretch to fancy suits then. The funniest thing about this latest craze is the way Sam, Bobby and Frank discuss it. They really are like three grumpy old men, complaining about the youth of today and the '48-hour millionaires' as they're locally known.

My work at the factory is going well, and Sam has now taken full control over the Sally Ann after Bobby's retirement last month. Our bills are still high, not least because we're paying back the loan for the boat, but he's had a bump in wages since becoming skipper, which has eased the financial pressure.

Do you know, Grace, it's so good to pour my thoughts out like this. I hope my letters don't bore you, or offend you with my talk of money, but honestly, there is no one else I can speak so openly with. I hope you know how much I appreciate our correspondence.

How is Aunt Helen since her fall last month? Has she fully recovered yet? It's hard to see those we love growing frail. I've noticed a change in Frank since he retired. I thought retirement would put a spring back in his step, but he seems unsure what to do with himself when not tending to his garden. Honestly, the amount of veg he's producing is enough to feed the entire street and my kitchen counter is groaning with carrots and potatoes! But when in the house, he seems to wander around aimlessly and I can tell it irritates Mum, not that she admits it aloud.

Please send Aunt Helen my love, and pass on the photograph I've enclosed. It was taken at Frank's birthday dinner last month and I think he and Mum look rather distinguished! I'd better end this letter here, for I only recently returned from work and need to be getting on with supper. I'll look forward to hearing from you soon,

All my love,

Your friend,

Annie

Chapter 15

March, 2018

Elle scrubbed at the limescale around the taps. She grabbed a clean tea-towel and began furiously polishing the metal until it gleamed. In her fitful state of mind, cleaning seemed the only thing that could distract her from anxious thoughts.

When they'd spoken that morning, Jago had agreed to her taking a few days off. But a few days didn't solve the longer-term problem of how to care for Grace. While her wrist healed, and until the knee operation happened, Grace would need care. A lot of care. Elle couldn't risk her having another fall.

As she scrubbed and polished, selling the cottage was the only viable option to present itself. They could buy an elderly-friendly bungalow and have enough change left over to pay for regular carers. The thought broke Elle's heart, but she couldn't think of another way.

A car horn sounded, and Elle rushed outside to find Jago jumping out of his van. A grey-faced Grace sat in the passenger seat, clutching a brown paper bag filled with what Elle guessed to be medication.

"Do you need a hand?" Elle asked Jago.

"Nah, I can manage. I'm sure Grace could do with a cup of tea, though. Fancy putting the kettle on?"

"Yep."

Elle ran back into the kitchen and filled the kettle with water from the gleaming taps. She cast anxious glances out of the window, looking out for the familiar form of Grace. Elle was beginning to wonder if Jago did in fact need help when he appeared on the path, a frail-looking Grace clutching his arm.

Elle opened the door and ushered the pair inside. She waited for him to prop Grace up in a chair and tucked a blanket over her legs.

"No need for all this fuss," said Grace.

"There's every need," said Elle. "You gave us a fright the other night."

"Yes, I'm rather embarrassed about that," said Grace, picking at a loose thread on the blanket.

"Embarrassed? You've no reason at all to be embarrassed. You'd be fit as a fiddle if it weren't for your dodgy knee. Now this has happened, I'll write to our local politician again. God, I'll set up camp outside his office if I have to."

"That's my girl," said Grace, managing a weak smile.

Elle made the tea and set a cup down beside Grace.

"Do you know, I think I may be too tired to drink that? I don't suppose you'd help me upstairs, would you, Jago? I'm sure I'll be right as rain in no time, but today I could use some help."

"Of course," said Jago. "I just need to grab something from the van."

He ran out to his van and reappeared, carrying a large plastic contraption. "Now, don't be cross with me, Grace, but I thought this might be useful."

"Whatever is it?"

"It's the toilet from my van. Only a temporary measure, till you've got your strength back."

"Yes, I suppose that could come in handy."

Elle was shocked at how easily Grace agreed. A woman so proud should not be reduced to using a porta-potty, when the condition which left her so disabled was so easily remedied by one operation. "Are you sure? I don't mind helping you to the toilet when you need to go?"

"You need to work, love. Besides, it's not so different from the chamber pot Uncle Richard kept under his bed, is it?"

"No, I suppose not."

"Well then. Jago can haul me up the stairs, and you can have the pleasure of carrying my chamber pot." Grace managed to chuckle.

"This is clean, isn't it?" Elle whispered to Jago.

"Of course it's clean. What do you take me for?" He shook his head in mock dismay and moved to help Grace to her feet.

With Grace happily settled in bed, and the porta-potty within easy reach, Jago and Elle headed back to the kitchen table.

"What did they say at the hospital?"

"They gave her some strong painkillers for the wrist, but they'll also help with her knee. There were the usual apologies about backlogs, and the usual promises that it would be her turn soon. To be honest, I felt sorry for all the hospital staff. They all looked wrung-out, like they either needed a holiday or a week-long sleep."

"Thanks so much for collecting her."

"No problem. She's like family to me."

"She feels the same about you."

"Take as much time off work as you need. Have you thought longer term about the care she's going to need?"

"It's so hard to make plans when we don't know when her op will be. There'll be some recovery time afterwards, but once that knee is fixed, she'll be as independent as she ever was. I have been thinking about the cottage. It seems like we'd be mad not to sell."

"Where would you move to?"

"We'd stay in town. Get a bungalow maybe."

"This place will need a lot of work if you want to get a fair asking price."

"Yeah, but the location alone is enough to earn us big bucks."

"True. I can't imagine Grace living anywhere but here."

"Me neither."

"God, Elle. I'm so sorry you're having to deal with all this. It sounds like things were going so well for you in Bristol and now you're stuck here with an invalid mother and a crumbling home. It must be hard to keep your chin up."

"It is. How are your parents?"

"Great, as far as I know. Off on another cruise somewhere. I don't even bother asking where they're going these days, I'm just pleased to have the house to myself for a few weeks."

Elle laughed. "We make a fine pair. Middle-aged and still living with our parents. What would our younger selves think if they could see us now?"

Jago looked down at his tea. "My younger self would be amazed you're talking to me." He looked up and his eyes were sad.

"Yeah, well, life's too short to hold a grudge. I'm pleased we're friends again."

"Me too. Listen, Elle. Maybe now's not the time, but do you think... we'll ever be more than friends? Do you think you'll ever be able to forgive me for what I did to you?"

"I forgave you a long time ago. But it's not a case of forgiveness. It's about trust."

"And you still don't trust me? After all I've done to help you?"

"All you've done? So, helping Grace was just a way to get into my good books, was it?" Elle felt anger rising in her throat. She swallowed it down, aware her voice was loud enough to risk waking Grace.

"I can't believe you'd think that. Of course, that's not why I've been helping you. I've done it because I love you, Elle, and I care about Grace. I can't believe you'd think that about me." Jago scraped his chair back, tipped his tea down the sink, and left the room.

Elle heard the revving of his van engine and the screeching of tyres as he pulled away from the cottage. Her mind was a melting-pot of thoughts and feelings, a swirling mass of emotion that made it impossible to grip on to any one thought. She pulled the photos Grace had found from their envelope and stared at them. The present was too complicated to think about. The past was safer. Had these black-and-white faces sat around the very table she was sitting at now? Had they had arguments, misunderstandings, and feelings of despair? *Give up your secrets*, thought Elle, before getting up and pouring herself a second cup of tea.

Chapter 16

March, 2018

Sophie was reading *We're Going on a Bear Hunt* for the thousandth time when the head teacher walked into the classroom. There was a time, early in her career, where the presence of a head teacher would cause children to still, straighten their backs and cease any mischief. These days a visitor to the class reignited the hyperactivity she had spent the past half-hour trying to calm.

"Settle down, children," said Miss Constantine, her feeble, ineffectual simper inaudible above the squirming rabble on the carpet.

"Quiet!" Sophie's own voice held an authority the head teacher lacked, and most of the children stilled, mirroring her raised hand. Only Zayn and his cronies continued to mutter and fidget. "How can we help you, Miss Constantine?" Sophie asked.

"I wonder if we could have a quick chat," said the head teacher.

"Beth, can you finish the story for me, please?"

"Sure," said Sophie's teaching assistant and friend. She had worked with many teaching assistants over the years, but none came close to Beth. She was one of the few things which made the job bearable these days.

Sophie followed her boss out into the corridor. From behind closed doors came the sounds of singing, the raised voices of teachers trying to be heard over their unruly rabble, and the whistle of an overenthusiastic P.E. coach.

Miss Constantine sighed. "Let's go to my office. We might hear ourselves think in there."

They walked down the long corridor, the smell of fried food filling the air around them. Hadn't a celebrity chef tried to make school dinners healthy not that long ago? Sophie had seen so many 'new initiatives' in her time, she did nothing but yawn with each recycled rabbit pulled out of the hat.

Inside her office, Miss Constantine sat down on a sofa and motioned for Sophie to take the armchair opposite. *Hmm,* thought Sophie, *so this isn't a bollocking. That would be done from behind the desk.* Miss Constantine twiddled her fingers and Sophie longed to shake her. The woman looked barely old enough to be out of school herself. All these young, ambitious career teachers made Sophie feel old and jaded. They strode in with promises to 'turn the school around', whilst regurgitating the same ideas she'd heard thousands of times before. Was there no one original left in education? It wasn't rocket science. In fact, Sophie could teach these managers a thing or two about the basics of running a school. If she could be bothered, which she couldn't.

"Was there something specific you needed to discuss with me?" asked Sophie, unable to bear the twiddling fingers and simpering smile a moment longer.

"Yes. I'm afraid I have some rather bad news. We received a call from your mother's nursing home. I'm afraid she has been taken into hospital."

"Hospital? What's happened?" *And why did you waste a whole five minutes before telling me?* Sophie shouted in her head.

"They think she's had a mini stroke, but the hospital will tell you more. I can cover your class for the rest of the day, as I'm sure you're anxious to get to the hospital."

"Thank you," said Sophie, wondering if she was too harsh with her boss. At least she had a heart, unlike some head teachers she'd worked with in the past.

She sprinted back along the corridor and grabbed her coat and bag from her classroom cupboard. She gave a rushed explanation to Beth, accepted a hug in return, then ignored the curious glances and questions from the nosier children as she hurtled back down the corridor.

Once at her car, Sophie allowed herself a moment to calm down. She leaned against the cool metal roof, allowing the news to sink in, whilst pushing away thoughts about the future. There was little point worrying until she knew what they were dealing with. She pulled her phone from her bag and called Ben.

"Mum? What's wrong? Why aren't you in class?"

"Your Gran's been taken ill. She's at the James Paget hospital."

"I'm coming with you. Can you pick me up?"

"I'll be there in five. Make sure you're ready." She clicked off the phone, put it back in her bag, and climbed into the car. Her hands gripped the steering wheel, trying to stop their shaking. Annie couldn't die now, she just couldn't. Not when there was the possibility of finding her long-lost sister. That would be too cruel a twist of fate.

By the time Sophie reached her house, Ben was waiting outside, a bag in hand.

"What have you got in there?" Sophie asked as he climbed into the car.

"Some stuff for Gran. A magazine, some chocolates, a book I found in the charity shop."

"How did you have time to get all that?"

"I was going to visit her at the nursing home, so I already had the bag packed. I doubt it will be much use to her now, but you never know. Any update on how she's doing?"

"No, nothing yet."

"Well, let's hope no news is good news."

"Yes, let's."

They drove to the hospital in silence, Sophie grateful for the presence of her son beside her. He reminded her of her dad, a good, kind man. It had been twenty long years since her father had died, and Sophie still missed him every day. Annie had been different while her husband was still alive. They'd had fun, been able to talk. She had seemed happy. Sophie could trace her mother's slow decline right back to the day her father died. It was as though part of Annie had died too, and however much cajoling and distraction Sophie tried, she could never get back the Mum she had known.

At the hospital, a distracted receptionist directed them to the ward they needed, and they walked the long corridors, Ben's trainers squeaking against the newly-mopped floor. An efficient, smiling nurse met them by the door to the ward. She updated them on Annie's condition, and Sophie's shoulders relaxed as she heard her mother was sitting up in bed eating a piece of toast. Ben placed an arm around her shoulder and gave it a reassuring squeeze.

Sophie was relieved to see Annie had a bed by the window. The view wasn't the best, but at least trees lined the car park, and Annie could look out at the sky. As the nurse had promised, she was sitting up in bed, munching on toast, while a lady in the next-door bed chatted about a love for oranges.

"And who is this handsome young man?" Annie asked as Ben pulled a chair up beside her bed.

"It's me, Ben, your grandson," he said, taking her hand in his.

Annie's face flickered with confusion, her eyes scrunching as she searched for a memory. Her features softened, her lips curling into a broad smile. "Ben! How lovely of you to visit me. I don't know why all these old fogies are in my bedroom. Be a love and ask them to leave, would you?"

"Mum," said Sophie, leaning forward in her chair. "You had a funny turn and you're in the hospital."

"The hospital? Don't be silly, love." Annie tutted and took another bite of her toast. "You tell her, Ben. Sophie has got herself in a muddle."

Sophie could almost see Ben weighing up his options. At least Annie was calm. Was it better to let her remain confused, or should he tell her the truth? In the end, he opted for neither option. "I've brought you some presents," he said, lifting his bag onto the bed.

"Oh, you're a good boy. What have you got here then?"

"I know this one's your favourite," said Ben, laying a copy of *Good Housekeeping* magazine on Annie's lap. She held out her plate of toast for Sophie to hold and began flicking through the pages. For several minutes, she was absorbed, unaware of anyone around her, even Ben.

A doctor entered the ward. He made for Annie's bed and her eyes lit up at the sight of him. "Goodness me, two handsome men beside my bed. Whatever will Sam say?" Annie giggled like a schoolgirl, and Sophie's eyes filled with tears. She wouldn't tell her Sam died twenty years ago. She'd tried that before, and each time grief hit Annie with full force.

"I promise not to do anything Sam would disapprove of," said the doctor, throwing Annie a winning smile. She giggled again. "Do you know why you're here, Mrs Thorn?"

"Of course, dear. I had a funny turn. An ambulance came and here I am."

Sophie raised an eyebrow and caught Ben's eye. He shrugged. There was no point trying to guess the workings of Annie's mind.

"Good. Well, I'm pleased to say all your test results are looking good. We'll keep you here for a few more hours just to be sure, then you'll be free to go home."

"Oh goody," said Annie, clapping her hands.

"Can I have a quick word?" asked Sophie.

"Of course. We can talk in the relatives' room. Could you give me half an hour? I need to finish my ward rounds, then I'll be free for a chat."

"No problem."

The doctor headed off to his next patient. Annie lost interest in her magazine and took a bite of the chocolate from Ben's bag. "Did I ever tell you about my time in Padstow?" she asked Ben.

He cast a look at Sophie and they both leaned forward. "No, I don't think you did."

"I was very young when we went. It was my first time on a train. Can you believe it?"

Ben laughed. "That must have been exciting."

"Exciting? I was sick as a dog. My poor mother, what a journey that would've been for her."

"I bet."

"Of course it was steam trains back then. Took us a whole day. I remember we had jam sandwiches and a flask of tea. Funny what you remember, eh?"

Sophie was amazed Annie could remember anything at all. "How long did you live there?"

"Will I ever get fed in this place?"

"Pardon?"

"Will I ever get fed in this place? I'm starving. Don't they have cooks in hospitals these days?"

"Here's your toast, Mum."

"Toast? I don't want toast. I want a decent hot meal."

"Gran, you were telling us about Padstow."

"Was I?" Annie looked at Ben with rheumy eyes. "Don't know why I'd rake up all that. Best left in the past, if you ask me."

Sophie suppressed a sigh. "You were talking about jam sandwiches on the train."

"Jam sandwiches? No, I want a good, hot meal. A pie, or bangers and mash. Why won't they feed me? What kind of place is this? When are you taking me home? I need a bit of sea air and I'll be right as rain."

"The doctor said you'll be going home soon."

"Good. I hope that no-good husband of yours won't be cooking again. He burns everything. Can't boil an egg, that man."

Tears filled Sophie's eyes. Old age could be a cruel mistress. It broke her heart to see her sharp-witted, sharp-tongued mother reduced to a mass of confusion and muddle. She looked at the small woman in the bed and wished she could turn back the clock to happier days. Would Annie tell them more about her time in Padstow, or had those memories been corroded by the disease that crept its way into her mind, creating cracks and crevices until memories fell away, lost forever?

Chapter 17

1967

My dear Grace,

I haven't been able to stop thinking about your last letter since it arrived yesterday, but it has taken me until now to find the courage to reply. I hold myself partly responsible for your situation, as I remember my words of encouragement when you voiced perfectly reasonable concerns about John. My only excuse is I was blinded by my own happy marriage, and wrongly mistook your concerns for pre-wedding nerves.

But, Grace, I of all people should have known better. It wasn't so long ago I fell for a man who could have ruined my life if it weren't for Sam stepping in to help me. I know how easy it is to fall for a man's charms, how easy it is to be manipulated, to question your own mind.

As requested, I shall send this letter to Aunt Helen's address, so John doesn't find it, but that alone rings alarm bells. It is wrong that he has made you cut off everyone in your life who cares for you. The only blessing about Aunt Helen's illness is it means he can't stop you from seeing her.

I don't say this lightly, Grace, but you need to get away from him. If you haven't already, tell Aunt Helen the truth about how he treats you. I know you worry about making her health worse, but she will know something is wrong, and the guessing and fretting will be far worse for her than the truth.

There is no failure in divorce if the alternative is staying married to a monster, and from what you have described, I'm in no doubt John is a monster. I know the law changed not that long ago, but divorce will still be a hard step to take. You need to visit the doctor and show him your injuries, and get them added to your medical records. Without evidence, it will be a much longer and more difficult process. My friend Mary went through something similar last year, and because she had no evidence of any injury, the whole process was extremely hard for her. In the end, she admitted to adultery she hadn't committed just to move things on. Many of her friends who sided with her husband ostracized her, thinking he was the injured party. Don't fall into that same trap, Grace. Get the evidence you need and don't see asking for help as weakness.

I'm sorry if my advice sounds extreme, but John won't change, and if you stay with him, you could end up with a child together, which will make the whole situation worse. Besides the other measures I've suggested, talk to Jack. I know he can have a short fuse, but if you make it clear he needs to stay calm for your sake, he will. Arrange for him to come to the house when John is at work and help you pack a bag. Then, stay at Aunt Helen's cottage. I suggest Jack stays with you, at least until things have calmed down.

The main thing, Grace, is you make yourself safe and get out of John's way. Please write to me as soon as you're able to let me know you are alright. And if you need to and can get away for long enough, I'll write my telephone number at the bottom of this letter, and you can call me anytime.

All my love and prayers,

Your friend,

Annie

Chapter 18

March, 2018

Somehow, Elle had found enough locals willing to help Grace to make a rota. Grace hated the thought of being cared for, but conceded that Elle must work, and in the short term, she would need help. The volunteers were mostly from the WI and had agreed to pop in for a cup of tea at regular intervals. It wasn't the most demanding role, and, unlike Grace, Elle felt no qualms in accepting their help.

Besides volunteers, an angry letter to the council had secured the assistance of a paid carer. Each morning and evening, Elle greeted the enthusiastic Tasha. The girl made Elle feel old. Tasha was young enough to be her daughter, but what she lacked in years and experience, she made up for in enthusiasm.

Grace had taken to Tasha from the start. Elle wondered if anyone could fail to warm to the broad, open-faced innocence of the carer. Each morning, Tasha appeared to help Grace dress and wash. Each evening, she returned to help Grace with her bedtime routine. There was no side to the girl, no hint of embarrassment as she dealt with the more intimate aspects of her role.

The arrival of Tasha had returned the sparkle to Grace's eye. Elle felt she owed the girl far more than the measly minimum-wage the council paid her. With no funds to top up her salary, Elle tried to find other ways to show her gratitude. When she had offered more cups of tea than was humanly possible to drink, she suggested Tasha and her friend come for a night out in the pub, using Elle's staff discount. She also cleared out her wardrobe, offering Tasha cast-offs that because of their expensive brands, Elle would never have call to wear while living with Grace.

Tasha's arrival also prompted an inescapable truth for Elle. She would have to return to work. Jago had signed off on her two weeks' leave via text message, and she hadn't seen him since the day he had brought Grace home.

"How are you feeling about going back to work?" asked Grace the morning of Elle's return.

"I'm worried about leaving you."

"What tosh. You're worried about facing Jago. Don't be using me as an excuse."

"Sometimes your sharp mind is a right pain in the bum," said Elle, sighing as she laid a cup of tea down on Grace's bedside cabinet. "Things were awkward the last time I saw him."

"I know."

"You know? How?"

"For starters, I heard you rowing the day I came back from hospital. Then I prised the details out of him when he visited me."

"Jago was here?"

"Yes."

"But when? I've barely left the house the past two weeks!"

"He popped in while you were out at the supermarket."

"Did he now?" muttered Elle.

"I must say, my girl, I'm rather ashamed of the way you spoke to him. Jago's a good man. You need to see him as he is now, not as the spotty teenager who made a poor decision and broke your heart."

"Jago was never spotty."

"You know what I mean. Don't we all make poor decisions in our lives? Look at you. I bet you didn't expect to be back living with your mother at forty. You've spent the past twenty years trying to avoid getting hurt, but at this rate, you'll end up an old spinster."

"You really know how to build a girl up, don't you?"

Grace laughed. "Sometimes it's a mother's job to deliver a few home truths. Now, shouldn't you be getting ready for work?"

"I don't start for another two hours."

"I know, but you want to go in there looking your best. And besides, you'll need a bit of time to work on your apology."

Elle sighed and left Grace to her tea. Up in her bedroom, she lay back on the bed, staring at the water-stained ceiling. Should she apologise to Jago? Probably. She hadn't been rational that day, and regardless of his feelings, he was her boss, so it was important to keep him on side.

A smell of damp wafted from the drawers as Elle opened them to find her work clothes. She sprayed some perfume on her T-shirt and jeans in the hope it would mask the musty smell acquired by everything in the cottage.

Elle pulled up her jeans and went to do up the button. No joy. She studied herself in the mirror. Her once flat stomach now bulged slightly, the jeans refusing to meet around her. *Great*, thought Elle. As if she didn't have enough to worry about, she was also now developing middle-aged spread. With her open button hidden by a belt, Elle called Jago.

"Hi, I wondered if we could meet up before my shift to clear the air?"

"OK. It's quiet now, so I can probably get away for half an hour. Do you want me to come to yours?"

"No. Tasha will be here any minute, and between her and Grace we won't get a word in edgeways."

"OK, how about the harbour?"

"Yes, let's meet outside mine and go for a walk."

"Sounds good. See you in five."

Jago put down the phone, and Elle checked her reflection in the mirror. It was just as well she wasn't trying to impress him, for her face screamed with worry and exhaustion. The purple rings beneath her eyes sat stark against her pale skin. Even her freckles looked as if they couldn't be bothered to make much of an appearance.

"I'm off early," called Elle, pausing on the stairs to check Grace had heard. "Do you need anything before I go?"

"No, don't worry. Tasha will be here any minute."

"OK. See you later. Love you."

"Love you too."

On her way out of the house, Elle bumped into Tasha. The girl's face lit up in a beaming smile, but she had bags under her eyes to match Elle's own.

"Hi, Tash. You OK? You look as tired as I do."

"Thanks," said Tasha, grinning. "I'm all good, just a bit knackered. The agency is so short-staffed I got roped in to a night shift last night."

"Oh no, you must be exhausted! I can sort Grace this morning if you need a break?"

"No, don't worry. I've got a few hours gap once I've seen to Grace, so I'll head off for a kip then."

"You're an angel."

"Tell that to my boss."

"I will," laughed Elle, feeling a rush of gratitude for the young girl. "I'm off, but shout if you need me. Grace seems good today, so leave early if you need to."

"Thanks, see you."

Elle waved and walked to the front of the cottage, leaning against the wall crying out for a lick of paint. She saw Jago before he saw her and felt a fluttering in her chest. It was silly to be nervous, but she felt wrong-footed. She had got used to the apologies coming from him and it didn't sit right that it was now her turn.

"Alright?" asked Jago.

"Yeah good. Shall we walk up towards the beach?"

"Fine by me, if we don't go far. I need to be back in about half an hour."

"Sure."

They followed the curve of the harbour in silence. It was only as they began climbing the hill that Elle spoke.

"I owe you an apology. I was a right cow to you the other day. But I didn't mean the things I said, I was just tired and stressed about Grace. I shouldn't have taken it out on you."

"Apology accepted."

Elle stopped and looked at Jago. "That's it?"

Jago shrugged. "Yeah. I mean, do you want me to hold a grudge?"

"No. I just thought you'd be more annoyed with me."

"Nah, I knew you were stressed about Grace. I was an easy target. I'm not going to lie, it hurts to know you don't trust me, but I've only got myself to blame, haven't I?"

Elle wasn't sure what to say to that, so they continued up the hill in silence. "Sorry, can we stop for a bit?"

Jago looked at Elle, his eyes full of concern. "Are you OK?"

"Just a bit out of breath. I'm so out of shape." Elle tried to laugh, but her heart pounded in her chest, and she tried to control her shaking legs.

"Sit down for a bit. We don't need to get all the way to the top."

Elle sat down beside him on a bench. “Sorry, I don’t know what’s wrong with me. I’m so unfit these days.”

“Hmm, maybe. But you spend all day running round the pub and I’ve never noticed you struggle before.”

“It must be these last two weeks stuck in the cottage, then.”

“Yeah, it’s probably nothing, but I’d like you to see a doctor.”

“That’s overreacting.”

“Elle, look how far we’ve come. You’d normally be able to run this far, and here you are, struggling to walk it. Please, for my peace of mind.”

“You shouldn’t worry so much.”

“I’m your boss, you know, health and safety and all that. You might have picked up a bug from somewhere. Are you sure you’re OK to work today?”

“Yes, I’m fine. Come on, let’s keep walking. I’d like to make it to the top.” She ignored the feeling of dizziness and got to her feet. Perhaps, if she could pretend she was fine, she would be. Grace needed her fighting fit. The last thing they needed was two invalids in the house.

Chapter 19

March, 2018

Sophie sat curled in the broad armchair beside Annie's bed, a copy of *Frenchman's Creek* in her hands. It had been a difficult couple of weeks since Annie returned to the nursing home. She had been agitated, even more confused than usual, with sudden outbursts of anger directed at whoever was close at the time. Apart from reruns of detective dramas, the only thing which soothed her old, battered mind was being read to.

It had been Ben's idea to read books set in Cornwall. His argument had been that they might jog Annie's memory sufficiently to recall more of her own Cornish adventure. So far, it hadn't worked, yet with each sentence Annie's face grew a little less creased.

Sophie finished the chapter and set the book down. Annie lay still, the blankets on her chest rising and falling with her breath. Sophie tiptoed around the bed and lifted a vase of flowers that had seen better days. The petals of the roses were crimping and turning brown, the water beneath a sludge colour emitting a slight odour. She crept into the ensuite, tipped the stagnant water away and threw the flowers out of the window. She'd ask Ben to bring fresh ones with him tomorrow.

"I'm sorry," came a whisper from the bed.

"Mum?" said Sophie, rushing back to her chair.

"I'm sorry. I shouldn't have gone near the water, Mum."

"Mum, it's OK. I'm here. It's Sophie, remember?"

Annie's eyes remained closed, her face twisted as she relived a memory from long ago. "I'm sorry he shouted at you, Mum. It was my fault. All my fault. I just wanted to see the water, get closer to the boats."

"Mum," said Sophie, giving Annie's hand a light tap. "Mum, it's OK. It's just a dream."

A tear slipped from the corner of Annie's closed eye. "I'm all wet, Mum. I'm all wet from the sea. I'm sorry. It's my fault. All my fault he's cross. I'm wet, Mum. I'm soaked to the skin."

Sophie lifted the blankets covering Annie. The pad beneath her was damp, an acrid smell of ammonia floating up from it. Sophie left the room, searching the corridor for a nurse.

"Everything alright, love?"

Sophie approached the smiling nurse and explained the situation.

"Ah, don't worry, these things happen. We'll have her sorted out soon enough."

The nurse went rummaging in a cupboard, returning with armfuls of clean sheets.

"Does this happen often?" asked Sophie, as they made their way back to Annie's room.

"More so since the stroke. We've tried to get her to wear her special pants, but she won't hear of it. Kicks up a right old fuss every time they come near her."

"Sounds like Mum," said Sophie, smiling at the nurse in sympathy.

"She's a fighter, all right. I've seen many residents decline fast after a mini stroke. But not our Annie. She's frailer than she was, but the feistiness is still there, more so even."

"I'm sorry about that. She can be an old battle-axe when the mood takes her."

The nurse laughed. "Trust me, I'd take a hundred Annies over the ones who fade away, any day. It breaks my heart when they slip off without a fight. Can't blame them though, I suppose. I wouldn't want to end up in a place like this."

"No, me neither," said Sophie, feeling a surge of guilt for dumping her mum in a home.

"Sorry, love. That was insensitive of me. Your mum needs the care we provide. I wasn't suggesting you should do it all yourself. I just mean it's a sad way to go, away from home, away from family. But sometimes there's no choice. At least we've got a good team here. You should see some of the places I've worked. The stories I could tell..."

Sophie was grateful they'd reached Annie's room, as she could do without stories of death and hopelessness. Annie seemed to have calmed, her memories, her dream forgotten. She lay curled on one side, sleeping like the child she'd once been.

"She's out for the count, poor soul," said the nurse, lifting the blankets to inspect the damage. "Her nightdress has risen and escaped the worst. I reckon we can change the pad and give her some fresh knickers without waking her, if that's OK?"

"Whatever you think's best."

"You sit beside her. She'll need you to keep her calm if she wakes up."

The nurse cleaned up after Annie with practised efficiency. A couple of times Annie stirred, but at no point did she wake fully, and within minutes the nurse was throwing the used pad into a bin and tucking blankets back around her legs.

"I'll change all the bedding tomorrow, but I think for now our girl needs her sleep."

"Thank you."

"All part of the service. Why don't you head home, love? Your mum's fine, kand if she slept through all that, she's unlikely to wake till morning."

*

By the time Sophie arrived home, it was nearing seven. Her stomach growled and her heart sank at the thought of having to cook. As she walked through the front door, a delicious smell of fried food and spices hit her.

"Ben?"

"Yeah?" Ben walked through to the hallway, a tea-towel slung over his shoulder.

"Have you cooked?"

A guilty look flickered across his handsome features. "Not exactly. I have got dinner though. I went out and picked us up a Chinese when I got your message to say you were on your way back."

"Thank you," said Sophie, walking to her son and throwing her arms around him.

"Hey, what's that for? It's only Chinese. Are you OK?"

"I'm just worried about Gran, that's all."

"How was she?"

"Same as ever. She wet the bed while I was there and seemed to be having bad dreams. The nurse was great. Despite my misgivings, I think she's in the right place."

"Of course she is," said Ben, tightening his arms around Sophie. "Now, are we going to eat? I'm starving."

"Me too," she said, letting him go and following him into the kitchen.

With plates piled high, they carried their dinner through to the sitting room. "Shall we break with convention and turn on the TV?" Sophie asked.

"Yeah, but can we have a talk first?"

"Sure. What's up? Are you planning to abandon me, too?" Sophie laughed, but the thought scared her. What would she do if she were left all alone?

"No, I wouldn't live with Dad in a million years."

"What is it then?"

"I've got a job."

"A job? You mean a gig somewhere?"

"No, I mean a proper job. Not that I'm abandoning the sound engineering, I'll still do that when I can."

"Well, where is this job, then?"

"At Gran's nursing home."

"What?"

"I've been chatting with the staff when I visit Gran. Sometimes I chat to the other residents too. It was the manager who approached me. I'd never thought of working in the care sector before."

"Then what's brought on the sudden change of heart?"

"Well, after I spoke to the manager, I got thinking. All this stuff going on with Gran has made me realise I want to do more to help."

"You already help. The amount you visit, it's practically your second home. How many times has your brother visited Gran in the last six months? Once? Twice? Don't ever think you don't do enough."

"Yeah, but there's more I could do if I was trained. Not just for Gran, but others like her."

"I think it's a very admirable ambition, but you know what they pay for those kinds of jobs?"

"Diddly squat."

"Exactly. I'd think hard before going into it. It's a lot of work for little reward."

"Little financial reward maybe, but I'd be rewarded in other ways. Anyway, you're a fine one to talk. If I added up all the hours you work teaching, you'd be taking home less than the minimum wage."

Sophie laughed. "Fair point. So, what will your job entail?"

"Well, obviously, I've got no training, so I'll be starting at the bottom. Quite literally, if you get my meaning. I'll be up to my elbows in adult nappies most of the time, I expect. It means I won't be able to afford to move out for a while, though. Sorry about that."

"You know what? For all my moaning, I love having you here. Especially these last few months. I've seen a real change in you since you started helping more with Gran. I think the nursing home will be lucky to have you."

"Thanks, Mum," said Ben, scooping a mouthful of food onto his fork. "You know, I may go into nursing eventually. It's something I've been thinking about, but I feel I need some experience in the care sector before I take that leap."

"Well, whatever you do, I'll be proud of you." Sophie turned on the TV but kept stealing glances across to Ben. Was her son finally growing up? She felt a surge of pride in the young man sitting by her side. However many times she failed in life, it seemed she'd got one thing right.

Chapter 20

1967

Dear Grace,

Thank you for your last letter, it's put my mind to rest because I've been worrying about you these past couple of weeks. It sounds as though Jack did a fine job of scaring off John, but I'm sorry you had to go through the ordeal of him turning up at Aunt Helen's.

I know getting the police involved must have been a difficult step, and you're right that without Jack beside you they may not have taken your concerns seriously, but thank goodness they did.

Did I ever tell you about my first meeting with Jack? We'd just arrived in Padstow, and I was very young. Mum took me to look at the harbour and I ended up falling in the water. I could have drowned, but Jack rescued me, then gave Mum a tongue-lashing for letting me out of her sight. So, it seems he's rescued both of us now, and it sounds as if that gruff side has come into its own in his dealings with John.

How has Aunt Helen been coping with all this upset? I remember her as a tough woman who takes everything in her stride, but I also remember her constant worry over Jack being out at sea and I'm sure that worried streak extends to you. It must be such a relief to her to have you between her own four walls where she can keep an eye on you. Please send her my love.

The thing to do now is to take some time to recover from all this. The divorce will probably be a lengthy process, and you're going to need to be fighting fit to get through it. Let Jack and Helen take care of you and be kind to yourself as you rebuild your life.

You know I'm always here should you need to talk to someone. Please keep me informed about how you're getting on. I've enclosed some of my recent knitting projects as summer is quickly slipping into winter and I remember the terrible storms you get down there. The pair of socks is for Jack, and the two sets of scarves and gloves are for you and Aunt Helen.

It has been good to take up knitting after so long and reminds me of when I first came to Padstow and Aunt Helen put a pair of knitting needles in my hands almost as soon as I'd arrived. We used to knit items for soldiers fighting in the war and by the end of my time in Padstow, I'd got rather good. These days I'm very rusty, but it's coming back to me slowly. I sometimes take my knitting over to Mum and Frank's and Mum tells me stories from her childhood on the island. I'm not sure I'll ever be able to go back there thanks to memories involving a certain Blaine McCloud, especially not with Sam, but I love hearing about the women knitting ganseys for men at sea, and Mum's stories connect me to past generations.

Speaking of the island, I'm not sure you'll remember them, but my Uncle Jimmy and Aunt Clara visited us last week. I hadn't seen them for quite some time, and it was a shock to see how much they'd aged, but they seem happy. In recent years, running the hotel has become too much for them, and they've now sold it and moved to a small cottage on the island. They seem as adventurous as ever, frequently travelling up to Edinburgh to take in a show, and to come and visit us down here, of course, but I'm not sure how many more years of gallivanting they'll manage.

Anyway, I shall leave my letter here. I hope my attempts at knitting provide some comfort during these difficult days, and you know you can write to me at any time,

All my love,

Your friend,

Annie.

Chapter 21

March, 2018

Sophie stepped out of the front door and found herself almost knocked to her feet. Bullets of rain tore at her skin, a fierce north wind yanking at her clothes. She set her bag down beside her and zipped her coat until it poked at her chin. From her bag, she grabbed a woollen hat Annie had made years ago and tugged it down over her ears.

Across the road, the sea swelled in anger, plumes of spray fighting their way to the edges of the sea wall. Thoughts of sandcastles and sea-swims were a distant memory. The beach was being consumed by a tide ready to fight. Even the hardiest swimmers had taken the day off and the scene before her was devoid of human life.

Only the gulls were hardy enough to brave the beach. They skittered along on changeable gusts, their cries barely audible above the howling north-easterly. Sophie wondered whether they were fighting the wind or revelling in it. How would it feel to be free to take off whenever you chose? She sighed, picked up her heavy school bag, buried her head in the wind, and made for her car.

In the few steps between the house and the car, Sophie became soaked to the skin. She climbed into the driver's seat, adjusted the rear-view mirror, and let out a barking laugh. She looked as though she'd had several buckets of water thrown over her head. Scrabbling around the car, Sophie found an old hoodie of Ben's and used it as a towel. Her plastered-down curls bounced back, freed from the water that had weighted them.

With a surge of reluctance, Sophie clicked the key around and started the car. The children would be wild today. They always reflected the weather, with their fundamental ties to nature that by adulthood had fractured. If it was windy, they'd be riled up like angry beasts. If it was hot, their sweaty faces spoke of lethargy, if it was rainy they'd be like caged animals, desperate to get out. Rain and wind combined signalled a tough day ahead.

"I'm getting too old for this," said Sophie to her car, eyeing the bag filled with paperwork that had kept her up until the small hours. The thermos at the top was tempting, but her lengthy to-do list wouldn't see to itself, and there were no elves on hand to get the classroom ready without her.

Sophie pulled into the school car park and parked alongside the only other car. The head teacher wouldn't arrive till eight-thirty, a privilege of being in management, Sophie supposed. By the time she'd hauled her bags into her classroom, the wall clock showed it was seven-thirty. Sophie set her bags down and raised her arms in a yawn.

Beyond the windows, the world lay in darkness. Sophie wondered if it would ever get light on such a miserable day. Rain pounded a drumbeat against the glass, the windows rattling against their frames. Sophie poured coffee from her flask and watched as the steam danced its way towards the ceiling. She thought back to the days when there'd been time to have a coffee in the staffroom at break. In the good old days, she'd known what a lunchbreak was.

By eight, the hall outside her classroom was noisy with the hungry mouths of the breakfast club. By nine, her class was destroying the activities Sophie had carefully laid out only an hour before. At twelve

Sophie tried to eat a salad at her computer while children yelled around her during wet play. By three-thirty, she was dead on her feet, dreading the prospect of another pointless staff meeting. At six, she finally left the school building and headed for home.

"Ben?" Sophie called as she walked through the front door.

Ben poked his head around the kitchen door. "You're late again."

"We were told at the staff meeting there'll be an inspection this week."

"Oh."

"Yes. Oh."

"Look, dinner's going to be another half-hour. Do you want me to run you a bath?"

"Who are you and what have you done with my son?"

"I'm practising."

"Practising?"

"Yeah, for my new job. I have my induction day tomorrow."

"Of course you do. Sorry, I'd forgotten. I know this may not sound very appealing, but do you fancy a quick stroll along the front?"

"You have seen the weather today, haven't you?"

Sophie laughed. "I have. But I've been stuck inside a fuggy classroom for close to twelve hours and could really do with blowing away the cobwebs."

"That's something Gran used to say."

"What?"

"Blowing away the cobwebs."

"Ah. So, are you up for it?"

"No. But I'll grab my coat."

Ben and Sophie linked arms as they fought their way across the road towards the sea. Salt stung their eyes as the North Sea directed its anger towards them. Each time they tried to speak, a petulant gust stole their breath. The newly painted beach huts rattled and creaked under the onslaught.

"How are you feeling about your new job?" yelled Sophie, moving her head close to Ben's ear.

"What?" he shouted back.

"I said...oh, never mind."

They bent lower, pushing against the wind. It wasn't long before the stinging mass of salt, sand and debris drawn up by the wind left them blind, and they turned their backs on the weather, ready to head home. With the wind behind them, progress was quick. They were buffeted along, grabbing hold of each other to steady themselves.

"Well, that was a good idea," laughed Ben, as they slammed the front door against the weather.

"Don't tell me you don't feel invigorated," said Sophie.

"Frozen to the bone is how I feel."

Sophie looked at Ben and laughed. The blond mop on his head stuck up here, there, and everywhere. "Let's get changed, then I can sample your culinary delights."

Mother and son rushed to their bedrooms to peel off the layers of damp clothes that pinched their skin. Once warm and dry, they reconvened in the kitchen.

"Something smells amazing. What is it?"

"Cottage pie."

"So, are you going to be cooking at the nursing home?"

"No, they have a kitchen team. But apparently, they're often short-staffed, so I thought there's no harm in broadening my skill set."

"Broadening your skill set, hey? Ben, I'm so proud of you."

"For taking on a minimum wage job?"

"Yes. The work you'll be doing is so important, it doesn't matter what you're paid."

"But it does matter, doesn't it? I'll never be able to get a place of my own. You'll be stuck with me for the foreseeable."

"You're having second thoughts?"

"About the job? No. About society? Yes. It's scandalous that those caring for the most needy should be paid so little. I'd like to see politicians trying their hand at the personal care of someone with dementia."

"All we can do is change what's on our doorstep. And you can live with me as long as you need to. I'm in no rush to kick you out."

"Really?" Ben raised an eyebrow.

"OK, so maybe it crossed my mind when you were playing Xbox all day. But it's different if you're working. Look, all I need is a bit of help with bills and food. The rest you can save for your future."

"Really?"

"Really."

Chapter 22

March, 2018

Elle felt tears roll down the sides of her cheeks. Beneath her, a paper sheet crunched and tore as it stuck like a limpet to her legs. She brushed away the tears and looked again at the grainy image beside her. Her head snapped back, and she closed her eyes. This couldn't be happening.

The room's air was thick and stuffy, drying out her throat and making her want to gag. Elle opened her eyes and looked up at the broken ceiling tile above. Another sign of the cuts that plagued the health service.

"Would you like a printout?"

Elle turned her head back to the smiling woman in an unflattering blue tunic and baggy trousers. She focussed her eyes on the woman's feet, smothered by thick socks and a pair of ancient Crocs. "I guess."

The woman handed Elle a paper towel to clean herself. She scrubbed hard at her stomach, trying to wipe away not just the clear jelly that covered it, but the knowledge of what lay beneath her skin. The tapping of a computer and the sound of a machine whirring filled the room.

"Here you are," said the chirpy nurse, placing a long stream of blurred images inside Elle's palm.

Elle clenched her fingers around the paper, refusing to raise it to her eyes. "Can you tell if... if..."

"No, not yet, but it won't be long until you can find out." The nurse went quiet, and Elle turned to look at her. A frown furrowed her brow, and she stared intently at Elle. "From the looks of this scan, I'd estimate you've just ticked over into your second trimester, but you have options, if this isn't an outcome you'd hoped for."

Elle sighed. If she only had to think of herself, she might have had a choice. But there was no way she could take this away from Grace, not after her lifetime of unanswered questions over her birth family. "Is my age a problem? Won't I be called a geriatric mother or something?"

The nurse laughed. "No. You'll be pleased to hear we no longer use that term. These days we prefer to say *advanced maternal age*."

Elle managed a small smile. "I'm not sure that sounds much better."

"At least it's not worse." The nurse kicked against the floor and her wheelie chair rolled close to Elle. She took her hand. "It is OK to be scared. You said this wasn't planned?"

"No."

"And the father? Is he likely to be involved?"

Elle sighed as she thought of Jago. She knew how he'd react. He'd be like an excitable puppy, making grand plans and promises he could not, or would not, keep. Of course, he had a right to know, but she needed to steel herself to deal with this alone. She couldn't let his inevitable enthusiasm blind her to the reality of what was to come. She was forty, about to become a single parent, living with her mother in a house falling down around their ears. "He's not all that reliable," was all Elle could manage.

"I see. Well, there is plenty of support out there. I'll signpost you to some charities who help single parents. Are you likely to need financial support? Here, this leaflet explains some options available to you if you decide to go through with the pregnancy."

Pregnant, pregnancy, preggers. When Elle had arrived at the doctor's earlier that morning, the P word was the last she'd expected to hear. She thought she was anaemic, or stressed, or worse, had some incurable disease that worried her when she woke in the small hours. The last thing she expected was to be told there was a human being growing inside her.

There was only one time it could have happened: the staff Christmas party. She couldn't even blame the drink or claim Jago had taken advantage of her. She was completely sober when it happened. It had been a moment of madness, a fumble in the cellar, a moment when her loneliness had been salved and she'd allowed herself to enjoy the brief contact of another human being.

Life is really unfair sometimes, thought Elle as she lay on the paper sheet, on a plastic bed, in a stuffy, airless room. People had sex all the time without getting pregnant. She'd done it once in the past two years and look where it had got her. A baby. A baby that would be half hers and half Jago's. It was unthinkable, impossible, but it was happening, as the photos in her hand proved.

"There's still time to think through all your options."

The nurse broke into Elle's thoughts, snapping her attention back to the room. "What do you mean?"

"I mean, you don't have to make any big decisions yet. You're only about twelve weeks. Anything could happen."

"You mean I could lose it?" Intense fear gripped Elle, and she instinctively laid a hand on her stomach.

"These things happen more often than you might think. But that wasn't what I meant. I meant you have time to decide whether to proceed with the pregnancy."

A thought struck Elle, and she looked the nurse straight in the eye. "I'm forty years old, single, and with no prospects of finding a long-term partner. This could be my only chance at motherhood."

"In that case, I'll assign you a midwife. Given your age, you'll likely be offered another scan in a few weeks, and we'll set up an initial midwife appointment where she can run you through everything to expect and answer questions."

"Thanks."

"Right, if that's all, I'd better get to my next patient."

"Of course. Thank you. You've been really helpful."

"Just doing my job."

*

As Elle stepped out onto the street, she wondered if anyone could tell. Did she look different? Was there a glowing sign above her head reading I'M PREGNANT? But no one noticed anything different about her. In fact, no one noticed anything at all. Passers-by bent their heads against the wind and rushed along the street in a hurry to get wherever they were going.

Elle wandered down the hill towards the lobster hatchery. The streets were quiet other than a few brave tourists cycling their way into town, the odd couple sitting eating seafood in a restaurant window. A warm glow of laughter and chatter spilled out of a pub entrance. Perhaps the tourists were still here, but only the foolhardy were braving the miserable weather.

At the harbour, Elle sat on a bench, clapping her hands to scare off the seagulls that flocked to the town in their droves despite the weather. Wind whipped salt into her eyes as she looked across the water to her home. Grace would be inside, reading, knitting or drinking a cup of tea. How would she take the news? She wasn't one to judge, but she might worry. Mind you, she was already worried about her daughter and Elle decided lying wouldn't help anything.

With a weary sigh, Elle stood up and walked the short distance back to the cottage.

"I'm home," she called as she walked through the door.

"Up here," Grace called back. "I've just made a fresh pot of tea."

"Great, thanks."

Elle poured herself a cup of tea and warmed her hands against the mug. There was no time like the present. She climbed the stairs to Grace's room.

Grace was sitting in an armchair looking out to the sea. A book hung on the arm of her chair and a cup sat steaming on the table beside her. "I saw you. Sitting on the bench, I mean. It's cold for sitting out, isn't it? How did it go with the doctor? I hope it wasn't bad news."

"That depends on your point of view."

Grace spun her head round and beckoned Elle to come close. "Pull up that stool and tell me all about it."

Elle grabbed the stool beneath Grace's dresser and sat down beside her mother. She took a sip of her tea, followed by a deep breath. "I'm pregnant."

"Pregnant?"

"Yes."

"Pregnant? But how?"

Elle smiled. "Do you need me to tell you about the birds and the bees?"

Grace grabbed her book and swatted it at Elle. "Silly girl. You know what I mean. I didn't think you had a chap. I'm guessing it's not an immaculate conception?"

"No, it's not, and no, I don't have a man in my life."

"Then you're going to have to explain this to me, Elle, as I'm very confused."

Elle had never enjoyed talking about her love life with Grace, and this was even worse.

"Is it that chap you were with in Bristol? What was his name? Brian?"

"Ryan. And no, we broke up two years ago, as you well know."

"Then who?" Grace took Elle's hand in hers and placed a gentle kiss on it. "Tell me, Elle. You know I won't judge you."

"I know. Jago's the father."

"Jago?"

"Yes."

"But when did you two get back together?"

"We didn't, we haven't, not really."

"Well, if making a baby isn't getting back together, I don't know what is." Grace huffed and picked up her tea.

"It happened once. At the Christmas party. It was a mistake, and we agreed to forget all about it and carry on as friends."

Grace chuckled into her tea. "From how the boy looks at you, I don't think he's all that happy with the arrangement. It's clear he's smitten."

"Don't be ridiculous."

"So, what did he say?"

"About what?"

"The baby, of course."

"I haven't told him. I literally just got back from seeing the doctor and came straight to you."

"But you will tell him?"

"I'm going to have to. I haven't decided when yet, though."

"The sooner the better, if you ask me."

"Yes, but it's complicated. I need to get my head around it first. And besides, given my age, I may miscarry."

"Oh, love. Don't talk like that."

"I have to be prepared."

"I know. But worrying won't help."

"Maybe. Anyway, what do you think about my news?"

A broad grin spread across Grace's lined face. "I think it's the best news I've heard in a long time. I think you will make a wonderful mother, and hopefully by then I'll have two working knees and will be the fun granny I'd always hoped to be. Come here." Grace pulled Elle into a tight hug. Held in her mother's arms, for the first time since she received the news, she felt as if everything would be alright.

Chapter 23

March, 2018

Sophie gripped Luke's hand and pulled him close to her. "You take care of yourself up there."

"I'm going to Scotland, Mum. Not the other side of the world."

"It's a mother's job to worry."

Luke gave her a tight squeeze, then turned to Ben, shaking his hand and slapping his back. "Look after the old girl for me," he said.

"Will do," said Ben.

Sophie and Ben watched as Luke slung his large backpack over his shoulder and made his way to the train. They stood in silence as his slim body disappeared into a carriage, his hand flying out in one last wave. Ben wrapped an arm around Sophie's shoulders.

"He'll be fine."

"I know. It's hard to say goodbye." Sophie brushed away a tear and turned to Ben. "It's just you and me now."

"And Gran."

"Of course. Shall we visit?"

"Yes, but let's grab some food first. I'm starving."

"You're always starving," said Sophie, following her son out of the station and onto the street beyond.

With Ben full of burger, they made their way to the nursing home. Ben was greeted like a local celebrity, smiles thrown from the female staff, fist bumps from the males.

"Looks like your first week here has gone well," smiled Sophie, her heart swelling with pride.

"They're just grateful for an extra pair of hands," said Ben, blushing.

"It looks more than that to me."

It took a long time to reach Annie's room. Ben kept stopping to chat to the residents. He crouched beside them, changing his tone for each patient. With some he was jokey, teasing them and laughing with them, with others he was gentle, speaking in low, soothing tones. It reminded Sophie of the sweet young boy he once was.

Annie sat propped up in bed, a trail of blues and greens spread across her legs. "She mentioned she used to knit," explained Ben, "so the nurse brought her some needles and wool."

"It's been a long time since you did any knitting, Mum," said Sophie, perching on the bed and running her hands across the wool.

Annie looked up with clear eyes. "Helen taught me."

"Helen?"

"Aunt Helen, in Padstow. I'll send this to her once I finish."

Sophie glanced at Ben, and he shrugged. "That's a great idea, Gran," he said. "You've chosen some lovely colours."

"Colours of the sea," said Annie, smiling down at her work. "You know, the Padstow sea was always such a different colour to Lowestoft's. Here it's mostly brown or grey, there it's turquoise, blue or navy." Annie's crepey hand ran up and down the rows of stitches. When she looked up, her eyes were clouded, lost in her memories. "When's Daddy coming?"

"Mum?"

"When's Daddy coming? I've been looking out for the boat but can't see it."

"He'll be here soon, Gran," said Ben, leaning over and taking Annie's hand in his own.

"You look just like him," said Annie, looking at Ben as though seeing him for the first time. "He was a handsome man, just like you."

"In that case, I'm honoured by the resemblance."

"Do you fish?"

"Pardon?"

"Daddy works the boats. He's the best fisherman in Lowestoft. Do you fish?"

"No, Gran. I work here now."

Annie looked around her in confusion. She shook her head and picked up her knitting. "I don't know what you're on about."

The room filled with the clicking of needles and the occasional tut from Annie when she dropped a stitch.

"Mum," said Sophie. "Can you teach me?"

Annie looked up, a frown creasing her papery skin. "I don't know. I don't want this spoiled. I'm making this for Aunt Helen."

"Maybe next time then," said Sophie.

Annie sighed and lifted her eyes to Sophie. "Well, if you must. Here," she said, holding out the needles. Sophie took them from her, her eyes filling with tears as Annie's instructions came out clear and certain. "I wouldn't say you're a natural," said Annie, looking down at Sophie's pitiful attempt. "Just like Mum, you are. She never had the patience for knitting."

"What was she like, your mum?" Annie was silent, and Sophie wondered if she'd registered the question or whether her mind had already moved on.

"Mum was Mum. Impatient, beautiful, strong-willed."

"Sounds like someone else we know," muttered Ben, and Sophie suppressed a smile.

"She wasn't like the other mums. Not a natural, if you know what I mean. She wanted to work. Nowadays that's what everyone does, but back then it wasn't the done thing. Perhaps she was foolhardy, perhaps she was ahead of her time."

"Well, whatever she was like, it sounds as though she would have had a few stories to tell." Sophie thought of the woman she'd seen in the photographs and wished she could go back in time to ask her all the questions swirling round her mind.

"We butted heads more often than we should have, but she loved me. She was very lovable, my mum, despite her strong-minded ways. After Daddy died, we lived with Nan. I enjoyed living with Nan, but she was my dad's mum, not my mum's, and Mum had to do a lot of looking after Sally, which must have been hard. I tried to help when I could. Nan used to work on the nets before her hands got too bad, and Mum did the same. Times were hard after the war, then there was that blasted flood which scuppered everything."

"Was your dad a fisherman?" asked Ben. "We thought Grandad Frank had always worked in an office?"

"Mind that stitch, young lady. We can't send a holey scarf to Helen. The wind will tear through it."

Sophie sighed, and Ben placed a hand on her shoulder. He pulled out a small notebook and scribbled down a few sentences with his pencil.

"What are you doing?" Sophie asked.

"Keeping notes. Every time she's lucid, I write down what she's said. That way, we can build a picture of her life. That's my plan, anyway."

"Sounds a good idea," said Sophie. "Ben?"

"Yeah?"

"I'm sorry I left it too late to find out all this stuff. I should have asked years ago."

"Why were you and Gran never close?"

Sophie sighed. "We got on OK before Dad died. I sometimes hear women describe their daughters as their best friends. It was never like that with me and Mum. We loved each other, don't get me wrong, but we were so different. She was feisty, unpredictable, exciting. I was more like Dad; calm, stable, staying in each night to do my homework. I think she found me boring.' Sophie smiled at Ben. "This is where you tell me I'm not boring."

Ben laughed. "You're many things, Mum. Boring isn't one of them."

Sophie leaned over and kissed his cheek. "I've not had adventures like Mum did, though. I opted to stay in the town where I was born. I've done the same job in the same school for nearly thirty years. I haven't exactly pushed myself."

"What are you talking about?" said Ben. "I see how hard you work. You push yourself every day. Just because you live your life differently to how Gran did, doesn't make it less valuable."

"I know, but she became more and more adventurous the older she became. By my teens, Mum was always off to some exotic location with her pals. Dad was a homebody, so stayed back to look after me. He said Mum was a free spirit, and it was his job to let her fly."

"Crikey, he sounds ahead of his time."

"I think he just wanted an easy life," laughed Sophie. "No, it wasn't that. He loved her, he loved her more than anything in the world. He once told me he couldn't remember a time when he hadn't loved her. They'd known each other all their lives. I sometimes wondered if Mum loved Dad as much as he loved her, but when he died, she was devastated. To be honest, I was surprised how badly his death hit her. She'd always been so independent, but without him, she crumbled."

"What are you going on about?" asked Annie.

Sophie threw a guilty look Ben's way. It was wrong to talk about Annie as though she weren't in the room. "Sorry, Mum. I was just telling Ben how much you enjoyed going off on adventures."

"Oh yes," said Annie. "You can't beat a bit of travel, boy."

"What was the best place you visited?" asked Ben, but Annie's eyes had clouded, her hands working on autopilot as she corrected Sophie's mistakes on the scarf.

"I think perhaps we should leave Gran to rest. This is a bit of a busman's holiday for you anyway," said Sophie.

"I don't mind," said Ben. "It's more interesting than spending my day off playing Xbox."

Sophie raised an eyebrow, marvelling at the change in her son. It was like one of the growth spurts he'd had as a teenager, only this time it was something inside growing rather than his limbs.

Chapter 24

1968

Dear Grace,

It was wonderful to receive your last letter and to hear you sounding so upbeat after all last year's trials and tribulations. What a relief it must be now John has moved away, although I pity his new wife, for surely, she doesn't know what she's letting herself in for!

I was very sorry to hear about Jack's death, but as you said, he lived to a ripe old age and the fact he was still fishing right up till the end is remarkable. All those years Helen feared losing him to the sea, to know he went peacefully in his own bed would hopefully be some comfort. It sounds as though the funeral was very well attended and I'm sure the entire community will miss Jack as he'd been such a regular fixture in the harbour for so many years. How is Aunt Helen coping? I'm sure it must have hit her hard, but you being there must also be a tremendous comfort.

I have my own news, which is both exciting and terrifying depending on your perspective... Grace, I am going to have a baby! As you know, Sam and I have been putting off starting a family until things were more secure with the Sally Ann, but this little one came along by chance, and as Sam said, if we'd waited there may never have been a right time. As you can imagine, my mum is beside herself and has already made a very dubious attempt at knitting a pair of booties.

He or she is due towards the end of the year, around November time, we think. The doctor was rather scathing about my age when he examined me, but thirty-three doesn't feel old to me. The thought of having to look after another human being terrifies me, but I'm certain Sam will make a wonderful father, and with so many family members close by, I'm sure we'll make a decent fist of raising a child.

Sam is already talking about our son joining him on the Sally Ann, which feels rather premature as we don't know we're having a son yet. For my part, all I want is for the child to be healthy, and to make it through the birth relatively unscathed. All my friends at the factory already have large families, and have been scaring me with horror stories from their own experiences of childbirth. My friend Beryl has six children, so whatever she says, it can't be all that bad or she would have stopped after one!

Now you're free of John, I hope you will find love and happiness again. I know you worry about the stigma of being a divorcée, but this is 1968, and any man worth his salt won't bat an eyelid. Twenty-seven is no age, so I'll hear no more of that nonsense about being past your prime. Goodness, I'm about to have my first child at the grand old age of thirty-three! It's a wonder Sam and I didn't bow to the pressure of family, friends and nosey neighbours sooner, but it's important to stick to your guns, and it's no one's business but your own when you hit life's milestones.

And enormous congratulations on your promotion to office supervisor! I know it's not your dream career and your colleagues frustrate you, but your boss must think a lot of you to have promoted you above all the other candidates. You always were a clever one, Grace, and I'm so proud of you. I'm sure Aunt Helen is too!

Speaking of Aunt Helen, how is her health now? From your last letter, it doesn't sound like she's doing too well. I know from experience how tricky it can be caring for an elderly relative, so make sure you ask for help if you need it.

I'd better go as I'm feeling terribly sick and need to nibble on a ginger biscuit. I'll write again soon,

All my love,

Your friend,

Annie

Chapter 25

March, 2018

Elle climbed the hill, shielding her eyes from the low sun. It was one of those perfect early spring days, full of hope that warmer weather was just around the corner. The sea beyond her sparkled like a bag of diamonds. Everything about the scene before her was soothing; the sweeping gulls, the crisp, pale sand, the grass-covered dunes across the water.

"I thought I'd find you up here." A voice behind her made Elle turn, and she saw Jago jogging to catch her up.

"Sorry, I thought I had a day off?"

"You do. I bumped into Grace, and she said you wanted to talk to me."

"She did, did she?" Elle would need to have a word with Grace later. "Well, she must have got the wrong end of the stick."

"Are you sure? It sounded important."

Elle waved a hand in the air. "Oh, it was probably just to check my shifts or something. I can't remember now."

Jago scrunched up his eyes, clearly not believing her. "Fine. If you don't want to talk, you don't have to. How about we walk instead?"

"Sounds good."

"How did it go at the doctors?"

Elle winced inwardly. She'd hoped Jago would've forgotten about her visit to the GP. "Oh, fine, fine. Nothing serious, just a few women's problems."

Again, he looked at her with questioning eyes but said nothing. They walked until the path split in two. "Shall we have a wander on the beach?"

"Sure."

"Have you said anything to Grace yet about the rumours Ned had heard?"

Elle shook her head. The truth was, since finding out about the pregnancy, the conversation with Ned had completely slipped her mind.

"Don't you think you should tell her?"

"Let's do a bit more digging first."

"OK."

They scrambled down a narrow path, Jago taking Elle's hand as they reached a steep shelf of slippery rocks. She accepted his help, feeling a jolt through her skin as his hand met hers.

"Nice to have it to ourselves," said Jago.

"Yes, need to make the most of it. It won't be long till the place is overrun, what with the Easter holidays just around the corner."

They walked slowly, their feet sinking into puddles of deep, soft sand. Further along the beach a man threw a stick to his grateful dog, who bounded after it, splashing through the shallows and returning to shake itself off on its master's legs.

"Have you had any luck finding extra staff for the summer?" In truth, Elle couldn't care less about the pub's staffing issues, but she felt it was a safe topic and better than silence.

"Not yet. I'm not looking forward to the season, to be honest. It's impossible to get staff at the moment, and if it's anything like last year, it will be a nightmare. I'm still short of at least two bar staff and at this rate it will be me cleaning the place as well as managing it."

"You're not enjoying being bar manager?"

"It has its moments. It's not something I'd ever planned on doing long-term. I was only supposed to be back for a year. Five years later and I'm still pulling pints."

"What had you planned to do once your year was up?"

"I wanted to go back overseas. Maybe Thailand or Australia again. I don't know, somewhere warm at least."

"And will you? Go travelling again, I mean?"

"I guess that depends if there's anything to keep me here."

Jago tried to catch Elle's eye, but she looked away. "You should do it," she said. "If that's what you want." She risked a glance at Jago, who seemed suddenly deflated.

"Yeah, I guess I should." He spoke quietly, his shoulders slumping as he hunkered down further into his coat. "Look, I'm getting cold. Do you mind if I head back?"

"No, not at all. I'll stay for a while. See you tomorrow."

Jago disappeared back up the path they had walked down, and Elle flopped down onto the sand. It was cold, and she felt dampness seeping through her coat and into her jeans. Why had she just encouraged the father of her child to move to the other side of the world? She pushed away the nagging voice in her head telling her she was a coward. The voice sounded remarkably like Grace's. *Just because you were hurt once, doesn't mean it will happen again*. But she couldn't take that risk. Last time she'd been so close to the edge it scared her. It had taken years to find the remnants of her self-esteem and force them back together until they resembled something like happiness. And now it wasn't just herself to worry about. What if Jago rejected her again? This time she'd have a baby to care for. A baby who'd need a strong, mentally sound mother, not a snivelling wreck who couldn't pull themselves together.

Elle grabbed a fistful of sand and threw it towards the sea. She let out a yell and threw another fistful, cursing as the wind blew some of it back into her face. The waistband of her jeans was digging into her skin, and she undid her top button. It wouldn't be long before her secret was evident for the world to see. She shouldn't have been such a coward. Hadn't today been the perfect opportunity to tell Jago her news?

Elle felt defeated and cold as she pushed herself up from the sand and began the slow trudge back to the cottage. Her steps slowed the nearer she got to the town, knowing Grace would give her the third degree as soon as she walked through the door.

"How did it go with Jago?" asked Grace, confirming Elle's worst suspicions before she could even close the door behind her.

"He found me. We didn't talk. Not about that anyway."

"By *that,* you mean the baby."

"You had no right sending him to find me." Elle turned on Grace, angry at her mother for interfering, and ultimately, for being right.

"If I don't nudge things on, I'm worried he won't find out till it's too late."

"What do you mean too late?" asked Elle, pulling off her damp coat.

"Someone's bound to notice something soon. It's far better if the news comes from you. Imagine how hurt he'll be if he hears about the baby from someone else."

"Yeah, well, it's not really any of his business, is it? He was talking today about going travelling again. I don't want to force him to stay, or hear false promises of commitment when I know at some point he'll give in to the wanderlust that drives him."

"I don't think you give that boy enough credit."

"You don't know him like I do."

"You know the old Jago. He's changed a lot since then. If only you'd open your eyes, you might see that for yourself."

"I don't need your advice or your help. It's not like you're one to be dishing out advice. You made a string of bad decisions where men are concerned and have no right to tell me what I should or shouldn't do. Please, just stay out of my business."

Elle stormed up to her bedroom, regretting her harsh words as soon as she'd thrown herself down onto the bed. None of this was Grace's fault. Elle pulled a pillow over her mouth and screamed into it.

Chapter 26

March, 2018

Sophie sat at the back of the hall watching a man who looked barely old enough to be out of school deliver an energetic PE lesson to her class. Even watching him made Sophie feel tired. She looked at the clock on the wall, counting the minutes till her planning time kicked in and she could retreat to the relative calm of the staffroom to get on with her work in peace.

"Here you go," said her assistant Beth, handing over a lidded cup steaming with tea. Sophie hated drinking tea from a plastic cup, it never tasted quite right, but the health and safety police would be onto her if she tried to smuggle a china cup out of the staffroom.

"Thanks."

"Why don't you go for your planning time now? That guy looks like he's got everything under control."

Sophie looked across at the instructor, the children hanging on his every word as he spoke to them in his kids'-TV-presenter voice. He began handing out hula hoops, and Sophie took that as her cue to leave. "Thanks," she said to Beth, knowing the young woman would enjoy half an hour staring at the good-looking man leading the class.

Sophie grabbed her bag and laptop and settled herself in the staffroom. She took a discreet look at her phone. Since Annie's stroke, she'd been sneaking glances whenever she was sure the head teacher wasn't around. Her screen flashed up with a message from Ben; *Call me when you can. It's about Gran. Nothing bad, so don't worry.*

Sophie slipped her phone in her pocket and made her way to the disabled toilet the staff used. Once safely behind a locked door, she took out the phone and called Ben.

"Hi."

"Hi, Mum. Why are you whispering?"

"I'm hiding in the toilet. Don't ask."

Ben laughed. "I hope I didn't panic you? Gran's fine. I didn't expect you to call back so soon."

"Oh, OK. I'm glad nothing's wrong. What did you want to talk about?"

"This really could have waited till you got home. I only messaged because I was excited."

"Hurry up, will you? If I stay in here much longer, they'll send out a search party."

"OK, well, I called Padstow Museum today. I gave them Gran's name, and guess what?"

Sophie sighed. "What?"

"They have a record of all the Lowestoft kids who came to Padstow with their parents and went to the local school. Gran's name was on there!" Ben's excited voice boomed from her phone and Sophie turned the volume down.

"Wow, great detective work, well done."

"Thanks. Anyway, they didn't have an address for her, but they're going to ask around and see if anyone remembers Gran and her parents. They said there are still a few families in town who lived there during the Second World War. They sounded almost as excited as I did by the time we'd finished chatting."

"That's great. Look, I'll talk to you about this when I get home. I really need to go. Thanks for letting me know, though."

"No problem. Speak to you later."

Sophie switched off her phone and flushed the toilet. When she came out, the head teacher was waiting outside the door.

"Everything alright, Sophie? I thought I heard voices in there?"

"Just me, talking to myself as usual. First sign of madness, I know."

The head teacher gave a wry smile and Sophie walked back to the staffroom as quickly as she could without arousing suspicion. She opened her laptop and pulled up her planning document for the following week. However hard she tried, Sophie found she couldn't concentrate on the screen in front of her. She sighed, clicked off the document and opened her internet browser.

An hour later Sophie had learned that a large community of Lowestoft fishing families used to descend on Padstow each year. She'd also discovered a memoir by one Lowestoft man who'd spent many years in Padstow as a child, teen, and finally as a grown fisherman himself. Sophie ordered a copy online, knowing that Ben, with his newfound interest in local history, would devour it.

A knock on the door caused Sophie to click off the internet and pull up her blank planning document. "Come in," she said.

"Sorry, not disturbing you, am I?" Brenda, the school secretary, appeared in the doorway, sheet of paper in hand.

"Not at all. Come in."

"I just need you to sign off on this letter about next week's visit to the zoo."

"Sure," said Sophie, taking the outstretched paper and scanning the text before scrawling her signature at the bottom.

"Looks like your planning's going well," said Brenda, leaning over Sophie's shoulder at the blank document on the screen.

Sophie held up her hands. "Guilty as charged," she said, laughing.

"So, what have you been up to all this time?" asked Brenda. "Not looking on any dodgy sites, I hope."

"What a dirty mind you have," said Sophie, pulling up the tab she'd been on. "If you must know, I got distracted by a bit of historical detective work."

"Oooh, tell all," said Brenda, pulling out a chair and sitting down.

"Don't you have work to be getting on with?"

"Don't you?" replied Brenda, raising an eyebrow.

"Fine," said Sophie, "but don't let on I've been wasting my much-needed planning time scouring the internet."

"My lips are sealed," said Brenda, a grin spreading across her face.

"You know my mum's been ill?" Brenda nodded. "Well, she's been saying some strange stuff. We think she may have had a sister we never knew about. And she's spoken about her family being in Padstow. Padstow in Cornwall, I mean."

Brenda laughed. "I know where Padstow is, Sophie. I go down there for my holidays every year. Have done since I was little. My family were fishermen and used to chase the herring that way, so it's always been a family tradition to go back once a year."

"Your family were down there too?"

"I think you'd find plenty of families in the town who were," said Brenda. "I've probably got some old photographs at home somewhere. I'll dig them out and bring them in for you."

"That would be amazing."

"And you should try the museum in town. They're helpful in there."

"That's a great idea. I might send my son down there. He's becoming obsessed with our family history."

"Good for him," said Brenda. "People forget what a rich history this town has. Everyone is always so quick to look at the negatives, but there's so much going for this place. I wish more people took an interest in the town's past. Those fishermen were a different breed. It was a dangerous job, fishing. I can't imagine the youth of today risking their lives every time they go out to work. They were ordinary everyday heroes, those men. Risking their lives to put food on their families' tables. They deserve more recognition than they get."

Their conversation was interrupted by the arrival of the head teacher. "Brenda, what are you doing in here? The office phone's been ringing off the hook."

"My fault," said Sophie. "I got her chatting."

"I'd appreciate it if you could gossip in your own time."

"Oh, we weren't gossiping," said Brenda. "Sophie's doing some research for a local history project she wants to do next term. My family have lived in the town for donkey's years, so I was just giving her a bit of help."

The head teacher sighed. "I'm sure all you've found out is very interesting, but you know we have a topic carousel to stick to. We can't deviate from that whenever the mood takes us. What would Ofsted think?"

Sophie inwardly groaned. When did education become about appeasing grumpy inspectors rather than making learning exciting for the children? Not for the first time, she wondered how much longer she could stick at the job.

Chapter 27

1968

Dear Grace,

I am delighted to announce the safe arrival of Sophie Rose Thorn, who was born after a very long labour and weighed in at a healthy seven pounds, six ounces.

Both Sam and I are smitten, and it was a huge relief to arrive home after spending a week in a hospital ward. I think the lack of sleep will take quite some getting used to, and we've yet to master the terry nappies, but we'll get there.

If it weren't for our mothers, I'm not sure what we'd have done. Our house looked like a bomb site, with baby clothes strewn all over the place and buckets full of soaking nappies blocking a route through the kitchen. Mum and Kitty appeared with a basket of dusters and cloths and gave the house a good spring clean for us yesterday. I would have felt embarrassed if I had the energy to care.

Kitty keeps saying we'd have had more energy if we'd started a family younger. I would have throttled her had Mum not stepped in to point out that she herself waited until her thirties to have me, so it was nothing more than a family tradition.

I'm not sure Kitty realises how tight money has been for us since Sam took over the Sally Ann. We've barely made a dent in the loan we took out to buy the boat, and now I'm not working things are even more tricky.

Mum and Frank have suggested we move in with them, but I think that would be hard, having had our own space for so long. I may see if I can take in some work making nets when Sophie's bigger or turn my hand to alterations and repairs. I've always been a competent knitter and can do a reasonable job with a needle and thread.

Anyway, it turns out all the horror stories my friends told me about birth are true! I won't make you feel ill with all the grisly details, but Sophie is now two weeks old, and I still can't sit down comfortably for longer than a few minutes at a time. It was a difficult birth, and the doctor has advised us to stop at one child. In the blur of having a newborn Sam and I are yet to talk about this rather shocking news, but to be honest, my heart is so full of little Sophie, I can't imagine having room for another child, even if I could have one.

I've enclosed a photograph of the little mite. It's a bit too early to tell, but she seems to have inherited my blonde hair and blue eyes, although apparently eye colour can change, so who knows? So far, she's proving a rather calm little thing, which makes me hopeful she'll turn out like her dad in temperament. Honestly, I didn't think I could love Sam more than I already do but seeing him with Sophie makes my heart swell. I've heard stories from friends whose husbands give a wide berth to anything to do with childcare, but not my Sam. He's a very modern man in some ways and has even stopped going to the pub in order to lie on his stomach beside Sophie, trying to make her smile. He's a natural parent, and I know she's going to grow up adoring her daddy. What a lucky little girl she is.

Seeing Sam with Sophie brought back memories of my dad, Tom. I'm ashamed of how little I think of him these days, but long-buried memories have flooded back. I haven't decided yet whether I'll tell Sophie about her grandad Tom. I'm not sure it would be fair to Frank, who dotes on his first grandchild, despite not being a blood relation. I'd hate to have their relationship overshadowed by a ghost. Perhaps I'll wait until she's an adult and then tell her about my darling dad. We'll see.

Sophie has just started crying, so I'll have to go and feed her. Write to me soon with all your news,

All my love,

Your friend,

Annie

Chapter 28

March, 2018

"Who do you love?" Jago asked, walking into the bar, brandishing a piece of paper.

"Um... Grace?"

Jago pouted and laid the paper down on the bar. "You might revise your answer when you hear where I've been."

"Oh yeah?" said Elle, raising an eyebrow.

"I've just got back from Padstow Museum."

"Right. And that's exciting because..."

Jago perched on a bar stool, grinning like an excitable child. "I had this idea to ask them about the people in the photo. They recognised Jack Tristan, Helen's brother, but couldn't remember anything about the woman, Marnie."

"Great."

"Hang on, this is about to get interesting."

"OK, go on."

"Right, well, they have records of all the kids who attended the local school. Lots of families came down here from Lowestoft, then went back at the end of the fishing season. During the wars, some families came down and stayed for longer, years even."

"But we don't know that the woman was from Lowestoft?"

"Of course we do."

"We do?"

"Yes, from those letters Grace received from Annie."

"Oh yes, of course," said Elle. She was still sceptical about the concept of *baby brain*, but there was no denying she'd struggled to retain information lately. At least Jago was still on the ball.

"Anyway, you're not going to believe this..." Jago's eyes shone with excitement, and he used his palms to make a drum roll on the bar.

"Come on, put me out of my misery."

Jago grinned. "OK then. So, this is crazy timing, but a man called the museum yesterday asking similar questions to me. He emailed them a photo..." Jago fished his phone out of his pocket and held it up to Elle.

"Oh my God. That's the same woman and child in the photos Grace found."

"Who do you love again?" asked Jago, smirking.

"You, of course," said Elle, adding "as a friend," before he could feel too smug.

"I asked for the bloke's email address, but they understandably didn't want to hand it over without his permission. They're emailing him today with your details so he can get in touch with you directly. Is it OK that I gave them your email instead of mine? I thought you'd want to hear any news first."

"Thank you, that's really thoughtful," said Elle. "I don't think I'll tell Grace about this just yet. I'd hate to get her hopes up for nothing."

"It's exciting though, don't you think? And it gives more weight to what Ned told us."

"Yeah, that's true, and yes, it is really exciting. It feels like we've been fumbling around in the dark and finally have a lead. Thanks so much for helping with this."

"No problem," said Jago. "Now get back to work."

Elle grinned at him, then turned back to the fridge she'd been restocking.

*

"Jago," called Elle. "Come and look at this."

He joined Elle at the table, where she was eating a sandwich. "What is it?"

"I've got an email from the man who contacted Padstow Museum."

"Already?"

"Yes, I know."

"He's keen. What does it say?"

Elle squinted at her phone. "He says his name's Ben, and he's been looking into his family history. His grandmother has dementia but has been talking about her time in Padstow as a child. They found the same photo we had in his grandmother's belongings, and he's been trying to find out more ever since."

"Wow, that's amazing. Imagine if he'd been looking a year ago. Chances are we wouldn't have made the connection so soon. This feels like fate."

"Yeah," said Elle, "it does a bit."

"So, are you going to tell Grace about this now?"

"Not right now, but soon. The man, Ben, has given me his mum's phone number. He says to call after six when she's back from work. I'll speak to Grace once I've spoken to this lady."

"Grace won't be pleased if she finds out you're keeping secrets from her."

"I'm just trying to protect her. However much she says she doesn't care about being adopted, I know it affects her more than she lets on, even now."

"OK. You know her best."

Elle smiled at Jago, grateful for his understanding.

The rest of the day passed slowly, the hands of the clock lethargically ticking round. When five o'clock finally rolled round, Elle said her goodbyes to Jago and headed home. She found Grace sitting in an armchair upstairs, watching TV.

"How's your wrist?"

"Good. The nurse came around to check it and said it's healing nicely. She was pleased with the movement of my fingers. Now if I could just get my knee sorted, I'd be back to a fully working human again."

Elle smiled. "I'm sure the op will happen soon. Hey, do you mind if we eat a bit earlier tonight?"

"Of course not. Do you have plans later?"

"Just a drink with one of the girls from work." Elle crossed her fingers behind her back. She hated lying to Grace, but couldn't make the phone call inside the house, and couldn't bear to raise her hopes if it all came to nothing.

"That sounds nice," said Grace, "but I'd be happier if you were meeting Jago."

"I thought we agreed that topic was off limits after the last truce was called?"

"Fine," said Grace with a dramatic sigh. "I've made my feelings clear, and I'll leave it at that. What are you thinking about supper?"

"Sausage and mash?"

"Perfect. I'm so sorry you're having to cook so much. Once I'm back on my feet..."

"Don't apologise, I enjoy cooking. I never bothered much when I was living by myself in Bristol. It's good to have someone to cook for."

Grace took Elle's hand and squeezed it. "Don't ever doubt how much I love you, and how grateful I am for all you do."

Elle batted away the compliment and went downstairs to cook. For the next hour, she was on edge. The sausages seemed to take an age to brown, the potatoes weren't softening as quickly as they should. When the meal was finally ready, Elle found she had little appetite, her hand shaking as she lifted the fork to her mouth.

"Are you alright?" asked Grace. "You seem a little jumpy."

"I'm fine, just tired."

"Perhaps you should cancel your drink this evening?"

"No," said Elle, too sharply.

Grace looked up through narrowed eyes. "It is a drink with a friend, isn't it?"

"What do you mean?" Elle knew her cheeks had reddened and the way Grace studied her she feared her lie would be found out.

"Now wouldn't be the time to be embarking on a new relationship," said Grace, directing a pointed look at Elle's stomach.

She laughed, relief washing over her. "You think I'm going out on a date? That's ridiculous!"

"You look guilty."

"Not guilty, just excited. I'd better go, or I'll be late. I'll take care of the dishes when I get back." Elle grabbed her mobile phone and rushed out of the room before Grace could quiz her further. As soon as she was out of the cottage, with trembling fingers she dialled the number for the woman who could change everything.

Chapter 29

March, 2018

Sophie yanked her heavy bags into the hallway and found Ben waiting for her on the stairs. "Is everything OK?"

"Yeah, I've been waiting for you to get back. I didn't want to share my news on the phone."

"OK... not bad news, I hope?"

Ben's lips spread into a wide smile. "Not bad news, but you may want to get yourself a drink."

"Now you're worrying me," said Sophie as she walked through to the kitchen and pulled a bottle of wine from the fridge. "Look," she said, holding up her glass to Ben, "now you can tell me what's going on?"

"Right, well, you know how I said I'd contacted the museum in Padstow?"

"Yes."

"Well, I wasn't the only one. They called me this afternoon to say someone else had been in asking for the same information as us. The guy didn't want to pass on my details without checking first, so gave me the email address of a woman called Elle."

"Elle?"

"Yes, Elle. I could be wrong, but I think she may be your cousin."

"What? You mean all the things Mum's been saying could be true?"

"Possibly. Anyway, I've given her your number and asked her to call you after six. Is that OK?"

"Yes, of course, but I'm not sure what I should say to her."

"Just compare notes. You can tell her all you've found out, ask her what she knows, and take it from there."

Sophie sat in her armchair beside the window, watching the minutes tick by on her watch. At one minute to six, her phone rang, and despite the fact that she was expecting it, the noise made her jump.

"Hello?"

"Hi, is that Sophie?"

"Yes, speaking."

"Hi, Sophie, my name is Elle. Your son Ben gave me your phone number."

"Ah, yes, he said you were going to call. It seems we may have a shared family history, not that I want to get ahead of myself. I'm intrigued to know why you have the same photo we do."

"The one of the women beside the harbour with a baby and a small girl?"

"Yes."

"My mum, Grace, found it when she was going through a box of old documents belonging to her Aunt Helen and Uncle Richard. They are both in that photo, along with Helen's brother Jack. Helen and Richard adopted Grace, and she never knew about her birth parents. Do you know the woman in the photo?"

Sophie's heart hammered inside her chest. "Yes, the little girl is my mum, Annie, and the woman is my gran, Marnie. My mum's not too well these days but keeps talking about another child. We've been wondering if Marnie may have had another baby while she was in Padstow, but as there's no record of it, we assumed the baby must have died."

"The baby in the photo is Grace."

"Really? Are you sure?"

"Certain."

"And she was adopted?"

"The story she was told was that her parents died in the Blitz, and she was evacuated to Padstow, but it's never really added up. We've been doing a bit of digging and came across a rumour about Marnie."

"What rumour?"

"That she may have had a baby while living in Padstow."

"But my grandad isn't in any of the photos we've found."

"No..."

Sophie had a feeling Elle was holding something back, but as this was their first encounter, decided not to press the issue. "So," said Sophie, taking a sip of wine. "Let me get this straight. If the rumour was true, and Marnie had a second child, I think we're safe to assume the baby, Grace, would be that child. Which would make my mum and your mum sisters."

"And it would make us cousins. Shit."

Sophie laughed.

"Sorry," said Elle, "I meant that in a good way. Did your gran ever talk about her time in Padstow?"

"I don't know," said Sophie. "I was really young when she died. My mum never said anything about it. It's only recently she's begun talking about Padstow and a baby. Unfortunately, she has dementia, so it's hard to follow her train of thought sometimes."

"I'm really sorry to hear that," said Elle.

"And your mum... you said she found the photo, so I'm assuming she's alive and well?"

Elle laughed, "Very much alive," she said, "and fairly well if you discount a dodgy knee."

Sophie let out a breath. "That's good to hear."

"You know your mum wrote to mine for years?"

"What? Are you sure?"

"Yes, she's shown me the letters. I've not read them, but they go back decades, right to the 1950s, I think."

"But surely if Annie and Grace were sisters, Mum would have said something before now?"

"Unless she had a good reason not to?"

"I'm not really sure what to do now."

"How do you mean?"

"Well, it seems like Annie's the only one who knows what happened, but if she's poorly..."

"Yes, we may never know. I guess we could do a DNA test. Or get both our mums to do one?"

"That's not a bad idea. It won't tell us what or why the sisters ended up in opposite ends of the country, but it would at least confirm that they are sisters."

By the time Sophie put the phone down, she was surprised to see an hour had passed.

"How did it go?" asked Ben, walking into the living room and handing her another glass of wine.

"Good, really good. In fact, I hope there is a family connection as Elle sounded lovely."

"So, what are our next steps?"

"A DNA test sounds like the best bet, but I'm not sure how we go about it."

"Hang on," said Ben, leaving the room and appearing moments later with his laptop. "I've been looking into DNA testing, just in case." He grinned at Sophie, and she shuffled over on the chair to make room for him. "Look, there are loads of sites on here offering DNA testing services. It sounds as though all you need to do is spit in a tube and post it off."

"Let's do it," said Sophie. "Order one for us and one for Elle."

"Are you sure?"

"Yes. If Mum has a sister, I want to find her before it's too late. It would give her some peace, don't you think?"

"Yes," said Ben. "I think it would." He put his arm around Sophie and pulled her close.

Chapter 30

1970

Dear Grace,

I'm afraid I'm writing to you with some very sad news. Two days ago, my lovely mum died very unexpectedly. We are all devastated, especially Frank, who is blaming himself. Apparently, Mum had been suffering from pain and exhaustion for quite some time but had refused to go to the doctor about it.

Frank feels he should have done more to get her medical help, but we all know how stubborn Mum was, and if she'd set her mind to something, there would be no changing it.

Sam has been a wonderful support and has been looking after Sophie for me so I can look after Frank. He's always been so stoic, it's strange to see him in such an emotional state. He's barely eaten in the past few days and sits in his chair staring at nothing.

I haven't had a chance to lose myself in grief, for between looking after Frank and organising the funeral, there has been little time to contemplate life without Mum.

We were unsure of Mum's wishes about where she'd like to be buried, but she must have known she was very ill, for she left detailed instructions for funeral arrangements. I thought she would want to be buried on the island, but Lowestoft had well and truly become her home, and she had bought burial plots beside Roy and Sally. Frank will also have a final resting place there when the time comes. It seems Mum thought of everything, even down to the hymns she would like us to sing.

I know she would want me to pass on her feelings for you, Grace. Although the time you shared in Padstow was brief, Mum always took an interest in your life and frequently asked me for updates on how you were getting on.

As you are currently in France, this letter is unlikely to reach you in time to attend the funeral. But, on the off chance you are back in the country, the funeral will be held at Christ Church, Lowestoft on Friday 20th at 3 p.m.

Jimmy and Clara are making the journey down, though I worry about them travelling all this way at their age. Thankfully, they are being sensible and spreading the journey over several days. They will stay with me and Sam, as I don't think Frank is up to hosting anyone now.

I had better go, as Sophie needs her supper and then I need to take some food over to Frank and try to tempt him to eat something.

I hope you are having a wonderful time over on the Continent and putting your French language skills to good use! Please write and tell me all about it when you get back. It will be a welcome distraction from all that is going on here.

All my love,

Your friend,

Annie

Chapter 31

March, 2018

"What's that you've got there?" asked Elle, finding Grace sitting on the sofa, surrounded by a pile of papers.

"Those letters from Annie. I've been going through them. I'm up to 1970." Grace brushed a tear from her eye and Elle walked over and wrapped an arm around her shoulders. "What's wrong?"

"I'd forgotten about this one. It was the letter Annie wrote when her mum, Marnie, died. I didn't read it until much later as I was away in France working as an au pair."

"Oh yes, I remember you telling me about that. Wasn't that after you'd divorced your first husband?"

"Yes, John." Grace grimaced. "Marrying him wasn't my finest hour. Going away for a while was just what I needed to clear my head, and I'd always been good at French when I was at school. Anyway, enough about me. How was your drink?"

Elle flopped down in an armchair. "I'm sorry, but I lied about that. There was no drink. I needed to make a phone call and didn't want you to hear."

A look of hurt flashed across Grace's face. "You could have just asked me to shut the door. I'm not one for eavesdropping. Who were you calling? Jago?"

"No, I was on the phone to a lovely lady called Sophie."

"Sophie? I've never heard you mention a friend called Sophie before."

"I'd never spoken to her before. Listen, Grace, I'm ninety-nine percent sure Sophie is Annie's daughter."

"Sophie..." Grace rummaged through the pile of letters until she found the one she needed. "Yes, Annie's daughter was called Sophie. Are you sure it's the same one?"

"As I said, I'm as certain as I can be at this stage. The thing is, me and Jago have been doing a bit of digging. We spoke to Ned Thomas."

"Pah, I wouldn't believe anything Nosey Ned has to say."

"Maybe not, but what he told us fits with other things we've found out." Elle explained about the museum and Ben, and everything they had learned so far. When she'd finished, she looked at Grace, but her face was inscrutable. "So? What do you think?"

"I think you should have told me all this sooner," said Grace, a frown clouding her face.

"But it was you who asked us to look into the photo."

"I know, but I expected you to tell me as soon as you'd found something. It's my life after all!"

"I'm sorry. Jago said I should have told you straight away, but I was worried about getting your hopes up and then it all turning out to be a wild goose chase."

"Goodness, Elle, I'm not a child! I appreciate all you've done for me, truly I do, but I don't need protecting. I'm an eighty-year-old woman, for God's sake!"

"I'm sorry."

Grace sighed and cleared away the letters. "Come here," she said, patting the sofa. Elle moved to sit beside her, and Grace pulled her close until Elle's head was resting on her shoulder. "You've always been so worried about doing the right thing, protecting me. But that's my job, not yours. Ever since your father left, it's like you wanted us in some sort of safe bubble, but that's not how life works, love. Life is messy, people are messy, they make mistakes, they hurt each other."

"So, what do you think, then? Are you angry?"

"Angry about what? Angry with whom?"

"With Marnie, with Annie, with Jack, with me?"

Grace surprised Elle with a laugh. "I'm a bit long in the tooth to be angry. Besides, most of the people on that list are dead. And yes, I'm irritated that you didn't tell me what was going on but look at all you've found out. How could I be angry about that?"

"Do you think the rumour about Jack could be true?"

Grace sat back in her chair and stared up at the ceiling. When she spoke, her voice was little more than a whisper. "Yes," she said. "I think it's true. Or at least, a lot of things would make sense if it were."

"Like what?"

"Well, aside from the fact I looked suspiciously like Jack, he was always extremely protective of me. He was a bit of a loner, not one for friends. He loved Helen and Richard, but he was a very private man and always kept himself to himself, even around them. But with me, he was different. Helen always used to say the sun came out from behind a cloud when he was with me, and it's true. I made him laugh and smile. I brought out a softer side to him. And when he found out how John was treating me, well, his reaction was rather strong, let's put it that way. He always looked after me."

Without warning, Grace burst into tears. Elle grabbed a handful of tissues and rubbed her back until the tears subsided.

"It's OK, Mum," she said. "Grace, it's OK."

Grace blew her nose and looked up at Elle. "You called me Mum," she said, smiling through her tears.

"A slip of the tongue."

Grace laughed. "I rather liked it. And I'm sorry about the tears. It's a shock, that's all, or rather, the fact it isn't a shock is a shock. All these years I've wondered who my parents were and one of them was right there all along."

"I wonder what happened between Marnie and Jack. Someone should have told you the truth long before now."

Grace shrugged. "Things were different back then. I'm sure everyone did what they thought was right. They would have kept quiet to protect me. Do you think Annie knew?"

"That's how I came to speak to Sophie. Annie has been talking about another baby, a sister."

Grace picked up the pile of letters. "All these years of correspondence and she never said a word. Do you know why she stopped writing?"

"She has dementia," said Elle, "so that could explain it. But listen, before we get ahead of ourselves, I think we should find out for certain if you and Annie are related."

"How can we do that? It sounds as if Annie's mind has gone, the poor thing."

"We can do a DNA test. It's very easy these days. Sophie's going to order you a test, if that's alright?"

"Of course it is. I want to know the truth more than anyone. Now, do you think you could pour me a small sherry? This has all been a bit of a shock."

Chapter 32

March, 2018

"That's me done," said Elle, stacking the final set of clean glasses on the shelf and letting out a loud yawn.

"I know you're tired," said Jago, "but can you stay for a quick chat?"

"Can it wait till tomorrow?" asked Elle, wondering if Jago had somehow learned the secret growing inside her.

"I'd rather chat to you now, if that's OK?"

"Fine," said Elle, pulling out a chair and plonking herself down. She covered her mouth as another yawn threatened.

"I haven't told anyone else about this yet," said Jago. "But I've been offered a job."

"A job? Where?"

"Sydney. In a bar I used to work at. I put a few feelers out after our last conversation, and it turns out a place I used to work is opening a second bar and looking for someone to run it."

"I thought you hated bar work?"

"It's a means to an end. It gets me in the country. Besides, there are worse jobs I could be doing."

"Hmm," said Elle.

"What? Do you think it's a bad idea? It was you who told me there was nothing keeping me here."

"I know," said Elle, her hand rubbing the tiny bump beneath her T-shirt. "Good for you, it's great news. I'm so happy for you."

"You don't look thrilled."

"I'm just tired."

"OK. You get going, I'll finish up here."

"Thanks."

"Oh, I forgot to ask, how did it go with the DNA thing?"

"No results yet. I'm still waiting for Sophie to submit her mum's test, but it shouldn't be too much longer before we hear."

"That's great. And Grace? How's she coping with all of this?"

Elle sighed and flopped into her chair. "It was a real shock at first, and she was cross that I hadn't kept her in the loop, then she became like a hyperactive puppy. I keep telling her not to get her hopes up, but she's not listening. I can understand why she's so desperate to have a sister. The only blood family she's got is me. But what if Annie isn't her sister? What then? And even if she is, she's ill, dementia. From what Sophie said, she's pretty bad."

"That's crap. Still, it might give her some answers she's been looking for. Oh, I forgot to tell you, and I hope you won't mind, but me and Ben have been emailing each other a bit."

"You and Ben? Why?"

Jago looked down at his feet, his cheeks turning pink. "I don't want you to think of me as a boring old man, but I find all the history he's dug up quite interesting."

"Why would I think any less of you for that? It is interesting."

"Yeah, I guess so. I suppose I'd never thought about the history of where I've grown up. I mean, I love traditions like May Day and stuff, but I had no idea about the links to Lowestoft. I'd not even heard of

Lowestoft until all this stuff with your mum came up. I went back to the museum yesterday and..."

"You went back to the museum?"

"Yes, you should go there, it's interesting. Me and Ben have both been doing a bit of digging and comparing notes. It would be cool to meet him if they ever come down here. He sounds like a really nice bloke."

"With your newfound love of history, it's a shame you'll be leaving here soon."

Jago pulled out a chair and sat down opposite Elle. "I don't have to take the job," he said. "Elle, look at me."

Elle forced herself to meet his gaze and tried to ignore the complicated feelings that proximity to Jago always dredged up. "It's your dream, and dreams are meant to be followed."

"Dreams can also change," he said quietly. "I'll see you tomorrow."

Elle stood and pulled on her coat. "Jago..."

"Goodnight, Elle."

Elle left the pub and, rather than going straight home, made her way to the harbour where there were still working boats moored up, just as there would have been in Jack's day. Despite a chill in the air, the night was still, and Elle sat on a bench, pulling her coat tighter around herself and listening to the gentle lapping of water against the harbour wall.

With thoughts of Jago too painful to contemplate, Elle turned her attention to all she had recently learned. She tried to picture Marnie and Annie walking beside the harbour, or Marnie and Jack. Were they in love? Did they have a torrid affair behind Marnie's husband's back? For, if Marnie had already had one child, she must have been married already.

Grace's reaction had come as a surprise, particularly where Jack was concerned. But the more she thought about it, the more Elle could understand. She knew who her own father was, but he'd been absent for most of her life, other than twice-yearly meetings, which were excruciating for all involved. At least Grace had spent time with her father and had had his protection. Elle's dad had been nowhere to be seen when she needed to learn to ride a bike, or stand up to bullies, or be given a lift to friends' houses.

Elle's breath caught in her chest. She'd been deprived of a father figure in her life and now she was about to inflict the same fate on her child. She and Jago didn't have to be together, but her baby needed its dad, and it wasn't up to her to deprive it of one. Elle jumped up from the bench and began running towards the pub. She had to tell Jago. It was the right thing to do.

When she reached the pub, the lights were off and although she knocked on the door for five minutes straight, there was no answer. Elle's resolve faltered, and she paused her knocking. Perhaps telling Jago wasn't meant to be. She turned to head home, but as she walked along the street, she heard a voice up ahead. Elle paused, and looking around a corner, spotted Jago, his face lit up by the screen of his phone.

"Yeah, great to speak to you. Yes, I know it's been ages. I know it's going to be amazing to be back there and hang out with you again. I've missed it so much. Yeah, I know, once you've lived in Sydney, nowhere else can quite measure up."

Elle swallowed down a sob. She shouldn't be eavesdropping on Jago's private conversations, but perhaps it was for the best. She'd been right all along. To tell him about the baby would be to trap him and she couldn't do that. No, it was best he found out the news when he was safely on the other side of the world.

Chapter 33

March, 2018

According to Ben, Annie was at her best just after breakfast. Unwilling to beg for time off, Sophie waited until Saturday to visit the nursing home with the DNA kit. It had been a painful wait. She'd been distracted at work and the children had picked up on it, running rings around her in a way she was not used to. Even the good, reliable, well-behaved kids had got in on the action. The head teacher had noticed too, making unannounced appearances in Sophie's classroom, supposedly to check she was alright but really, Sophie suspected, to spy.

On Friday afternoon, she had been called into the head teacher's office. In simpering tones, the woman had questioned whether everything was alright at home. Sophie blamed her poor recent performance on the stress of Annie's stroke and left the meeting with a thinly veiled warning to up her game.

Despite the week leaving her dog tired, Sophie woke at six on Saturday, eager for the day to get underway. She crept downstairs so as not to wake Ben, only to find him up, a freshly brewed pot of coffee in front of him.

"You couldn't sleep either?"

"No. I was lying there worrying so thought it was best to get up."

"You were worrying about Gran?"

"Yes. I don't know how well she'll cope with us coming at her with a plastic pot to spit in. There's no way she'll understand what's going on."

"Yes, I'd wondered about that. What do you think we should tell her?"

"The truth? You never know, it may sink in somehow. I can't see an alternative."

"Do you think we're doing the wrong thing, raking up old wounds?"

"No," said Ben. "It was Gran who started this. It's clearly unresolved for her. If we can get her some answers, she may find peace."

"Let's hope so," said Sophie.

Two hours later, Sophie and Ben pulled up outside the nursing home. Ben strode in purposefully, greeting various staff members as he went. She followed him to a staff room where he made them their fourth coffee of the day, then went off to explain to his manager what Sophie was there to do.

"We're good to go," said Ben. "I'll come with you in case Gran becomes distressed."

Sophie shuddered at the thought. As much as she told herself what they were doing was in Annie's best interest, the thought of coaxing her to share her saliva with strangers wasn't very appealing. Mother and son finished their drinks and made their way to Annie's room.

"Mum?" said Sophie, tapping on the door.

Annie smiled as they walked in, and Sophie felt tears spring to her eyes. Her mother was dressed and even wearing a touch of makeup. The thin hand lying on the armrest was decorated with bubble-gum pink fingernails.

"Ooh, these look lovely," said Sophie, sitting beside Annie and taking her hand.

"We have a nail technician come in once a month. I wasn't sure Gran would enjoy it, but she found the whole experience relaxing. She was given a hand massage, too. That sent you to sleep, didn't it, Gran?"

Annie smiled and reached out a hand for Ben to hold. "You're a good boy," she said. Turning to Sophie, her eyes twinkled, and her mouth curled into a smile. "This young man has been doing a fine job of looking after me until I'm well enough to go home."

"I'm very pleased to hear it," said Sophie. "Mum, I've got something to show you." Sophie pulled the DNA kit from her bag and explained the process to Annie. Annie's eyes stayed clear throughout, and Sophie prayed she understood what was going on. "Do you understand, Mum? This may help you find the other baby."

"My sister."

"Yes," said Sophie, glancing at Ben. "It will help find out if the baby is your sister."

Annie laughed and patted Sophie's hand. "She's a funny one, this girl. Of course, the baby was my sister." She continued to chuckle as Sophie prepared the kit.

"Mum, can you spit in here, please?"

"No, I jolly well cannot. What kind of woman do you think I am? Spit into a tube? Disgusting."

"It's for the doctor," said Ben, shrugging at Sophie as she raised an eyebrow. "It's not a complete lie," he muttered, "some of those scientists analysing the saliva will probably have PhDs."

"It's not her job to give me medicine," said Annie, poking a finger at Sophie.

"True," said Sophie. "Then what about Ben? See, he's wearing the right uniform."

Without a word, Annie turned to Ben, her mouth open wide. Ben took the kit from Sophie and held the tube to Annie's lips. She deposited a small amount of saliva inside it, then looked at him with a twinkle in her eye. "That was such a naughty thing to do. Don't tell Mum I've been spitting, or I'll be in trouble."

Ben gently dabbed a tissue across Annie's lips and she giggled.

"Well done, Mum," said Sophie. "You did very well."

Annie ignored Sophie and turned on the TV. Ben left to start his shift, and Sophie pulled her chair closer to Annie's. If she closed her eyes, she could pretend they were at home, watching TV together after dinner. Sophie jumped as a rough palm gripped hold of her hand.

"You will find my sister, won't you? We should never have left her behind. We need to bring her home."

Sophie stroked Annie's hair with her free hand. "Of course, Mum. I promise."

Annie nodded, turning her eyes back to the programme she was watching.

On her way out, Sophie bumped into Ben. "Well done," she said. "I couldn't have done that without you."

"Was she OK after I left?"

"She was unsettled, but she soon forgot all about it and kept asking why I was there."

"I suppose that's a good thing. What do we do now?"

"Send this off to the lab and cross our fingers the result is the one we're hoping for."

"And if it isn't?"

"We'll cross that bridge when we come to it. Whatever the result, I've arranged to go to Padstow next weekend. Regardless of if Mum has a sister, we know from the school records she lived there during the war, and I'd like to see the place for myself."

"I'd love to come with you, but I'm rostered on to work next weekend. I could see about swapping shifts?"

"No, don't do that," said Sophie. "I'll be fine on my own, and I promise to take you with me the next time I go."

"You'd better. Now get that test in the post. The wait's going to be unbearable as it is."

"Yes, sir," said Sophie. She pulled her son into a hug and left the building, the precious envelope clasped in her hand.

Chapter 34

1970

Dear Grace,

It was wonderful to receive your letter, and I felt I was travelling around France myself as I read your words. What an exciting adventure you've been on, and I must say very much deserved after all you've been through. Paris sounds particularly special, and you've inspired me to do a bit of travelling myself once Sophie is a little older. The Louvre sounds magnificent, as does seeing the sights by bicycle, particularly if the guide is as dishy as you described.

I'm pleased you could stay with such a kind family, and it's a shame you couldn't accept their offer of a longer stay. How is Aunt Helen? It must have been such a worry knowing she'd had a fall when you were so far away. Please send her my love.

How does it feel to be back in Padstow? Do you know, I still dream about the place, and would love to take Sophie there for a holiday one day, although she'd need to be older as I don't fancy travelling that far with a feisty toddler! I remember all the things I enjoyed about living there as a little girl, despite the fact the beaches were covered in barbed wire for much of my time there. The estuary was magnificent on a bright summer's day, and although we have lovely beaches here, the sea never quite matches the blue of Padstow. I'm so pleased I got to spend part of my childhood there, despite the circumstances. It must have been so hard for Mum travelling all that way with me on her own. Now I'm a mother myself, I realise what a challenge it must have been.

Speaking of children, after a slow start with speaking, Sophie now doesn't stop. She's such a little chatterbox and we even hear her talking to herself at night after we've put her to bed. Her first word, unsurprisingly, was 'Daddy', and I'm in no doubt who her favourite parent is. It sometimes rankles, given how much of the humdrum caring I do, but I also love to see the bond between father and daughter, and try not to begrudge their closeness. At least Sophie has taken her looks firmly from my side of the family, and I've lost count of the times folk have stopped us in the street to comment that we're two peas in a pod.

When I look at Sophie, I see my mother in her, and it brings me so much comfort to know Mum lives on through the younger generations. Thank you for the beautiful flowers you sent and for your kind words of condolence after Mum's death. I knew you were probably still in France and would be unable to make the funeral, so you have nothing to apologise for, the invitation was extended out of courtesy, not expectation.

Frank continues to struggle with Mum's death, so me and Sam have decided to move in with him. It makes sense, as he has more space than we do, and it means I'll be able to keep an eye on him without leaving Sophie in the care of others. Frank doesn't have any living relatives, so I'm all he has left. Grief has left him so frail, but I'm hoping having Sophie in the house will bring back some of his old spark.

Do you remember I told you my Uncle Jimmy and Aunt Clara were coming to the funeral? Well, they made it here in one piece. I must say, for a pair of seventy-five-year-olds they seemed remarkably sprightly. Their retirement from running the hotel suits them, although they've not been idle. Clara spends a lot of her time looking after her brother Ben's children, who are now aged sixteen, fourteen, ten, and five. From what

Clara's told me, their youngest, Jane, was a surprise arrival, and came as a shock to Ben, who is no spring chicken himself. Clara says, looking after Ben's brood keeps her young! Jimmy volunteers at the local school helping children learn to read. There are only ten pupils, so it's not too strenuous a task for him, but his eyes lit up when he was telling me about being back in the classroom.

Recently I've been considering taking a trip back up to Holy Island. Frank has mentioned wanting to create some sort of memorial to Mum there, and I think it may be good for him to visit a place she loved so dearly. He often looks at photographs from their wedding day on the island, and planning a trip would give him something to look forward to. Sam isn't keen to go, for obvious reasons, so I'll probably leave Sophie here with Sam and Kitty.

I still sometimes wonder what happened to Blaine McCloud. After Sam and I married, I wrote to his wife, as enough time had passed for me to feel detached from the whole debacle, and I felt she had a right to know the truth. She wrote back to say Blaine had briefly returned to the family home, but his crimes soon caught up with him and at the time of her writing he was detained at Her Majesty's pleasure. She sounded pleased to be rid of him, but I wouldn't be surprised if he charmed his way back into her affections on his release. I never told Sam about the letter. He never mentions that difficult period in our relationship, so I decided it was best to let sleeping dogs lie.

Sorry, I have really rambled on there, haven't I? I'd love to hear more about France in your next letter and let me know how Aunt Helen is. Tell her we're all thinking of her and hope her recovery is swift.

All my love,

Your friend,

Annie

Chapter 35

April, 2018

"What's that thing you always tell me?" asked Elle. "I know, a watched pot never boils."

Grace humphed and stuck out her tongue. Elle laughed. "Speaking of pots," said Grace. "I don't suppose you could put the kettle on?"

"If I didn't know you better, I'd think you were enjoying ordering me around."

"Then it's just as well you do know better. I'd give anything to stride over to that kettle and make one myself."

"I know," said Elle, squeezing Grace's arm. "You know the postman never gets here before eleven?"

"He may be early today."

Elle sighed. "How was Tasha today?" she asked, changing the subject. She was as nervous waiting for results as Grace, and could do with taking her mind off the imminent arrival of the postman.

"As lovely as ever. The poor girl's so overworked, though. I've a mind to write to her boss."

"You know she's asked us not to. If I ever find myself a better job, I'll make sure she's properly rewarded for her work."

"I know you will. You're a good girl. Have you had any luck with the job hunt?"

"No, and I doubt I will. It's hard enough to find work, let alone while pregnant."

"Can't you do that home-working thing that's becoming increasingly popular these days?"

"That's the dream."

"Well, don't give up on it yet. Something will come along soon enough."

Elle hoped so. She wasn't sure how long they could live in a house falling down around their ears. When she'd opened her last pay slip from the pub, her self-esteem had taken another nosedive as she compared her salary now to what she had been earning two years previously. It was all very well being around for Grace, but for every month she spent not working in the profession she'd trained for, the prospects of ever returning to a job in PR became less and less. Working at the pub didn't bring in enough to sustain them long-term. She needed a better solution.

The landline rang, and both Elle and Grace jumped. No one used the landline anymore, even Grace favoured her mobile these days. Elle grabbed the phone and listened to the voice on the other end. Grace studied her, wondering what had caused her daughter's eyes to fill with tears.

"Well?" demanded Grace as soon as Elle had put down the receiver.

"That was the hospital. They've had a cancellation and can do your op first thing tomorrow. They want me to take you in as soon as possible for pre-op tests."

"It's happening?" asked Grace, her eyes filling with tears.

"It looks that way."

"I won't believe it until I'm on that operating table."

"Me neither. I'll call Jago and see if I can borrow his van. You'd better pack yourself a bag."

"What about the post?"

"The post can wait till you're back home again."

"No," said Grace. "I want to know the results as soon as they arrive. If they come while I'm in hospital, I want you to open them and ring me."

"Are you sure you don't want to open them yourself?"

Grace sighed. "I just want to know."

"Fine," said Elle, "but right now there's a bed waiting for you at the hospital and I suggest we get there quickly before someone else jumps the queue and you get pushed to the back again."

It was late afternoon before Elle finally returned to Padstow. She parked the van in Jago's drive and walked through the narrow lanes to the cottage. As she opened the door, it caught on a pile of papers behind it. The letter. Elle had tried telling Grace they could get the results sooner if they looked online, but Grace was insistent that she wanted to hold the information in her hand.

Elle picked up the pile of post, rifling through bills and more bills until she found what she was looking for. She considered FaceTiming Grace but decided against it. It would be better to know the results so she could break the news gently should it be bad. Grace was already anxious in her hospital ward. She didn't need any further upset.

Elle sat at the kitchen table and turned the brown envelope in her hands. With a deep breath, she tore the paper, pulling a series of sheets from inside it. At first, she wasn't sure what she was looking at, then she understood, letting the realisation seep in.

"Hello?" Grace sounded frail and scared on the other end of the phone.

"I've got the results."

"What does it say?"

Elle took a deep breath. "It says you have a sister."

The line went quiet, and Elle wondered if Grace had lost the signal. Then came the unmistakable sounds of Grace's tears.

"Are you OK?"

"Yes," sniffed Grace. "Just overwhelmed. This is turning into quite the day. You'd better call Sophie and let her know."

"She'll have had the results sent to her phone. She's on her way to Cornwall as we speak."

"Oh gosh, I forgot she's supposed to be visiting today."

"Don't worry, I remembered. I've not been able to get hold of her yet, but that will be because she's driving. I've left a message and asked her to find alternative accommodation for tonight and to come across and meet me in the morning. I felt dreadful changing our plans, but I'm sure she'll understand."

"Do you think you'll be able to bring her to the hospital?"

"No, I'm sorry. You'll be in recovery tomorrow and she has to be back at work on Monday."

"That's a shame," said Grace, her voice laced with disappointment.

"Don't worry, as soon as you're back on your feet, I'll drive us up to Lowestoft so you can meet her. And your sister, of course."

"That sounds like a good plan. Oh, the doctor's here. I'd best get off the phone."

"I'll speak to you later. And, Grace?"

"Yes?"

"I love you."

Chapter 36

April, 2018

The line of traffic inched past Stonehenge, a fat worm of vehicles slithering along the tarmac at two miles an hour. The last throes of the evening sun glinted against windscreens, a visual reminder to drivers behind of how far was yet to go, and how slow progress would be.

Cramp threatened to overwhelm her right leg, and Sophie stretched it out as best she could, massaging into muscle with her knuckles. She yawned and banged her hands against the steering wheel, swearing inwardly at the journey's pace. Her skin felt sticky to the touch, her mouth dry. The can of coke in the cup holder was tempting, but with her bladder fit to burst, Sophie couldn't risk drinking it.

At least I'm not stuck on the motorway, thought Sophie. Ben had programmed the route into her satnav the previous evening, and at her insistence, had avoided all motorways between Lowestoft and Cornwall. At seven that morning, her predicted journey time was eight hours, but here she was, still in Somerset, with the sun slinking to bed at six p.m.

Sophie leaned back and clicked the bones in her neck. To her left, the sun caught the ancient stone, and Sophie understood for the first time what all the fuss was about. She had never had the slightest inclination to visit the stone circle, but swathed in the amber beams of a setting sun, the stones rose majestically from their resting place. A shiver went through her body as she thought of the intrepid souls who had dragged the stones from Wales, of the centuries of pagans who had worshipped at their craggy feet.

The persistent beeping of a horn burst through her thoughts and Sophie realised with a start that the traffic had moved forward, leaving a gap of several hundred precious meters between her and the car in front. Sophie raised her hand in apology, flicked her indicators on and off, and set off to close the gap.

From inside her bag came the chirpy chimes of her phone's ringtone. Whoever was calling seemed keen to get hold of her. The phone had been ringing on and off throughout the journey, but she'd not wanted to stop to check. Ben had helped her set up a special ringtone for him and the nursing home, so she knew there was no urgent news about Annie. As the traffic crawled along, Sophie reached into her bag to check the screen, but as she did, the line of cars in front edged their way forward, and she dropped the phone back in her bag.

In hindsight, Friday was a stupid day to travel, but with a training day at school and on the pretext of working from home, it seemed a good way to gain an extra day. Clearly most of London's residents had made the same plan, and her battered Corsa was sandwiched between grey and black four-by-fours, duvet covers pressed against the back windscreen, expensive mountain bikes strapped to the back.

At the first sight of a layby, Sophie pulled the car in and switched off the engine. It would mean losing precious minutes of driving time, but the call on her phone could be important. Sophie retrieved the phone from her bag and saw Elle's name flash up. She clicked on the message icon.

"Hi, um, it's Elle here, um, my name probably flashed up, so you probably know that already, um, sorry. Crap, I need to stop mumbling.

So, yeah, I'm really sorry, but Grace got a call saying there's been a cancellation, and she can go in for her knee op. I've just dropped her off at the hospital and the op is first thing tomorrow morning. She'll be nil by mouth today and they need to check bloods and stuff before she goes under the knife. That's a very long-winded way of saying everything is now up in the air and I can't guarantee I'll be home later when you arrive and, in all the excitement, I forgot to leave a key. I'm so sorry. I've got friends who I'm sure you could crash with if you can't find somewhere. Anyway, let me know, but maybe text rather than call as I'll be driving for the next hour or so, and I may be able to pick up, but you never know, crap, I'm out of..."

Sophie threw her phone down on the passenger seat and fought back tears. *Don't be stupid,* she told herself, i*t's not a big deal, you're just tired*. It was true, sitting in heavy traffic for eleven hours had sucked all the energy from her body, but so had the nerves and anticipation of meeting Elle and Grace for the first time. Now it looked as though her journey to Cornwall would be wasted. Was it even worth completing the rest of the drive? The traffic looked temptingly sparse on the opposite side of the road. Perhaps she could just turn round and forget all about her long-lost relatives? Sophie picked up her phone again.

Great news about your mum! I hope the operation goes well. Let me know how she gets on. Wondering if it would be better for me to go home and come down a different weekend when she's had time to recover?

Sophie clicked the send button, and a reply came back almost instantly.

No!

Three dots appeared showing that Elle was still typing.

Don't go home! Grace will be in theatre all morning tomorrow and won't be up for seeing anyone till the evening. Come over to mine first thing and we can hang out for the day. I don't want you to have a wasted trip and I've been dying to meet you!

P.S. Let me know if you need somewhere to crash. X

Somewhere to crash sounded like something Ben would say, and Sophie wondered what the age difference was between her and Elle. She typed out a message, then opened up her Airbnb app.

No, don't worry, I'll find somewhere. I've been stuck in traffic for hours, so would have been very late getting to yours, anyway. I'll find somewhere between here and Padstow to stop over and will meet you in the morning xx

The thought of sleeping on a stranger's sofa filled Sophie with dread. She scrolled through Airbnb, trying to find somewhere that wouldn't cost the earth. Most places wanted a booking of at least two nights, and she was giving up hope of finding anywhere to spend the night when a picture of a terraced house caught her eye. A double ensuite room for thirty-five pounds. Bodmin, the name rang a bell, but Sophie was ignorant about the geography of Cornwall and had to look it up on the map. It didn't look all that far from Padstow and would mean a shorter drive that evening.

Once booked in, Sophie waited for a gap in the traffic and pulled back onto the A303. Dusk was setting in and the twilight brought with it a renewed pace. Impatient to reach her bed for the night, Sophie revved her rust bucket of a vehicle and used a rare patch of dual carriageway to overtake the many caravans making their way west.

By nine o'clock, Sophie finally took a turning off to Bodmin. Being so central to the small town, the Airbnb was easy to find. Sophie pulled up outside and turned off the engine with a sigh of relief. She hated driving. It was fine when she was married to Will as he loved it and never minded doing the lion's share. Now, though, driving was another in a long list of tasks she had to get on with alone. Sometimes she longed for someone to take some of the load.

A front door opened, and warm light spilled out. A small woman who reminded Sophie of a pixie stood looking towards her car. Sophie waved and opened the door, stretching her tired bones as climbed out.

"Are you looking for number 21?" the woman asked.

"Yes, I'm Sophie. Are you Kate?"

"That's me, Kate Trenain. Nice to meet you. Do you need any help with your luggage?"

"No, I've only got a small bag. Thanks though."

Sophie grabbed her bag and followed the woman into the house. She walked straight into a cosy sitting room, tidy but with hints of family life dotted around its peripheries.

"Sorry about the mess," said Kate. "I wasn't expecting guests this evening, so I let Rosie play in here today. I thought I'd removed all signs of a child, but seems I've missed a few." She picked up a one-legged Barbie doll and shrugged apologetically at Sophie.

"Oh, don't worry, I'm just grateful you accepted the booking. I was beginning to think I'd need to sleep in my car tonight."

"I wish we could offer a longer stay, but I've got more guests coming tomorrow. Will you be alright finding somewhere for the weekend?"

"Yes, don't worry. I'm staying with family, but there was an emergency, which meant I couldn't be with them tonight. Nothing bad," added Sophie, seeing a worried look cross Kate's face, "I'm fine to stay with them tomorrow."

"That's great," said Kate. "I'll show you to your room. It's up here."

Sophie followed her host up a narrow staircase to her room. It was a pleasant surprise to find she had a sitting room in addition to a bedroom. "This is a very generous space," she told Kate.

"Thanks. I like guests to be comfortable. We live downstairs, though we've had to extend the house since Rosie arrived."

"Well, this accommodation is very welcome. It was a hellish drive, and I'm ready for an early night."

"I'll leave you to it," said Kate, "but come and find me if you need anything."

"Thanks," said Sophie, flopping down onto the bed as soon as her host had left the room. She fired off a quick text to let Elle know she had finally arrived in Cornwall, then another to Ben. Sophie wished he'd been able to come with her. She would have felt proud to have her son by her side, but some things had to be done alone. There would be plenty of time for Elle to meet Ben if things went well tomorrow.

Through the floorboards, Elle heard the comforting sounds of family life. Looking out of the window, she saw a large man carrying bin bags through the garden. She watched as he turned and blew a kiss to someone in the house. A little girl ran into the garden and the man dropped his bags of rubbish, scooped her up in his arms and spun her around.

"Not just before bed, Bob," she heard her host cry. The man shrugged an apology, the little girl running back inside to find her mother.

Sometimes, Sophie missed those days, when life was dominated by the schedule of bedtime stories and early starts. But she tried not to think about it. It hurt too much. Had Will been plotting his escape while mundane life carried on around him? Had he longed for his sons to grow so he could leave them without the weight of guilt that came with abandoning a child? Sophie sighed, pulled her toothbrush from her bag, and began getting ready for bed.

Chapter 37

April, 2018

Elle yawned and refilled her coffee mug. A tap on the window made her jump, and she looked up to see Jago's face pressed against the window.

"What are you doing here so early?" she asked him through the glass.

"I knew you'd be worrying about Grace, so thought you could probably do with some breakfast." He held a bag aloft, and Elle could almost smell the pastry through the single-glazed window. "Are you going to let me in?"

"Sorry," said Elle, unlocking the back door. Grace spoke of a time when no doors in the village would be locked, when everyone knew their neighbour, no one owning anything worth enough to steal. How times had changed.

Elle turned her back on Jago, pulling two chipped plates from the shelf and pouring him a black coffee. "Thanks for this, it was a long night. I couldn't sleep for worrying about Grace."

"How's she doing?"

"She's scared, not that she'll admit it. I wanted to stay longer at the hospital, but she kept saying she was fine. Crazy about the DNA results, isn't it?"

"Yes, crazy amazing. Hopefully, that will have given Grace a helpful distraction. I can't imagine her being scared of anything."

"It's not a sight I've seen often, that's for sure."

"When's the op happening?"

Elle checked her watch. "Hopefully in the next half an hour. I can't believe it's actually going ahead at last. I'm trying not to get my hopes up in case there's another cancellation."

"It will be fine," said Jago, pulling Elle into a hug that she was too tired to resist. "You've got today off, haven't you?"

"Yes. I'm meeting my long-lost cousin today."

"I assumed you would have cancelled with all that's going on."

"I would have done, if she hadn't been halfway to Cornwall when Grace got called in."

"She didn't stay here?"

"No, she found an Airbnb in Bodmin. She's coming over here this morning. I need to have a bit of a tidy before she gets here."

"The place looks fine to me," said Jago, looking around the kitchen over the top of Elle's head.

"That's such a man thing to say," said Elle, pulling away from him and appraising the state of the kitchen. "There's a load of washing up in the sink. I haven't cleaned the bathroom since last weekend. The washing basket's overflowing, and the entire house needs a vacuum."

"Where is it?"

"What?"

"The vacuum cleaner. Come on, I've got a few hours till I'm at the pub. We'll each do half an hour on the house, then we'll reward ourselves with those croissants. I'll hoover. You do the dishes."

"You sure?"

"Of course."

"Thanks," said Elle, retrieving the vacuum cleaner from the under-stairs cupboard.

Half an hour later, the cottage was presentable. Elle and Jago took their croissants outside and perched on the wall in front of the cottage.

"Remember when we used to hide behind here and pelt tourists with pebbles from our slingshot?"

Elle groaned. "We were proper tearaways. Poor Grace, the number of times she had people at the door complaining about us. It's a wonder she didn't ground me for life."

"She was probably cheering us on from behind the curtains." Elle turned and smiled at Jago. They were on safe ground, the time before things went wrong, the time before he stopped being her best friend.

"Why don't you bring your cousin to the pub for lunch? I'd love to meet her."

"Bit of a busman's holiday though."

"I'd treat you to lunch..."

"You're on. But no embarrassing stories about me, OK? I want to make a good impression."

"Fine," said Jago, dramatically sighing and jumping off the wall.

"I'd better get going. Good luck with your cousin."

"Thanks, see you later."

Elle sighed in frustration. Another opportunity to talk to Jago had been missed. If only he hadn't announced his plans to leave the country, she might have summoned the courage to break the news. Now it seemed pointless. She'd only be holding him back.

Elle climbed off the wall and walked inside. She tried looking at the cottage with fresh eyes, feeling a wave of embarrassment as she did so. In their emails, Sophie had said she was a teacher. What would a professional woman make of the rundown cottage? Would she be ashamed of the family she had inherited? Elle didn't have time to worry, as her phone vibrated against the wooden worktop, Sophie's name flashing up on the screen.

"Hi, I think I'm nearby, but not sure exactly which is your house."

"Where are you right now?"

"By the harbour, trying to avoid the dive-bombing seagulls." Sophie laughed, and Elle felt more at ease.

"Hang on," said Elle, running through to the sitting room and looking out of the window. "Are you wearing a navy duffle coat?"

"That's me."

"Great, I can see you. I'll come and find you."

Elle slipped her boots on and walked over to where her cousin stood. Shyness threatened, but she reminded herself that she was on home ground. This was her territory; Sophie was likely to be far more nervous than she was.

"Sophie?"

A woman with blonde curls and bright blue eyes turned, her dimples deepening as a smile creased her face. "Wow, I can't believe we're finally meeting. Should we hug?" Sophie held her arms wide, and Elle walked into them, feeling ungainly against Sophie's slim frame.

"That's our place," said Elle, pointing across to her cottage, patches of green moss creeping across weatherworn paint. She felt ashamed at the state of her home, her cheeks flushing as she remembered the letters from the town council and second-home owners suggesting she improve the *frontage of her property*.

"Wow, what an amazing location. I can't believe I've never been here before."

"You've never been to Cornwall?"

"No, we tried once when the boys were little, but a combination of a flat tyre and whining children caused my husband to turn back when we'd just reached Devon. Ex-husband, I should say."

Elle laughed and led Sophie to the back of the cottage. She opened the door and was hit by the smell of damp that she had grown used to. "I'd give you a tour, but you can see most of it from where you're standing. You can sleep in Grace's room. Because of her age, they're keeping her in for a couple of days."

"Sorry, that should have been the first thing I asked you. How is Grace? Did the operation go OK?"

"I'm still waiting for the call. Fingers crossed everything's gone to plan, and the hospital calls me soon."

"Are you sure it's OK me staying? I don't want to get in the way, given all you've got on your plate."

"You're a welcome distraction, trust me. I'm just sorry the accommodation's not up to much."

"What are you talking about?" said Sophie, wandering from the kitchen to the sitting room. "This place is adorable, and those views are incredible."

"Thanks, you're very kind."

"Not kind, honest. This place is charming. It reminds me of a house we used to stay in when we went on holiday to the Norfolk Broads. I feel very at home." Sophie flopped into a faded armchair and smiled up at Elle.

"Tea? Coffee?"

"Tea would be great, thanks."

"You must be tired after your long journey?"

"A bit, but not as tired as if I'd been at school. The Airbnb I stayed at was lovely. I haven't slept that well for months."

"That's good. I'm sorry about the last-minute change of plans."

"Stop saying sorry," laughed Sophie. "I've got a weekend in a sought-after part of Cornwall, with a generous host, in a gorgeous cottage. People pay thousands for those kinds of weekends."

Elle smiled at her cousin. Sophie was good company, her tinkling laugh and ready smile putting Elle's nerves at bay.

"Do you think our gran ever stayed here?"

"Yes, I think it's likely she did. You saw the photos I emailed?" Sophie nodded. "I think she lodged here with your mum. Quite how they all fitted in, I've no clue, but I guess standards were different in those days."

"I guess so. I wonder what she'd think if she could see us here now?" Elle grabbed the pile of photographs from the bookshelf and held one out so Sophie could see. "If only walls could talk," she said, looking around the cottage. If only.

Chapter 38

April, 2018

Sophie insisted on a tour of Padstow, oohing and aahing at the quaint shops, turning pale at the prices on restaurant menus. “What’s it like living here?” she asked Elle. “This place seems like paradise.”

Elle laughed. “It probably is paradise if you’re a second-home owner. It’s not such plain sailing for locals.”

“How do you mean?”

“Inflated house prices and minimum wage seasonal work aren’t a good recipe for a stable local community. You’ll struggle to find any locals living in town these days. Most live on the outskirts.”

“You live as central as you can get, though.”

Elle laughed again. “We’re clinging on by the skin of our teeth. You should see the stack of offers we’ve had for the cottage.”

“You’re not tempted to sell up?”

“Tempted, yes. Will we do it? Not if I can help it. I wavered a bit when Grace’s knee got bad, but now she’s having the op, I want to keep her in her home. It sounds ridiculous wanting to keep the cottage, but it’s the only constant Grace has had in her life. First there was the uncertainty over her adoption, then a series of unsuccessful encounters with men. The cottage has always been there, always been home. I’ll keep her in it as long as I can.”

"Good for you. The view you have from the cottage is priceless."

"What about you? Do you live close to the sea?"

"Yes, I live opposite the beach. I take it for granted, but I'm very lucky."

The two women stopped at the quayside. "Do you fancy an ice cream?" asked Elle. "It's an essential experience while on holiday."

"Why not?" said Sophie.

Elle popped into a café and emerged with two cones. They sat down on the quay, their legs dangling down, watching the fishing boats bobbing on calm water.

"Is it always this busy?" asked Sophie.

"This is nothing. We've not even hit the Easter holidays yet. In summer, you can barely move for crowds."

"Urgh," said Sophie, "that doesn't sound like much fun."

"Where you live must get pretty busy too," said Elle, "what with you being so near the beach?"

"Hmm," said Sophie, "Lowestoft's something of a hidden gem. It gets busier in the summer, but nothing like you're describing."

"Maybe I'll come and spend the summer with you," laughed Elle.

"You're welcome anytime," said Sophie, surprised at how easy it was to be in Elle's company. It was as though they'd known each other for years rather than hours. "Where to next?" Sophie asked, popping the remaining ice cream into her mouth.

"Is it too early to get lunch?" asked Elle.

Sophie grinned. "You're just like I was," she said.

"What do you mean?"

"When I was pregnant with my boys, I had to eat every two hours or God help those around me."

Elle went pale, ignoring the ice cream melting around her hand. Sophie's palm flew to her mouth. "Oh my God," she said. "I'm so sorry. I thought you were pregnant." She slapped her hand to her mouth, her eyes widening. "I honestly didn't mean any offence. You're really slim, you don't look fat at all. Please accept my apologies."

To Sophie's dismay, Elle lifted her cuff and brushed tears from her eyes. "You haven't offended me," she said, turning to look at Sophie. "That's not why I'm crying. How did you know?"

"So, you are?"

Elle nodded.

"Phew. Well, aside from the fact you stroke your stomach every couple of minutes?"

"I don't..."

"You do. There was also the way you reacted to the smell in the lobster hatchery. I couldn't smell anything, but you turned green. Then there was the way your eyes were drawn to the baby clothes in the shop window."

"Anything else?" asked Elle, open-mouthed.

"Well, it was true when I said you don't look fat, but there is a small round belly beneath your shirt. I saw it when you were walking into the wind."

"Are you always this observant?"

"It's a useful skill as a primary school teacher," said Sophie. "You need eyes like a hawk."

Elle's eyes filled with tears once more. "You have no idea how good it is to talk to someone about this," she said. "It's been my little secret for months."

"I don't think you'll be able to keep it a secret for much longer," said Sophie, looking down at Elle's stomach. "Doesn't Grace know?"

"Yes, but I don't like talking to her about it. She has certain opinions that I don't share."

"Ah. Why don't you tell me all about it over lunch?"

"Good plan. But, Sophie?"

"Yes?"

"Please don't mention it again till we're alone. It would only take one person to overhear, and the news will be all around the village in no time."

Sophie pretended to pull a zip across her lips. Elle linked her arm with hers and led her towards the pub. The day was warm and bright but held an early spring chill, and walking into the pub felt like being enveloped in a thick blanket.

"So this is the mysterious Sophie?" said Jago, as the two women walked to the bar.

"Sophie, this is my friend, Jago," said Elle. Jago leaned over the bar and held out a hand for her to shake.

"A pleasure to meet you," he said.

"Likewise," said Sophie.

Elle noticed Sophie blush as their hands touched. A shot of jealousy ran through her as she pictured all the svelte young Aussies he'd be mingling with in his new life.

"Why don't you two ladies find a seat and I'll bring over some menus and your drinks? What will it be, Sophie?"

"A glass of merlot, please."

"Elle?"

"Just a lemonade, thanks. I've got a banging headache." Elle avoided catching Sophie's eye.

"It will be all the stress with Grace," said Jago, reaching out and squeezing Elle's hand. "Have you heard from the hospital?"

"Not yet. Hopefully, they'll call me soon."

"I'm sure they will. Now you two go and chill. I'll bring your drinks over in a sec."

"Thanks," said Elle, leading Sophie to a table at the far side of the room.

"It's lovely in here," said Sophie as they sat down. "Is this where you work?"

"Yes, for the time being. I'm trying to find something better paid, but no luck so far. Sorry," said Elle as her phone buzzed in her pocket. "I need to take this."

"No problem," said Sophie, as Elle took her phone outside.

"She's abandoned you already, has she?" asked Jago, setting two drinks down on the table in front of Sophie.

"Her phone rang. Maybe the hospital?"

"Oh wow, I hope it's good news." Jago pulled back a chair and sat down. "So, what do you make of Padstow so far?"

"I love it," said Sophie. "You're so lucky to live here."

"Yes, I guess we are. Although I won't be living here much longer."

"No?"

"I've been offered a job in Australia. To be honest, I was worried about leaving Elle here by herself with Grace, but now she has you, I feel better about it."

"Is Elle struggling?"

"I think things have been tough. She moved home not that long ago and has been juggling caring for Grace while working here and trying to keep the cottage standing. I help where I can, but it's not easy for her. Hopefully, if it's good news from the hospital, things will settle down for her a bit."

Sophie smiled and nodded, not trusting herself to open her mouth. With a baby on the way, she doubted things would get easier for Elle any time soon.

Elle walked back into the pub, her face lit up with a grin.

"Good news?" asked Jago, pushing his chair back and walking to her.

"Yes," said Elle. She promptly burst into tears and Jago pulled her into a hug. "Sorry about that," she said, removing herself from his arms and returning to the table. "It's the relief of it all. The op went well. Grace has been moved to recovery and should be home in a couple of days."

"That's fantastic news," said Sophie.

"Wait there, ladies," said Jago, "this calls for a proper celebration."

He returned moments later with a bottle of prosecco. "I couldn't stretch to champagne, unfortunately," he said, pouring out two glasses.

"Not for me," said Elle, pointing to her head.

"Sod the headache," said Jago.

Elle smiled and took a small sip from her glass.

"Thank you," said Sophie.

"No problem. Just shout when you're ready to order."

With Jago back behind the bar, Sophie turned to Elle. "Is he the father?" she whispered.

"Is it that obvious?"

"It's obvious he's in love with you."

Elle laughed. "No, not Jago. We're just good friends."

"I can't imagine wanting to have a baby with any of my good friends," said Sophie, smirking behind her glass.

"It was an accident."

"And he doesn't know?"

"No. He's leaving soon, and I don't want to tie him down."

"Are you sure you're not just scared?" Elle frowned, and Sophie winced. "Sorry," she said, "I'm overstepping the mark. We've only just met and I'm dishing out advice. Ignore me."

"Don't worry," said Elle. "You're probably right. It's too late now, anyway. His flight is booked, his new job awaits. Before long, all I'll be to him is a fond memory."

"And the mother of his child."

"Can we change the subject, please? Here, let's look at the menu. I'm starving."

Chapter 39

1970

Dear Grace,

Thank you for your last letter and the photographs of Paris. What a shame you couldn't bring Pierre home in your suitcase! It may have only been a holiday fling, but how romantic, and what a contrast to your time with John. You never know, you may find a handsome Frenchman knocking on your door one day with a baguette under his arm, wearing a beret, demanding you make an honest man out of him. Alright, so perhaps I'm getting carried away, but now I'm a wife and mother, I must live vicariously through you.

I've recently returned from my own adventure, not that Northumberland is as exciting as France! I travelled to the island with Frank last week and it proved a very cathartic trip for us both. It was a long journey, but we stopped over in Durham for a night to break it up, and what a treat it was to drive over to the island on the not-so-new causeway! We arrived early and had to wait for the tide to depart, and it was so exciting watching the road emerge from beneath the water. Neither of us could quite believe our eyes.

Jimmy met us on the mainland side once the water had cleared and was keen to point out the recent improvements to the causeway, including better signage, turning areas, and improvements to the refuge box. There have been several casualties after vehicles became trapped by water in the previous few years, so it's hoped the new measures will improve things. We stopped to look at the refuge box, which is like a small wooden shed on stilts. Most impressive was a newly installed telephone that connects directly to Berwick police. I can imagine stranded travellers being most grateful for this technological advancement should they become trapped and need to escape the encroaching tide!

These days, Jimmy and Clara live in a small cottage, so rather than squeeze in with them, we stayed at the Lindisfarne hotel where Amy still works, now as the general manager. It felt very luxurious having a large bedroom all to myself, but Frank insisted on paying and he was keen to make the trip as comfortable as possible. We visited Ben, Amy, and their children, and I had the pleasure of catching up with my old friend, Genie Guthrey. You may remember me telling you about her hopelessness at ever finding a husband? Well, she needn't have worried, as she caught the eye of a lovely man called Roger who came to the island for a holiday, and they married a year to the day after first meeting. They now have three beautiful daughters and run the post office together since her parents died. It was wonderful to see her so happy and we spent a fun evening reminiscing about our summer spent together.

Frank decided to dedicate a bench to Marnie's memory. Jimmy organised to have one delivered to the island, and we positioned it overlooking the harbour and castle. We had a brief ceremony where we all said a few words in memory of Mum, and then we went back to Jimmy and Clara's cottage, where we planted a rose bush in memory of my grandmother Rose.

I think the best thing about our trip was seeing the change in Frank. He'd already shown glimmers of his old self since we moved in with him, but being on the island brought colour back to his cheeks and put a spring back in his step. I was worried the change would be temporary, but since we've been home, he's been much more like his old self. I still catch him staring at photographs of Mum, but that's to be expected. From experience I know the complexities of grief, but for a while it felt as though I'd lost them both, so the improvement in Frank has been very welcome.

We were only away for a week, but I swear Sophie had grown an inch during that time. I missed her more than I thought I would, and I was rather pleased to hear from Sam that she also missed me. I'd expected her to delight in a week with just her daddy, but he said she cried several times and kept asking when I was coming home. Hearing that news was the best welcome home I could have received.

Speaking of my daughter, I'd better go and spend some time with her, but I look forward to hearing from you soon.

All my love,

Your friend,

Annie

Chapter 40

April, 2018

Elle wished Grace had waited longer before insisting on the long drive east. Despite the hire car's seat being pushed back as far as it would go, Grace's face flickered with pain as the drive took its toll on her knee.

"It's a shame we couldn't have come in Jago's van," she said for the fiftieth time that day.

"The step up would have been too tricky with your knee."

Grace humphed. "My knee is healing nicely, according to the doctor."

"Yes, but did you tell your doctor you were planning on sitting in a car for nine hours three weeks after your operation? I know the nurse told you it was possible, but that doesn't mean it's wise."

Grace humphed again and turned to look out of the window. "It's very flat around here, isn't it?"

"And they have far too many roundabouts," muttered Elle, wondering if they'd ever make it past Ipswich. She yawned, opening her window to let the fresh air in. The drive felt endless, more so due to the frequent stops to allow Grace to stretch her legs.

After what felt like a lifetime, Ipswich was behind them and the car wove along a twisting road flanked by thatched cottages and pretty villages.

"This is more like it," said Grace, "what charming houses." She smiled as she stared beyond the window, excitement pushing tiredness and aching bones to the backs of both their minds.

"Not long now," said Elle, sneaking a glance out of the side window as they passed what looked like a vast lake.

"I suppose my mother must have done this journey by train."

"A far more sensible idea," said Elle. "If we'd taken the train, we could have had a few G and Ts on the journey."

"I'm sorry," said Grace. "It's my fault you've had such a long drive."

"Don't be silly," said Elle. "I'd rather a long drive than have you stumbling up and down staircases and squished into packed tube trains."

"We could've taken a taxi across London."

"We could," said Elle, deciding the next time they made the journey, it would be by train. She'd tried to refuse Jago's offer to hire a car for them, but with money so tight, she'd been forced to accept. Elle adjusted her seatbelt and shuffled to get comfortable.

"You're starting to show," said Grace.

"It's OK. Sophie knows about the baby."

"You told Sophie?"

"Yes. She guessed, and I could hardly deny it. Is that a problem?" Elle glanced across at Grace, whose lips were pursed in a thin line.

"I would've thought telling the father was more of a priority than sharing the news with a woman you barely know."

"Sophie's family."

"So's Jago. He just doesn't know it yet."

"He's moving to Australia."

Grace slammed her hand against the armrest. "You silly, silly, girl. Do you think he'd be off to Australia if he knew about the baby? It's like you're deliberately making life hard for yourself."

"I don't want to trap him. I don't want him to resent me for making him stay."

"And what about what Jago wants? You're not giving him a choice."

"Can we change the subject, please?" asked Elle. "I need to concentrate on the road."

Grace muttered something under her breath, then fell quiet. Elle found the silence worse than any of Grace's rebukes. This trip should be an exciting moment to share, not a moment shrouded by awkward silence.

As they arrived in the town, Elle followed signs to the seafront. They drove along a road flanked by tall terraces, the sea lying in a ribbon on the far side of the road.

"I think this is the one," said Elle, pulling up outside a tall four-storey house.

"You didn't tell me Sophie was rich," said Grace.

"I don't think she is," said Elle. "Not everywhere costs as much as Padstow."

"True. Oh goodness, isn't it exciting to see the sea?"

Elle laughed. "We see the sea every day."

"But not this sea. This is the North Sea. And anyway, what we see is technically an estuary leading to the Atlantic Ocean. It isn't, in fact, a sea at all."

"No need to be so pedantic," said Elle, grateful the awkward silence had been broken.

"Can we take a quick look at the beach?" asked Grace.

"Why not?"

They climbed out of the car, the wind whipping their hair into their eyes. Elle took Grace by the arm and helped her across the road.

"This is magnificent," said Grace, squinting against the sun and staring up and down the beach. "Look at those beach huts, such pretty colours. And all this space. Ah," she said, throwing her arms wide. "Isn't it just wonderful to be able to breathe, to be able to walk in a straight line and not dodge thousands of people in your path?"

"Lowestoft does seem to have its advantages."

"Isn't it strange that Jack never came here? I mean, if he'd had some sort of relationship with Marnie, you would have thought he might have visited?"

"Not if theirs was a clandestine affair."

Grace winced.

"Sorry."

"Have you found any answers in those letters you've been reading?"

"No, not yet. I'm still only up to 1970. I'm taking my time with them, trying to savour all the news Annie shared and picture the people and places she mentioned. In the last letter I read, she'd just been to visit Holy Island."

"Holy Island?"

"Yes, Marnie's family were islanders, from what I gather."

"Another puzzle piece to slot into place."

"Precisely. Now, how about we meet this niece of mine?"

Chapter 41

April, 2018

Grace was not what Sophie had been expecting. Given her age and recent health problems, Sophie was prepared for a frail old lady. Grace was nothing of the sort. Sophie watched as a sprightly woman with waist-length curls near enough jumped out of the car and took a big gulp of sea air. Elle climbed out of the car, stretching her arms above her head and opening her mouth wide in a yawn.

Sophie knew she should move from the window, open the front door, and welcome them into her home. Instead, she stayed out of sight, judging the mother-daughter dynamics and comparing them to her own experience. Elle looked up at the house, checking her phone to make sure she had the right number. Across the roof of the car, Grace and Elle entered into a discussion, Elle pointing back at the house, Grace towards the sea. Sophie watched as Elle's shoulders flopped down in a sigh, before walking round to Grace, handing her a walking stick, checking both ways, then crossing the road.

Sophie pulled herself away from the window, running into the hall and pushing her feet into slipper boots. She grabbed a key from its hook and let herself out into the evening light. Just above the promenade wall, she could see the heads of her cousin and aunt. By the time Sophie caught up with them, they were sitting on a bench, looking out across miles of golden sand. The sun tinted the sea and sky pink, making the scene before them more California than Suffolk. Grace and Elle looked up in surprise as Sophie walked over to them. Elle jumped up, pulling her into a bear hug.

"Good to see you again," Elle said into Sophie's hair.

"Good to see you too," said Sophie. "I saw you from the window and thought I'd come out and say hello."

"Sophie, this is my mother, Grace. Grace, Sophie."

Grace stood up, clutching Sophie's hands and looking deep into her eyes. "I always thought it was just me and Elle. I never expected to have any other family. You have no idea what a pleasure it is to meet you, my dear."

"Likewise," said Sophie, taking in the details of Grace's face, the deep lines in places that showed she had lived a life full of smiles. Her eyes were as bright as a teenager's, glinting like sun on water.

"Do you want to stay out here for a little while? I can bring you over a cup of tea?"

"Oh no, no, it's alright, we'll come inside now. I just wanted to glimpse the sea before the light fails us."

"Oh, don't worry about that," said Sophie. "It takes forever to get dark at this time of year. Being the most easterly part of the UK, the sun never sets for long once we approach summertime."

"How weird is it we both ended up living within a stone's throw of the beach?" said Elle, linking arms with Sophie.

"I guess it's in our blood," said Sophie, leading her cousin and aunt across the road towards her house. Having spent time in Elle and Grace's cottage, she felt no nerves showing them her own home.

"This place is massive," said Elle as they stepped through the door and into a large entrance hall.

"You get a lot more for your money here," laughed Sophie. "Lowestoft is a hidden gem."

"It sure is, love," said Grace, wandering across to the large bay window and staring out to the sea. "How long have you lived here?"

"Over twenty years. I bought the place with my ex-husband before we had children. We thought it would be a good place to raise a family."

"And was it?"

"Yes, it was. Unfortunately, it's not such a great place to be a twenty-something looking for work. My eldest son recently moved to Scotland to live with his father."

"And your youngest?"

"Still living here with me. He works at the nursing home where Mum lives."

"I can't wait to see her," said Grace, "and your son, of course."

Sophie managed a sad smile. "I wish you could have visited Mum when she was still Mum. So often these days I feel like I don't know her at all. I'm afraid it may confuse her meeting you. She may struggle to understand who you are."

"Don't worry, dear. I'm prepared for what I may find. Of course, it would have been wonderful to visit your mother before that evil disease took hold, but as the saying goes, better late than never. Besides, I have all the letters she wrote over the years to remind me of the woman she once was. It's strange to think we've not laid eyes on each other for over sixty years. I imagine we've both changed a lot in that time. Will we be going to the nursing home tomorrow?"

"I wondered about meeting on the quay. I thought it may help unlock some of her memories. And I know my mum, she's a proud woman. Whether she's aware of it, I know she'd rather you didn't see her in the home. It's a good place, but not where she would have wanted to end up."

"I understand," said Grace, reaching across and squeezing Sophie's hand.

"Sorry," said Sophie. "I haven't offered you a drink. And you must be starving after your long journey."

Elle laughed. "Not with all the snacks Grace packed. But a cuppa would be lovely."

"Are you sure you don't fancy something a little stronger?" asked Grace, pulling a bottle of champagne from her bag.

"Don't tell me you've been carting that round every service station we stopped at?" asked Elle, tapping her head with her palm.

Grace grinned. "This is a celebration," she said. "I think champagne is the drink of choice on such occasions."

Elle shook her head, wondering how Grace had got hold of a bottle of champagne. Jago. It had to be.

"Why don't I put that in the fridge to chill," said Sophie. "We can start with tea, then move on to champagne."

"Very civilised," said Grace, sinking down into an armchair.

Ben arrived home and Sophie looked on in admiration as he chatted easily to Elle and Grace. Her heart swelled with pride as he described his work at the nursing home and spoke of his desire to one day train as a nurse. They spent a pleasant evening sharing stories, looking through old photographs and getting to know one another. Sophie bathed in Grace's warmth and humour, enjoying the playful dynamic between mother and daughter. She wished Annie could join in the reunion and prayed the meeting the following day would go well. Only time would tell.

Chapter 42

April, 2018

Sophie pulled the car up as close as she could to the harbour. It had been a long time since Annie had walked anywhere without the aid of a Zimmer frame. She was nervous; this moment could go either way. In a rare lucid moment, it had been Annie who insisted on meeting Grace here, rather than the nursing home where she was comfortable and in familiar surroundings. Sophie worried she'd forget the decision she'd made, but a week later Annie's mind was still set. She had even written it down on a piece of paper in scrawling, spidery letters, so different from the neat loops and joins that characterised her handwriting in younger years. The carers had gone to a lot of trouble to get Annie ready. Her hair had been blow-dried, and she had on a two-piece that Sophie hadn't seen before. The carer must have bought it, for there was no way Annie was up to walking round the shops.

Annie leaned her weight against Sophie, not that she weighed more than a small child these days, she was all skin and bone. They walked in silence, slow shuffling steps disturbing seagulls who protested with angry squawks. Sophie wondered how many meetings, how many goodbyes had happened beside this harbour. She thought of the fishermen from long ago, leaving their families for weeks, if not months on end. She thought of the arrivals, all those people from foreign lands, from further up the coast, all come to share in the riches of Lowestoft's spoils.

Sophie spotted Elle and Grace before they spotted her. They were sitting on a concrete wall which barred the sea from the town. Their legs swung below them, Grace's bright red sandals startling against the grey concrete and murky brown of the water below. Sophie called their names, and they looked up, shielding their eyes against the sun. Elle leaped up onto her feet and rushed over to Sophie.

"Who are you, dear? Who are you? Who are you?" asked Annie, distressed at the touch of Elle's hand.

"Mum, this is your niece, this is Elle. Remember? I told you about her."

"I don't know nothing about no Elle. Who are you? Why are you touching me?"

"Mum..."

Sophie looked at Elle and gave a shake of her head. Elle let go of Annie's arm, hanging back a couple of paces from mother and daughter. They walked to where Grace sat, hand still shielding her eyes, as though frozen in time.

Grace slowly climbed to her feet and stepped towards Annie. "Annie, we haven't met in such a long time. I'm your sister Grace, from Padstow."

"Padstow? I don't have a sister. I live in Lowestoft, not Padstow."

Sophie pulled the photograph of Marnie, Annie and baby Grace standing beside Padstow harbour. "Look, Mum. That's Gran, your mum, that little girl is you, and that baby, well, that baby is Grace." Sophie pointed from the photograph to Grace and back again.

"Grace? Is it really you?"

"Yes, Annie," said Grace, tears streaming down her face. "It's me. Your little sister."

Annie let go of Sophie's arm, lifting her hands and placing them on Grace's cheeks. "But you're all grown up. You're old."

Grace laughed. "Yes, I'm not so little anymore."

"Your hair should be red."

"It hasn't been red for a long time now, Annie."

Annie took hold of one of Grace's curls, letting it slip gently through her fingers. "Red," she whispered. "Just like Jack's."

Grace's eyes filled with tears. "And yours was blonde, like Marnie's."

Annie nodded, a smile tugging her lips as tears filled her eyes. "I wanted to see you long before now. All those years we wrote to each other and so many times I wanted to say yes, come and see me, but I was scared I wouldn't be able to keep Mum's secret if I saw you. I worried it would have been cruel to Aunt Helen. Once Helen and Mum were gone, I should have spoken up. But... oh, where am I?" Annie's eyes grew cloudy, and she looked around her, trying to decipher where she was and why.

Grace took Annie's hands and said in a gentle voice, "you're here with me, Annie. You're with your sister, Grace. Please don't feel any guilt about not telling me the truth about Marnie. Helen and Richard raised me as their own and I grew up surrounded by love."

"But I wanted you with me. I wanted to have a sister." Her voice had become a distressed whine, and she whipped her head from side to side as if trying to shake off the past. "Mum said I could tell you the truth if I wanted to, but it would have hurt too many people." Annie let out a sob, collapsing onto Sophie, who wrapped her arms around her mother and held her tight, stroking her hair. When Annie had calmed down, she looked up again at Grace. "You know, sometimes I used to talk to you, as if you were an imaginary friend." Annie's cheeks turned pink and she looked down at her shoes.

"I'm not imaginary anymore," said Grace. "And I'm here, with you, in Lowestoft."

"But look at us," said Annie. "We're too old to play. You've come too late."

"It's never too late," said Grace, stroking her thumbs across the papery skin on Annie's hands.

"I'm tired," said Annie. "Where's my boy?"

"Do you mean Ben?"

"Yes, that's the one. Where is he?"

"He's here," said Sophie, as Ben came to stand beside Annie.

"Are you alright, Gran?"

"I'm tired. I don't know who these people are." Annie looked up at Ben with wide, frightened eyes.

"It's OK, Gran. Let's get you home, shall we?"

Ben helped Annie begin the slow walk along the harbour side, Sophie, Elle and Grace walking behind.

"I'm sorry," said Sophie. "I'd hoped you might get more out of Mum."

"You've nothing to apologise for," said Grace. "We met, she knew me, I knew her, that's all that matters."

Ben and Annie stopped walking and Annie lifted an arm to the boats. "My dad used to go out on his boat. He'd be gone for days on end, weeks sometimes. It was the sea that took him from us. I've never trusted the sea since."

Chapter 43

1976

Dear Grace,

Congratulations on your engagement! I'm so pleased you have a second chance at love (or third if you count Pierre!). It sounds as though you and Arthur are a good match, and you're right that after your experience with John, steady and stable must make a nice change.

Will you both live in the cottage when you're married, or will you make a fresh start somewhere else? I'm sure Arthur's current home in Wadebridge is nice enough, but it would be hard to beat the views you have and I'm sure moving inland would be a big change, having lived by the sea your entire life.

It must feel strange living in the cottage without Helen. I've thought of her often over the past year and wish I had tried to visit before she died. You've coped remarkably well, but it must be lovely to have someone to look after you now. I'm sure Helen would have approved of your choice of husband, and it would have brought her much joy to know you've found a second chance at happiness.

It's been two months now since we lost Frank, and the house still feels strange without him in it. Sophie has moved into what was Frank's bedroom, as it's much bigger than the box room she was in before. She chose yellow for the walls, although I'm not sure why we bothered painting them as she's covered them in posters pulled out from Bunty *magazine.*

Sophie keeps crazing to read Jackie, *but I won't let her anywhere near those magazines until she's a lot older! She already seems too grown up for my liking, and we frequently butt heads, although Sam can do no wrong in her eyes.*

Frank kindly left us some money in his will, and we have been able to pay off the loan we took out on the Sally Ann, update the bathroom with a more modern suite (in a lovely avocado green), and there's still a little left over. I wanted to go on a family holiday at Easter, but Sophie is off on a pack holiday with the Brownies (somewhere near Bungay so not too far from home) and Sam says he's too busy with the Sally Ann to take time away. He suggested I go away for a few days with a friend, and when I mentioned it to Beryl, she jumped at the chance.

We've been adventurous and have booked a few days away over in Holland. From where we are, it's very easy, as there are regular ferries from Harwich, and then we'll take a coach to Amsterdam. It will be the first time either Beryl or I have left the country, and we're both as nervous as we are excited.

I know I'm lucky to have a husband who'll encourage me to go away with friends. It's hard to imagine I ever doubted my love for Sam. We've lost some of the passion we had in our early years of marriage, but what's grown in its place is a far deeper love, and he truly is my best friend. I hope you find the same deep love for Arthur. It sounds as though he's like my Sam; quiet, unassuming, but with a kind heart. Who knows, you may even welcome your own bundle of joy soon.

Speaking of Sam, he's begun talking about leaving the fishing industry. I never thought I'd see the day, but apparently the North Sea oil rigs have been hiring trawlermen as standby safety vessels. There's no doubt Sam is qualified, what with his naval experience, volunteering with the lifeboat, and the number of times he's come to the aid of other vessels, but

I worry how he'd feel leaving fishing behind. It's always been his passion, and I can't see working for the oil rigs will hold quite the same appeal, or perhaps I'm being too romantic about it. It would certainly be a safer job, I'm sure, but I'd still have nights worrying about him being out in the middle of the sea in all weathers.

Anyway, I'd better leave this letter here but let me know all about your wedding plans and if you've chosen a dress yet. And, Grace, I am so happy for you,

All my love,

Your friend,

Annie

Chapter 44

April, 2018

"Do you mind if I head upstairs for a nap?" asked Elle. "I'm sorry to be feeble, but ever since I found out I was pregnant, all I've wanted to do is sleep."

"Of course I don't mind," said Sophie. "Would you like to take a cup of tea up with you?"

"No, I'll grab a glass of water on my way up. Will you be OK, Grace?"

"Of course I will. I don't need babysitting."

Elle rolled her eyes and waved as she walked towards the stairs.

"If you'd like a rest too, please feel free," said Sophie. "You had a long day of travelling yesterday and I know how tiring that journey can be."

"Actually," said Grace, "I rather fancy a walk along the seafront, if you'd like to join me? I can't go too far as my knee is still healing, but my handsome physiotherapist tells me it's good to move it and build strength gradually by taking short walks."

"I'd love to join you," said Sophie. "I'll grab my coat."

The two women crossed the road, Sophie linking arms with Grace, worried about the state of her new knee. It was only a few weeks since the operation, and the last thing Sophie wanted was to set back her recovery.

"I'm sorry it didn't go so well with Mum earlier," said Sophie, as they ambled along the seafront.

"Nonsense. I've already told you how special it was to see Annie again. The last time I saw her in person was shortly after her eighteenth birthday."

"Goodness, that long? Was there a reason she visited you then?"

Grace looked at Sophie and narrowed her eyes. "How much do you know about your mother's life before she married your father?"

"Very little. She never talked about her past when I was younger, and by the time I was old enough to be interested, I had my own family to worry about. One of my biggest regrets is that I never asked her questions when I could. We were never especially close, you see."

"Oh dear, that is sad to hear."

Sophie smiled. "It wasn't that bad. I was a daddy's girl, that's all. Me and him were so similar in temperament, even though I look like Mum. I always got the impression I was a disappointment to her."

"Why on earth would you have been a disappointment?"

"I don't think she wanted me to move back to Lowestoft after university. I think she saw it as a backwards step. And the fact I got pregnant so young, well, I don't think she liked my ex, Will, although it turns out that was for good reason."

"She probably just wanted what was best for you. That time she visited us in Padstow just after her birthday, she seemed so lost."

"Why would she have seemed lost?"

"You know she lived in Padstow during the war?"

"Yes, but I've only found out recently. Was she an evacuee?"

"In a sense, yes, but she came to Padstow before the war. Your mum and Marnie were meeting Tom there."

"Tom?"

"Your grandfather."

Sophie smiled. "No, my grandfather was called Frank."

"Frank was your grandmother's second husband."

"What?"

"Let's sit," said Grace, pointing to a bench overlooking the sea and shooing away seagulls with her walking stick.

The two women sat down and for a few minutes Sophie closed her eyes, enjoying the warmth of the sun on her lips and the gentle breeze against her cheeks. "Why have I never heard about Tom?"

"Your mother once told me in her letters it would have felt disloyal to Frank to tell you about Tom. I think she always planned to tell you when you were an adult, but she wanted you to see Frank as your grandfather, nothing more and nothing less."

"Can you tell me about Tom?" she said, opening her eyes and turning to Grace.

"He died before I came along," said Grace, "so everything I know is second-hand, either from Annie or my Aunt Helen."

"That's alright, it's a lot more than I know."

Grace reached out her hand and squeezed Sophie's. "Tom was a Lowestoft fisherman. He had his own boat, the *Sally Ann*, which had been passed down to him by his father, Roy. Each winter and spring, fishermen from the east would head west, in search of more abundant fishing grounds. According to Helen, in previous years Tom had come alone, but in 1939, with war looming on the horizon, he decided to bring Marnie and Annie with him. They took the train, while Tom and his crew sailed down the coast. On the way, somewhere off the coast of Cornwall, Tom's boat hit bad weather. He was washed overboard, and his body was never found."

"Oh, God, that's awful," said Sophie, tears filling her eyes. "Why wouldn't Mum have told me about this?"

Grace shrugged. "It was a very traumatic time for her. She was only five years old. By the time Annie returned to Lowestoft at the end of the war, Marnie had met Frank. They married in a joint ceremony with Jimmy and Clara up on the island."

"The island?"

"Yes, Holy Island, Lindisfarne."

"Oh, yes. I remember Mum going up there a few times when I was young, but she never took me with her."

Grace shifted on the bench, and the muscles in her face twitched.

"What aren't you telling me, Grace?"

"The island held mixed emotions for your mother. Shortly after she came to visit us in Padstow, she travelled up to the island to spend the summer working at Jimmy and Clara's hotel."

"Hotel? What hotel?"

Grace shook her head. "Goodness, Annie really kept you in the dark, didn't she?" Sophie shrugged and Grace continued. "They were an island family, the Watsons. Your grandmother Marnie, her brother Jimmy, and Jimmy's wife Clara were all born and grew up there. Jimmy and Clara left the island in 1913 to follow the herring down to Lowestoft, although from the little I know, each had a complicated family situation that left them little choice. Eventually, Jimmy and Clara ended up back on the island and ran a hotel until they retired."

"So, they must have retired before I was born?"

"Yes."

"And my grandmother? She never wanted to go back?"

"She'd made her home here in Lowestoft and was happy to settle here. Anyway, as I said, at eighteen Annie was a little lost, searching around for where she belonged. Whatever she was looking for, she didn't find it in Padstow, so continued her search up on the island.

Now, at the time, I was unaware of what was going on up there. I was still at school, you see, but I found out later that Annie met a man."

"But I thought my mum and dad were childhood sweethearts?"

"They were, but with one, um, what should I say… blip, yes, blip will do."

"As in a 'cheating on my dad' sort of blip?"

"Oh, I think Annie had broken things off with Sam before she took up with Blaine McCloud."

"Blaine McCloud? What sort of name is that? He sounds like a villain from a historical fiction novel."

Grace chuckled. "You're not far off the mark. He tricked Annie, left her even more broken than when she arrived. Your father forgave her and took her back, but the experience left a sour taste in both their mouths. Sam was a forgiving man, but he never returned to the island after all that happened. Your mother wrote to me after each of her visits, and I got the impression she was torn between a love for the place and memories of her own foolishness and hurt."

"I wish she'd taken me with her at least once."

"After Jimmy and Clara died, I suppose she felt she had no reason to visit again. Her only remaining relatives were a cousin, Ben, his wife, Amy, and their children. But when Amy's mother became ill, they moved to the mainland."

"I vaguely remember Jimmy and Clara. They came to visit us a few times when I was little. I remember being scared of Jimmy at first as he had all this long white curly hair and I thought he was a wizard, but then he gave me sweets and suddenly didn't seem frightening at all. And Clara, she must have been at least eighty when I last saw her, but I remember she didn't look like any other old ladies I'd met. She wore wide-legged trousers and a silk shirt, and I thought she was a film star."

Grace laughed. "Yes, I remember Annie telling me Clara was always well turned out and still turned heads, even as an older woman. Her mother was beautiful too and Annie was named after her."

"There's so much about my family I don't know," said Sophie, shaking her head. "I have a vague recollection of Mum curled up on her bed crying, and when I asked Dad what was wrong, he told me Jimmy and Clara had died, and Mum was very upset by the news."

"Yes, their deaths were as romantic as their love story. They were born on the same night in 1895 and died within three days of each other in the spring of 1978. I remember it as it was around the same time Elle was born."

"It wasn't..."

"Oh no," said Grace, taking hold of Sophie's hand, "they died of natural causes. Clara was the first to go, and everyone said Jimmy then died of a broken heart. Their path to love wasn't a smooth one, and I suppose once they'd found each other again, they never wanted to be separated, even by death."

"Do you know their story? How they got together?"

Grace smiled. "I know bits and pieces, but not the full picture."

"Well, given how good we've been at uncovering family secrets so far, I'd say if anyone is able to find out Jimmy and Clara's story, it's us."

Chapter 45

April, 2018

A soft knocking on the door woke Elle. She rubbed her eyes and pulled herself up to sitting. "Come in."

"Sorry, I didn't realise you were still sleeping," said Sophie, walking into the room carrying a tray.

"What's that?"

"Tea and ginger biscuits. I remember they were the only things I could stomach when I was pregnant."

"Thank you, that's so thoughtful. Why don't you sit down and join me?"

Sophie perched herself on the edge of the bed and looked around, frowning. "I'm sorry, this room is a bit scruffy. It was my son Luke's bedroom until he moved out, and I've never got around to redecorating."

Elle looked around the room. The cream walls could do with a freshen-up, the tell-tale circles where Blu Tack had secured posters to the wall still visible. But it was a large room, with light pouring in from the tall window and views out to the sea. "It's a gorgeous room," said Elle truthfully. "It's a treat to stay in a room with such high ceilings and so much space. I forget how cramped our cottage is until I stay in other places."

"Your cottage is delightful," said Sophie.

"It would be if I could afford to do all the repairs needed," said Elle with a grimace. "Anyway, I'm not going to think about that. Is Grace OK?"

"Yes, fine. She's downstairs with her feet up reading the paper."

"Is her knee bad?"

"No, we went for a walk along the seafront, so I suggested she rest it now she's back. She seems sprightly for someone who was in hospital so recently."

"She's a trooper alright," said Elle with a smile. "Did you have a nice walk?"

"We had a very interesting walk. Grace was filling me in on all sorts of family history I had no clue about. It was fascinating."

"She's a great storyteller, that's for sure."

"She's quite a closed book when it comes to herself, though, or is that just with me?"

Elle smiled but couldn't make the smile reach her eyes. "She's embarrassed about her own life."

"Embarrassed? Whatever for?"

"She feels she should have made more of her life, I think."

"In what way?"

"She didn't have the best luck with men. Her first husband was abusive, then she married my dad, and he was just, well, Dad. Neither relationship worked out, and I think she's always blamed herself, as though because she was adopted, she somehow couldn't hold down a healthy relationship. It's complete nonsense. In both of her marriages, it was the men who were the problem."

"Even your dad?"

"Don't get me wrong, I love my dad, but he's so flaky. And he was a real shit to Mum. He cheated on her when I was four, then buggered off to London to start a new family with his mistress. Mum was left to raise me alone and went from crappy job to crappy job just trying to make ends meet and keep a roof over our heads. It's another reason I'm so passionate about not selling up, if there's any other way. If Mum could keep hold of the cottage as a single parent, I should be able to help her now."

"It sounds like she had rotten luck with men."

"Yes. I'm not saying she played no part in the breakdown of her relationships, but at the end of the day, all she wanted was a loving family, and it makes me so sad that she ended up alone."

"She had you."

"True, but it can't have been easy."

"Why do you call her Grace, not Mum?"

"It was just what she was used to. She always called Helen and Richard by their first names, and said it made her too sad hearing the word mum as it reminded her of the gaps in her family history."

"Perhaps things will be different now?"

A wide smile spread across Elle's face. "I know Grace, and I can see how happy she is to have finally found a family to be part of. It's such a shame your mum's so poorly, but it's meant so much to Grace to see her."

"I hadn't realised how well your mum and mine knew each other, or even that it's possible to be that close to someone just through letters. Grace knows so much more about my mum and her family than I do. It makes me ashamed when I think about it. I should have taken more of an interest."

"Hindsight is a wonderful thing. Come on, tell me what you found out. I'd love to hear."

For the next hour, the two cousins talked through all Sophie had learned from Grace. By the time they had worked through an entire pot of tea, a plan had formed in their minds, and both had grins on their faces resembling excitable children.

As Sophie rushed downstairs to look for something, Elle walked to the window. The sea glistened beneath an ever-warming sun, a handful of families braving the cool temperatures to venture onto the beach with buckets and spades. She wrapped her arms around herself and looked down at the tiny bump protruding from beneath her T-shirt. Would she bring her own child here to play on the beach? Her pregnancy felt far less scary now she knew the child would be born into a loving extended family. Jago might be moving to the other side of the world, but rather than leaving her and Grace in a bubble of two, they would have back-up. The new and tentative bonds between the two sides of the family would grow stronger in time. The Watson family name had been lost by the last few generations of females, but its spirit lived on.

"I've got what we need," said Sophie, bursting into the room and spreading a large map across Elle's bed. The two cousins pored over it, their fingers running up and down the paper now soft with age. "Here it is."

"Do you really think we can do it?" asked Elle, staring at the tiny dot in the North Sea that Sophie's fingertip rested beside.

"Of course we can. Next week is the school holidays, so I'm free as a bird, other than the thirty reports I need to write." Sophie grimaced. "Don't worry though, I'm used to tackling those last-minute. As long as you can take the time off, and you think Grace's knee will cope with the distance, there's nothing stopping us."

"I texted Jago, and he's fine with me taking the week off. Given it's the holidays, there are local kids he can draft in for waitressing, and a couple of students are back for Easter and looking for bar work."

"And Grace's knee?"

"I think it will be fine, but let's ask her." Elle reached out and took Sophie's hand. "Thank you."

"What for?"

"For inspiring me, for taking my mind off all that's going on, for being family."

"Yes, I'm afraid you're stuck with me now. Come on."

The two cousins walked downstairs and found Grace dozing in a chair. As they walked in, she opened her eyes, then promptly narrowed them.

"What have you two been up to? You look as thick as thieves."

"We've had an idea. You may think it's mad, and if you think it's too much, please say so."

"What is it?"

"How would you feel about going to visit the island?"

"Holy Island?"

"Yes."

"Hmm, it's an interesting idea, but will take some planning, as it's a rather long way."

Elle glanced at Sophie, who nodded in encouragement. "The thing is, we were wondering about going next week."

"Next week?"

"Yes."

"It's a lovely idea, girls, but can we afford it?"

"I had too much wine at Christmas and booked a holiday on the spur of the moment," said Sophie. "When Mum started going downhill, I cancelled it and got a refund. I'd like to put the money towards this trip. We've had a look and found a cheap holiday cottage on the mainland."

"That's a very kind offer," said Grace, "but what about your mum?"

"Now Ben's working at the nursing home, I feel better about leaving her."

"But wouldn't you rather treat yourself to a holiday in the sun?"

"No," said Sophie, "I'd rather visit the island with both of you. But I completely understand if you think it's too far."

"How long would we go for?" asked Grace.

"I don't think we could go for longer than a few nights. I'll need the second week of the holiday to catch up on all the paperwork I've been ignoring, and you'll need to take a couple of days to travel back to Cornwall, as it's such a long way. Rather than you having to come back here, we could travel north in your car. I'd be happy to drive, then I could get the train back down to Lowestoft and you could do the journey back to Cornwall in stages."

Grace grinned. "I think it sounds like a fabulous adventure. I'm in."

"Really?" asked Elle. "Are you sure?"

"Stop asking in case I change my mind."

Elle and Sophie squealed and hugged each other tightly. "Northumberland, here we come!"

Chapter 46

1978

Dear Grace,

Enormous congratulations on the birth of your little girl and thank you so much for the photograph you sent. You and Arthur look pleased as punch and what a beautiful little dot Elle is. I can understand why you considered naming her after Helen, but Elle is such a pretty name for a little girl, and I laughed a lot to read it derived from a week of calling the baby 'her' and 'she' unable to agree. I knew your French language skills would come in handy one day!

The birth sounds rather dramatic, but at least it was quick. Thank goodness you have a midwife living in the village or poor Arthur would have needed to do more than simply hold your hand, and it doesn't sound like he's got much of a stomach for anything gory. I can't believe he fainted! Men are ridiculous sometimes, aren't they? And isn't it funny that despite all the scaremongering that goes on about homebirths, your little girl left you no choice and came out as perfect as can be? It sounds like Elle is going to grow up to be a woman who knows her own mind, that's for sure.

I've enclosed a blanket I've knitted. It's yellow, as I wasn't sure if you'd have a boy or a girl and thought yellow would be a passable colour for either. I'm afraid it's a bit of a rushed job as looking after Sam's parents is taking up more and more of my time, but I finished it just in the nick of time. I've also started work on a pair of pink booties, but goodness knows when I'll get them finished. Kitty likes to knit with me when she's feeling well enough, so I take my knitting with me each time I go round there as it's a good distraction from her pain.

Can you believe my own little girl turned ten last month? I remember when she was a baby everyone told me to treasure those early years as they pass so quickly, but that's hard to do when you're knee deep in nappies and surviving on next to no sleep. But I'm going to reiterate that advice to you, Grace, for now my little girl is growing up so fast and I miss those days when she'd curl up on my lap with a thumb stuck in her mouth.

Sophie is as much of a daddy's girl as ever but is stuck with me a lot of the time as Sam is so busy these days servicing the rigs. It's good money, and between the oil rigs and factories, there is now more than enough work to replace the fishing that once employed most of the town. I'm considering increasing my hours at the factory once Sophie starts secondary school. It's a shame Lowestoft Grammar School merged with Lowestoft Secondary Modern, as Sophie would have been more than bright enough to pass the eleven-plus. I'm sure this new comprehensive education system benefits some children, but I can't help feeling my Sophie will miss out.

Anyway, you have plenty of time before you need to think about schools for little Elle. Is she feeding well? Are you feeding her formula milk, which seems all the rage these days? I was considered old-fashioned to breastfeed Sophie even in 1968, so I can only imagine how that is viewed these days. If it wasn't for Kitty, practically forcing me to use my own milk, I suspect I would also have used a bottle, but it is certainly a lot cheaper to use your own natural resources if money is tight, which it was for us back then.

Anyway, while all this talk of babies is lovely, I must pass on some sadder news. My Uncle Jimmy and Aunt Clara died a couple of weeks ago, within three days of one another. I'm still coming to terms with the news and can't quite believe they are gone. I loved them dearly, and they were my last connection to the island and that part of my family history.

Last week, I travelled up to the island for their funerals. Just like how they shared their wedding day with Mum and Frank, they shared their funerals with each other. The church was full, but other than Ben, Amy and their children and the Guthries, I didn't know any of the mourners. Ben and Amy are talking about moving away, so there shall no longer be any reason for me to visit the island. It was rather traumatic, not only saying goodbye to my beloved aunt and uncle, but also to a place that holds such mixed feelings for me, but always felt like home.

While I was there, I spent a day by myself just walking around the island, sitting with my memories, and enjoying the distance I feel between my life now and the person I was during the summer I spent there. I even went to the old tumbledown cottage where Blaine used to paint me, but I think someone must have bought it as there was scaffolding up and a couple of trucks parked outside.

The interesting thing about this visit was how my own memories seemed to jumble with a far lengthier family history. I pictured Jimmy and Clara in their youth, strolling through the dunes, and Clara's mother, my namesake, sitting outside her cottage threading mussels onto a fishing line. You probably think I am very fanciful, but as well as saying goodbye to the place, it felt important to say goodbye to the people.

Perhaps one day Sophie will visit the island. Part of me wishes I'd taken her up there myself, but how could I explain all that happened there to a ten-year-old? It's better she discovers the place for herself and makes memories of her own.

Anyway, I'd best go as I've a cottage pie in the oven and I'd like the top browned, not burned to a crisp! Let me know how you're faring with motherhood, and I look forward to hearing from you soon.

All my love,

Your friend,

Annie

Chapter 47

April, 2018

"I see it!"

Sophie glanced out of the driver's side window, wishing she could get a better look at the view Elle and Grace had their eyes glued to.

"It's so strange seeing it in real life after hearing so much about it in Annie's letters," said Grace.

"And even weirder to think we all have island blood running through our veins," said Elle.

"Do you think we should have made badges?" asked Sophie. "To identify us as locals?"

Elle laughed. "Something tells me no one would believe that as soon as we open our mouths. The accent is so different up here."

"I remember it vaguely from Clara and Jimmy's visits when I was little," said Sophie. "Uncle Jimmy only had a hint of it, but when Clara spoke, I used to think it sounded like she was singing."

"We'll be hearing a lot more of it over the next few days," said Grace. "I know we need to get to our accommodation, but do you think we could drive down to the edge of the causeway to have a quick look?"

Sophie glanced at the clock on her dashboard. "I don't see why not. We've got another hour yet before we can check in and we're only fifteen miles from Berwick."

"Perfect," said Grace, sitting back in her seat, a contented smile on her face.

Sophie spotted a sign to the island and turned off the main road onto a narrow country lane. Grace's suggestion of a stop was welcome. It had been a long drive, and she'd done the lion's share. Rather than spend more money on an overnight stop, Grace had insisted her knee would be fine if they did the drive in one go, and despite the copious amounts of coffee she'd drunk, Sophie needed a break.

The narrow road curled downwards, and they had it to themselves, no other cars bothering to make the journey with the causeway closed. They crossed a railway line and passed what must once have been a small station, then as they turned a corner, the island came into view.

"Oh my goodness," said Sophie, slowing the car so she could get a proper look. "Isn't it beautiful?"

"No wonder your great-aunt and uncle moved back there," said Elle.

"*Our* great-aunt and uncle," said Sophie.

Elle laughed. "This shared family history is going to take a bit of getting used to."

They all fell silent as the car approached the causeway. Sophie pulled the car to a stop and turned off the engine. She turned to Elle and Grace. "Shall we?" Elle and Grace nodded, and they all climbed out of the car.

The day was still, swallows and gulls darting across a clear blue sky. The only sound was the lapping of water against the road, and the occasional cry of seabirds in the distance. Grace linked arms with Sophie and together they walked to the water's edge. Across the water, the island stared out at them, the shapes of houses visible to the naked eye.

"Look," said Sophie, pointing to a rescue hut halfway between the mainland and the island. "That must be for when people get stuck."

"I remember Annie telling me about that once," said Grace. "They'd just installed a telephone so stranded visitors could call the local police station for help."

"What year was that?" asked Elle, walking to stand beside them.

Grace shook her head. "I can't remember exactly, but probably sometime around 1970. Annie and Frank came up here for a visit after Marnie died. I think they positioned a bench somewhere in her memory."

"It would be good to find that while we're here," said Sophie. "And I expect we'll find a fair few Watsons buried in the churchyard."

Elle shivered. The toe of her boot clipped the water's edge, sending ripples across its still surface. "There's a strange feel to this place, don't you think?"

"I find it very peaceful," said Grace, taking a deep breath of fresh sea air.

"Yes, me too, but there's also something almost mystical about it. I've been reading up about the island and some people believe it's a thin place."

"Thin place?"

"An idea taken from Celtic spirituality to describe a place where the physical world is closer to the spiritual realm."

"Goodness," said Grace, "I've never seen this spiritual side to you."

Elle shrugged. "It's interesting, that's all. I wouldn't say I believe it, but I believe some places are special, whether that's their history, beauty, or something more other-worldly, who knows?"

"There's definitely something about this place," said Sophie. "I can't remember the last time I felt so calm."

The three women found a large rock to sit on and a hush descended as they took in the view. Sophie had seen her fair share of seascapes, but there was something so intriguing about the road signs just visible above the water, and the wooden posts marking a road that was currently submerged. She wished Ben was with her to see it, but if he had been there would have been no feelings of peace, just a constant nagging worry about whether Annie was alright. Sophie resolved to bring Ben with her one day. Luke could travel down from Edinburgh, and they could make a family trip of it.

"As lovely as this is," said Sophie, "we should probably make a move. I for one could murder a hot cup of tea."

As they turned their back on the island and made their way to the car, Sophie felt a strange sensation. It was as though something was tugging her back. She turned and gazed once more at the island. *It's all in my head*, she told herself, and yet even as she climbed back in the car and began driving away, she couldn't shake the sensation that this was a homecoming, that the island somehow knew they were here, and was ready to welcome a few more Watsons back into its fold.

Chapter 48

April, 2018

"Morning," said Elle.

"Morning."

Elle giggled and rubbed her eyes. "Doesn't this feel a bit like when you went to a sleepover as a kid?"

"I was just thinking the same," said Sophie.

"Maybe tonight we should have a midnight feast?"

"Now you're talking."

Despite Grace's protests, Elle and Sophie had insisted Grace take the double room and that they'd share. Elle was so used to being on her own it had felt strange at first to be bunking in with a cousin she was only just getting to know, but in the end, she'd thoroughly enjoyed their first night as roomies. They'd talked late into the night, too late if Elle's foggy head was anything to go by. But along with the tiredness was a deep sense of relief. To unburden her worries about the baby and Jago had lifted a weight from Elle's shoulders she hadn't been aware she was carrying. Sophie proved a good listener, and a wise counsellor. Elle felt as if she'd finally gained a big sister, and the thought brought tears to her eyes.

"Are you alright?" asked Sophie, pulling herself up against the headboard.

"Yes, I'm just so grateful to be here with you. Growing up as an only child was kind of lonely."

"I know what you mean. It's why I had two children of my own. I would have loved to have someone to share things with when I was younger. And now, with Mum so ill..."

Elle rubbed her bump. "I feel guilty when I think this baby will be an only child like I was."

"There's no reason they have to be."

Elle laughed. "I'm a forty-year-old single woman. I'm lucky to be having one baby never mind any more."

"I still don't think you should give up on Jago just yet. And as much as I'm here for you, on this point I agree with your mum. He needs to know the truth about the baby."

Elle rolled her eyes, then sank down into her bed and pulled the covers over her head. Sophie crossed the room and yanked the duvet off Elle.

"Come on, I'll stop trying to boss you around. Get in the shower and there'll be breakfast waiting for you when you're done."

"You don't need to cook for me, you've already done so much arranging this place for us." Elle looked around their large twin room with its own ensuite and views out to Spittal beach beyond. The cottage was recently refurbished, and Elle felt a pang of jealousy as she took in the smooth new plaster, tasteful paint colours, and luxurious furnishings. "If I had the money, I'd do our cottage up just like this. It's beachy, but without being twee."

"I know what you mean. It was a very lucky find, especially during the Easter holidays. I suspect we may have found ourselves a hidden gem with Spittal. Shall we explore the seafront after breakfast? The causeway won't be open until midday, so we may as well make the most of the morning."

"That sounds like a great plan. I'll quickly check on Grace, then get washed and dressed."

"Leave Grace to me," said Sophie. "You're going to be spending the next eighteen years looking after other people. At least while you're pregnant, let us look after you for once."

Elle climbed out of bed and wrapped her arms around Sophie. "Thank you."

"You're welcome."

As warm water cascaded down Elle's skin, the smell of bacon reached her, causing her stomach to rumble. She looked down and placed a hand on the bump, which was now a defined, solid bulge beneath her skin. A fluttering sensation caught her by surprise, and she placed a second hand against her stomach. "Is that you, little one? Are you enjoying our adventure?" Tears filled her eyes, and she let them fall, joining with the water from the shower head. Rather than anxiety, Elle felt a wash of gratitude. The baby was a wonderful, unexpected gift and whatever happened in her future, she would always make sure her child knew it was wanted, even if it hadn't been planned.

Elle stepped out of the shower and dried her eyes and body on one of the fluffy towels provided. She wrapped a spare towel around her head and pulled on jeans, a T-shirt and a jumper. Although it was now firmly into spring, this far north they were yet to experience any proper warmth, and a chill still hung in the air that required extra layers than she would have needed in Cornwall.

The smell of bacon and coffee lured Elle downstairs, where she found Grace sitting at a table in the smart kitchen, and Sophie slaving over a hot stove.

"Breakfast's nearly ready," said Sophie, her cheeks pink from the pan's heat.

"Thank you so much for this. How did you sleep, Grace?"

"Like a log. Although I feel bad taking that glorious bed for myself."

"Don't feel guilty," said Elle. "It's fun sharing with Sophie, apart from her snoring."

"Oi, I don't snore!"

"I was only joking," said Elle with a grin, "please don't poison my food, it smells so good."

Sophie laughed and began plating up bacon and eggs.

"Sophie suggested we explore the seafront this morning," said Elle.

"Yes, she said. I might leave you girls to it," said Grace. "My knee's holding up very well, but I'd rather save my energy for when we get to the island. Is that alright with you?"

"Of course."

Once breakfast was eaten and the dishes cleaned, Elle nipped across the road to the local shop and bought a paper for Grace, then joined Sophie, who was waiting by the front door. It only took them a minute to walk to the beach, past rows of neat terraced houses and children on their way to school.

"They have a different Easter holiday up here," said Sophie. "I looked it up. That must be why the cottage was such a bargain."

"Do you enjoy your job?" asked Elle, as they stopped to let a mother and her three small children pass.

"I love working with the children, but I could do without all the paperwork and bureaucracy."

"The lack of paperwork is definitely something to recommend bar work over my old job in PR."

"Do you miss your old job?"

"I miss the money," said Elle. "But yes, on a serious note, I do. I miss using my brain, and the buzz I'd get from solving a problem, or knowing I'd helped a client. I miss being part of a team. The people I work with at the pub are great, but apart from Jago they're all half my age. And some customers we get can be really rude. They make assumptions about me based on the job I'm doing, and I sometimes want to get all my qualifications and shove them in their faces."

"I can imagine," laughed Sophie.

At the beach they stopped and leaned against railings, enjoying the view out to sea one way, and across to the town of Berwick in the other.

"I wonder if Mum ever came here?"

"She probably did if she spent an entire summer on the island."

"I wish my dad was still alive. He's been gone twenty years, but I still miss him every day."

"You were lucky to get on so well."

"You don't get on with your dad?"

Elle gave Sophie a small smile. "He's OK, but a bit of a pain. I hated him after he left me and Grace, and although we get on OK now, we're not close. I suppose there are some advantages to him having a second family. I'm not sure I could have coped with two elderly parents to look after."

"That's true. What about your half-siblings? Do you see much of them?"

"No, they've never really seen me as family, probably thanks to their mum, who was keen for Dad to cut all ties with me and Grace once he'd left. I know they're blood relations, but they don't feel it. We've got nothing in common, and to be honest, I don't think they're very nice people. I'm quite pleased they live far enough away that I don't have to pretend to like them."

They walked down a slope that led to the beach and began walking across the sand toward the estuary.

"It's sad when families break up. I often wonder what effect my and Will's divorce has had on my boys."

"Nothing too bad from what I've seen of Ben. You must be so proud of him."

Sophie smiled. "He's certainly grown up a lot in the past few months. He reminds me of my dad in some ways."

"Tell me about your dad. His name was Sam, right?"

"Yes, Sam. What to say about Dad? Well, for starters, he adored Mum, and I mean adored. She was never all that openly romantic, but he'd leave little notes around the house for her to find, telling her she was beautiful, that sort of thing. She pretended to find them irritating, but she loved it, really. Dad was born into a fishing family and was happiest when out on the water. He gave up fishing when I was quite young to work servicing the oil rigs. I guess these days he'd have been working for the new wind farms popping up all over the place. He never retired and worked right up to the end, literally. He was onboard his boat the Sally Ann when he had a heart attack. He was only sixty-four." Sophie stopped and dabbed her eyes with the corner of her sleeve.

"I'm so sorry, I didn't mean to dredge up sad memories."

"They're not sad, well, apart from the heart attack bit," said Sophie with a smile. "When I think of Dad, I get this rush of warmth. He was such a kind, thoughtful man. I idolised him. Will always said he could never measure up to my dad's ghost, and he was probably right. But enough of that. Dad was a Thorn. We're here for the Watsons."

"True," said Elle. "Goodness knows what we're going to discover today, if anything, but I can't wait to get over to that island and find out."

Chapter 49

April, 2018

No one spoke as the car wound its way across the causeway, water glinting in puddles on the sand. To their left, a stream of walkers was crossing the sand on foot, their path guided by a row of tall wooden posts that stood proud against the sky.

"I think they must be pilgrims," said Elle from her position on the back seat.

"That would make sense, I guess," said Sophie. "It is nearly Easter. Perhaps we should have gone for the authentic experience and walked like they are."

"My knee is holding up well," said Grace, "but I can only imagine my physio's face were I to tell him I'd been walking barefoot across miles of sand." She let out a little chuckle and continued staring out of the window at the island looming ever larger.

The car met land, hugging sand dunes, but the tell-tale seaweed strewn on the road signalled this part too would at times be submerged. Sophie turned a corner and revved the car to get up a small hill. She joined a queue for the car park, surprised by how many other visitors there were to this remote part of Northumberland.

It took a while to find a space, and even longer to walk the short distance to the village, the crowds of families and groups of adults making progress painfully slow. A couple of times, Grace let out a frustrated sigh, tapping her walking stick harder on the ground, hoping to make a path through the masses. As they reached the village, the crowd thinned out a little, and some of their tension dissipated.

Grace walked up what she assumed was the main village street, blinking, trying to get her bearings. She wished she'd brought Annie's letters with her, for fragments of information passed down through their correspondence flitted in and out of her mind, jumbling together.

"I thought the post office was on this street," she said, turning to Elle and Sophie with a frown. "That's the way Annie described it in her letters."

"I think I saw it as we were walking into the village," said Elle. "Back that way. Did you need something from there?"

Grace shook her head. "No, not really. It just seemed like a good place to start. Annie used to talk a lot about her friend Genie. I wondered if the current owners might remember her."

"Then let's start there," said Sophie, linking arms with Grace and giving her a reassuring smile.

A bell rang as they pushed open the door and walked into a modern-looking shop with a post office counter tucked in one corner. "Morning," called a smiling woman from behind the counter. "Do you need any help, or are you just browsing?"

"I... um... we..."

Elle squeezed Grace's hand, then stepped forward. "Sorry," she said, "it's overwhelming being here. We recently found out we're descended from an old island family, so have come on a bit of a recce to see what we can find out."

"Oh, right, I see. Well, I've lived on the island for the past ten years, but I'm afraid I'm still getting to grips with its history. It's hard to find the time for research when you've a busy shop to run. The lady we took over from might be able to help you, though."

Grace's head snapped up and she took a step forward. "What was the previous owner's name?"

"That would be Mrs Williams. A lovely lady. She recently moved back to the island after a few years away."

"Oh, that's a shame," said Grace. "I was hoping we might find a lady named Genie Guthrey still living here. My friend, my sister, used to mention her in her letters to me."

The shopkeeper's face spread into a wide smile. "Genie Guthrey, you say? Well, Mrs Williams' first name is Genie, and I can't imagine there are too many Genies on one small island. Guthrey must have been her maiden name."

"And you say she's still living on the island?" Grace felt alert, any confusion or uncertainty gone, and in its place an eager curiosity.

"Yes, she lives in a little cottage up on Front Street, just before you get to Marygate."

"Do you think she'd mind if we called in?"

"I'm sure she'd be delighted. It's Cuthie's Cottage. She has a red front door and a green metal bench outside. Mrs Williams loves to sit outside her cottage and watch the world go by." The shopkeeper bent her head and looked out of the window. "You might find her out there now, given it's such a lovely day."

"Thank you," said Grace. "Thank you so very much."

"My pleasure."

As they stepped back out onto the street, Grace realised her legs were shaking and she leaned against a wall for support.

"Are you alright?" asked Sophie, taking Grace's arm.

"Yes. I don't think I realised how important coming here would be to me. When we first arrived, I'd lost all hope of finding any family connections, but now I think our change in fortunes has left me rather wobbly."

"Why don't we go back inside and have a cup of tea?" asked Elle. "There was a café next to the shop."

Grace shook her head. "No, I want to see if we can find Genie."

"Alright, but if at any point you feel unwell, you're to tell me."

"I should be mothering you, Elle, not the other way around."

"Come on," said Elle, rolling her eyes and taking her mother's hand.

As they emerged onto Front Street, Grace stopped and pointed. "Look. I think that's her."

A short distance away, a hunched lady with a shock of white hair was sitting on a bench, leaning against a wooden walking stick. Grace rushed forward, stopping in front of the woman and taking a deep breath.

"Hello."

"Hello yerself. It's a fine day for a visit to the island. Ye'll be here for the pilgrimage, no doubt." The woman smiled and showed a full set of teeth. Up close, she looked younger than from a distance, her eyes bright, a faint trace of colour on her lips.

"I was wondering whether you are Mrs Williams?"

"Aye, that I am. Who's asking?"

Grace, her legs still a little shaky, sat down beside Mrs Williams on the bench. "My name is Grace, and I think we may have a mutual acquaintance. Was your maiden name Guthrey? Genie Guthrey?"

"Goodness, nae one's called me that in many a year. But aye, I'm Genie Guthrey. Who's yer friend?"

Grace let out a long breath, then turned to Genie. "My friend's name is Annie, Annie Thorn, née Hearn."

Genie's eyes widened. "Annie Hearn? And you say your name is Grace?" Her cheeks flushed, and Grace smiled.

"You know, don't you?"

"Kna what?"

"That I'm Annie's sister."

Genie shook her head, her eyebrows raised. "Aye, I knew that, but I didna think ye did. When did ye find out?"

"I've only known for a short while. This is my daughter, Elle, and Annie's daughter, Sophie."

"Blimey, I should have realised sooner," said Genie, pointing at Sophie. "Yer the spit of Annie."

"So people tell me," said Sophie, holding out her hand. "Pleased to meet you."

"And ye, pet. And how's yer mam? Is she nae with ye? It's decades since she was last here. We kept in touch for a long time, then about ten years ago, her letters stopped. Oh, good Lord, she's not dead, is she?"

"No, but she's poorly. Dementia."

Genie leaned back and closed her eyes. "No," she whispered. "Poor Annie. I went through that with my husband, Roger, and kna all too well what a cruel disease it is. How bad is she?"

"She sometimes remembers me," said Sophie, "and lately she's been talking more about the past."

"Hence us finding out the secret she'd kept all these years," said Grace with a sad smile.

"Ah, that ate her up, so it did. Poor lass poured all her woes out in her letters. The number of times she wanted to tell ye, but she was scared it would do more harm than good."

"Given how bad Mum's dementia is, she's unable to tell us much about the past," said Sophie. "Part of the reason we're here is to find out where our family comes from. I don't suppose you know anything about the Watsons?"

Genie's eyes twinkled, and she tapped her walking stick on the ground. "I'd say ye've come to the right place. Knew Jimmy and Clara right until they died. I didna kna Marnie so well, but I know enough. How do you fancy a trip down memory lane?"

"Really?" said Grace, her eyes shining. "You'd be willing to tell us about the Watsons?"

"I'll dee more than that, lass," said Genie, pushing herself up to standing. "Come with me and I'll show ye."

Chapter 50

April, 2018

"Let's start in here," said Genie, leading them through into her cottage. "Take a seat."

Elle raised her eyebrows as they walked into an open-plan kitchen/dining/living space that whilst still keeping a cottage feel also exuded modernity. The kitchen was tucked at one end of the room, grey Shaker-style cupboards sitting against fresh white walls, a wooden worktop and Belfast sink adding to the style. Next to the kitchen stood a wooden table and four chairs, and beyond them a small grey velvet sofa and two matching armchairs covered in colourful cushions.

"I struggle with an armchair these days," said Genie, pulling one of the kitchen chairs over to the sitting area. "Once I'm in, I canna get out again."

"I know that feeling," said Grace.

"Help yerself to a dining chair if ye'd be more comfortable."

"No need," said Grace, tapping her knee. "I've finally got myself a new knee, thanks to the NHS."

"Good for ye. I had my hip done last year and I can't tell ye what a difference it made."

Elle caught Sophie's eye, and they shared a smile. It wasn't often Elle felt young now she'd reached her forties, but with all the talk of joint replacements, she felt like a spring chicken.

"Can I interest any of ye in a cup of tea?" asked Genie.

"That would be lovely, thank you," said Grace.

"Would you like a hand making it?" asked Elle.

"Na," said Genie, batting away the suggestion, "there's plenty of life in this old dog yet." She walked to the kitchen and filled the kettle. "Ye're probably wondering why we're starting here?"

"No, not at all," said Elle. "We're grateful for you sparing the time to talk to us, and your beautiful home is a lovely place for a chat."

Genie laughed. "Aye, my home is canny enough, but that's nae why yer here. This," she said, waving her arms around the room, "used to be in the Watson family. And if I'm nae mistaken, it's likely both Jimmy and Marnie were born here."

"Oh my goodness," said Sophie, looking around the room with fresh eyes. "This was my grandmother's home?"

"Aye. And yer Aunt Clara was born just across the road in that cottage there." Genie pointed out of the window at another stone-built building that was double-glazed and had a sign attached to the wall advertising it as a holiday cottage. "Of course, when I bought this place, it was in a right state. It's had no end of tenants over the years, some who took little care of the place. I think the lord of the manor must have got fed up with a revolving door of people moving in and out, so ten years ago, put it up for sale. I was looking to move back here, so when my estate agent rang me, I put in an offer there and then."

"You moved away from the island?" asked Grace.

"When my lovely husband died, yes. We'd run the post office together for years, but I didn't want to carry on without him. Annie was always encouraging me to spread my wings and travel, so when Roger died, I thought, why not? I sold up my cottage and post office and spent five years travelling all around the world. After that I tried living close to my grandchildren down in Newcastle, but as Dorothy would say, *there's no place like home.*"

"Do you have any regrets about moving back?" asked Elle, thinking of her own decision to return to Padstow.

"None. The grandchildren come to visit all the time, and this is where I belong. How much do you know about the Watson family?"

"Very little," said Grace, "only the snippets Annie told me in her letters."

"Right, well, Marnie was one of ten children. Her mam, Rose, lived at the hotel with Jimmy and Clara in the last few years of her life, but while her family was young, they all lived here. Of course, it would have been very different back then. This room we're in was all there was to the place. These days it's been extended out back and a second storey added for the bedrooms, but back then they would have cooked, ate, worked and slept all in this one room, all twelve of them. They would have had a privy out in the yard, but that could have been shared with several neighbours. We don't know we're born these days, do we? So, not only was Rose living in a tiny space with a lot of other people, but she also had Alex Watson to contend with. You kna much about him?"

Grace, Elle, and Sophie all shook their heads. Genie carried a tray with a teapot and cups over to them and set it down on the coffee table.

"Right, well, Alex Watson, Rose's husband, Annie's grandad, was still being talked about long after his death. He was a nasty piece of work, what these days you'd call abusive. And he didna spare the children his fists either, although he mainly saved them for poor old Rose. From what I've heard he swaggered around the island like he was lord of the bloody manor, when in fact he was a violent drunk, who let his boat go to rack and ruin and who drank himself into an early grave, much to his family's relief, I might add."

"I had no idea my grandmother had grown up in that environment," said Sophie. "It explains why she left the island so young."

"Aye, but that was also to care for Jimmy, who'd had an accident down in Lowestoft. You kna about that?" The three women shook their heads, and Genie sighed. "Ye'd better settle in, as this could be a long story."

An hour and several cups of tea later, they emerged back onto the street with Genie, who was insisting she give them a tour.

"Are you sure you don't mind?" asked Elle.

"Of course not. If I get tired, ye can carry me home."

"Deal," said Elle, grinning at the woman she was growing very fond of.

"Let's start down by the harbour and work our way back from there. There's a lot to show ye, and we've only a couple more hours before the tide comes in again, so let's get going."

Chapter 51

April, 2018

Elle cupped her hands around her bump and took a deep breath of fresh sea air. She turned at the sound of footsteps crunching against gravel and smiled as Sophie came to stand beside her. Glancing round, she saw Grace and Genie huddled together on a bench, their heads bent as they chattered away, barely pausing for breath.

"It's done her a lot of good coming here," said Elle.

"Grace?"

"Hmm. I think it's brought her some peace."

"Yes, I can't imagine what it's like living your whole life not knowing where you came from."

"It certainly puts my own problems into perspective. Finding out how our relatives lived all those years ago really makes you think, doesn't it?"

"How do you mean?"

"I've been so absorbed with trying to fix up the cottage and so worried about my future, I've not stopped long enough to draw breath and look at what I have. Yes, the cottage is falling down around our ears, but we still own a piece of prime real estate in one of the country's most sought-after locations. We have options. Those poor chaps spending their whole lives at sea, and the women working their fingers to the bone. They just got on with it, didn't they?"

"I suppose there is something to be said for that. I'm prone to a little introspection from time to time, too. My life hasn't exactly been a success. I'm envious of you, you know."

"Me?"

"Yes. You had such a good job, and you're still so young, you can turn your hand to anything you like."

"But you've sustained a career for thirty years!" said Elle, her eyebrows raised. "Think of all those children you've helped. It's amazing what you've done."

"Maybe, but I'm fifty, single, and have recently started hating my job. That doesn't scream success to me."

"In our ancestors' day, fifty would have meant old age, but things are different now. You could be only halfway through your life. There's nothing to stop you making a change, if that's what you want."

"Yes, I suppose you're right. What about you? Have you thought any more about what you'll do next?"

Elle shrugged. "My thoughts are all a bit of a jumble at the moment. Since I've been pregnant, my future feels very limited."

Sophie squared her shoulders. "Perhaps, but anything is possible. Just think about all those women in our family Genie has been telling us about; Clara, going from herring girl to hotelier, Marnie, leaving all she knew behind to help her brother and make a life for herself in an unfamiliar town, Anna, running away from home to be with the man she loved, even Rose, who never lost her fighting spirit however much Alex Watson tried to quash it. We're from excellent stock, Elle. We're the last in a very long line of strong women, and I think it's about time we started using them as our inspiration."

Elle turned to Sophie and held out her hand. "Shake on it?"

Sophie grinned. "To seizing life by the horns wherever it may lead us."

Elle laughed. "I'm worried about the effect this island and Genie are having on us. The next thing you know, we'll be burning our bras and marching for women's rights."

"I think we've missed the boat on that front," said Sophie. "Come on, let's find out what other inspirational stories Genie has to tell."

"Sorry, pets," said Genie when Elle and Sophie reached her. "Me and Grace have been having a good old chinwag and time's got away with us. We'd better get a move on as the tide waits for no man."

"How's your knee, Grace?" asked Elle.

"Fine, remarkably pain free, in fact. The physio told me it's best to keep moving, and it seems he was right."

"We've a bit of a hill ahead of us. Will you manage that?" asked Genie.

"As long as we take it slow, I'll be fine."

"Grand, follow me."

Genie led them around the curve of the harbour, pointing out the herring houses where Rose would once have gutted and packed herring, and the current fishermen's sheds with their creels and lobster pots stacked up outside. "There's still some fishing goes on here," said Genie, "but nothing like in the old days."

"Sounds like Lowestoft."

"And Padstow."

"Aye, it's the same everywhere now. And it doesn't look like that blasted Brexit is going to do much to change things. But let's not get talking about politics. I'd hate for us to fall out." Genie threw them a wicked grin and pointed to a gentle slope. "We'll head up there to what's known as the Heugh. You get wonderful views up there. It's where folk used to go to look out for silver darlings back in the day."

Elle linked arms with Grace and helped her navigate the grassy slope. "Are you OK?"

"Yes, fine."

"You're amazing, you know. Most people would still be chilling on the sofa at this stage."

"When you get to my age, Elle, you have to make the most of each day, as you don't know how many more you'll get."

Elle shook her head. "I hate it when you talk like that. Anyway, tell me if you experience any pain and we'll take a break."

"It's a gentle slope, not Mount Everest."

"Fine."

When they reached the top of the Heugh, they gazed around them, enjoying widespread views across the island on one side and the mainland on the other.

"Here," said Genie, "this is something I wanted you to see." Genie walked to a weather-worn wooden bench and rubbed a brass plaque with her scarf.

"Oh, my goodness," said Grace, leaning in to read the plaque. "This is the bench Annie told me about. She and Frank brought it here after Marnie died. Can you read what it says, Elle? I haven't brought my glasses with me."

Elle stepped forward and read the inscription, her voice catching. "In loving memory of Marnie Watson, home at last. 1900 – 1970."

Grace slumped down on the bench and looked out over the view. Elle sat down beside her and held her hand.

"Are you alright?"

When Grace turned, her eyes shone with tears. "Yes, but it suddenly feels real. Marnie was my mother, and yet also a stranger. I wish I could go back in time and get to know her. At least I have Annie's letters, I suppose."

"I'm so sorry for all you've missed out on," said Sophie. "Mum should have told you the truth years ago."

Grace shook her head. "She did what she thought was right. There's no point in blaming anyone now."

"If it helps, she really agonised over the decision," said Genie. "You know she ran away?"

Grace nodded.

"Well, that was all to do with that awful Blaine McCloud, but it was around the same time she found out about you, Grace. When Sam eventually brought her back to the island, she was a real mess. I think keeping her mother's secret has haunted her all her life."

"Which would explain why it's all coming out now," said Sophie. "There's so much Mum has forgotten, but you're one of the few things that remains, Grace."

"Thank you, all of you. Now, there's a tide on its way in, so what would you like to show us next, Genie?"

Chapter 52

April, 2018

"You see that building over there?" asked Genie.

"The white one?"

"Aye, that's it. That was the hotel Clara and Jimmy used to run."

"Where Annie stayed the summer of 1953?" asked Grace.

"Aye, the very same. Of course, the place is very different now. They ripped it back almost to a shell a few years ago and gave it a proper makeover. It's nice now, but I can't help feeling it's lost some of its former charm. Goodness knows what Clara and Jimmy would have thought of it if they were still alive. Speaking of Clara and Jimmy, shall we go and see them?"

"Go and see them?" said Sophie. "I thought they died years ago?"

"Aye, that's right, pet. I mean, visit them in the churchyard. There's plenty of Watsons down there."

"Good idea. Perhaps we could visit the ruined priory while we're here, too?" asked Elle.

"Hah," scoffed Genie, "not likely. Follow me."

They followed Genie further along the Heugh, to where they had a better view of the priory. It was hard to spot a patch of grass for all the bodies that were packed between its ruined walls.

"What's happening down there?" asked Elle.

"It's all the pilgrims. Come every year, they do. Fill the place up, sing a few hymns, then traipse back over the sand with their spiritual cup full to the brim, or so I'm told."

"You're not tempted to join in?" asked Grace.

"Na, I'm a woman of faith, but I like to keep my conversations with God private, whilst kneeling in front of a pew in church on a Sunday morning. This lot seems to get a lot out of worshiping en masse, but it's not for me. Each to their own, I say, live and let live and all that."

The path down from the Heugh was rockier than the one they'd previously taken, and it took both Sophie and Elle to support Grace, making sure no harm came to her new knee.

"There's caves cut into the rock just down there," said Genie. "Some folk call them the prayer caves, but none of the goings-on I've heard of sound very religious." As Genie chuckled to herself, Elle caught Sophie's eye and tried not to laugh. "We won't look at them as the path to get there is treacherous enough for a young'un, let alone us oldies, hey, Grace?"

Grace lifted her eyes from the path in front to smile at Genie. There was nothing to dislike about the plain-speaking, warm woman who'd given up her afternoon to take them on a trip down memory lane.

"It's so strange to think of Mum spending a summer here," said Sophie, as they reached the bottom of a path and found themselves on a shingle beach.

"We used to come to this beach together sometimes," said Genie. "I remember it like it was yesterday. We even had a barny here once." She tutted and shook her head.

"What did you argue about?" asked Sophie.

"The only thing we ever argued about. Blaine McCloud. Goodness me, I could have throttled that man for leading Annie astray like he did.

The only good thing about the whole sorry saga was that she found out his true colours before it was too late. Mind you, he tainted the island in her eyes, and she was never that comfortable coming back here."

"That's so sad," said Elle.

"Yes, but it all turned out for the best," said Genie. "Annie got her happy ending with Sam. I always knew he was the love of her life; it just took her a little while to realise it."

"Thank goodness my dad stuck by her," said Sophie. "I guess it's a lesson that if you find a good man, you should do everything you can to keep him."

"Well said, love," said Grace, throwing a pointed look Elle's way.

"Let's go to the churchyard, shall we?" said Elle, ignoring Grace and heading off toward the church that looked over the beach.

At a small wooden gate, Elle waited for the others to catch up, and used the moment to let her heart rate settle. Thoughts of Jago were never far away, even when she took herself to the other end of the country.

"Are you alright, pet?" asked Genie when she reached the gate. "We've all been so worried about Grace and her knee, but you need looking after too in your condition."

"My condition?"

"The baby," said Genie.

"Grace told you."

Genie frowned. "No, no one told me. It's plain as day you're trying to hide a bump under that baggy jumper."

Before Elle could reply, Genie had let herself through the gate and was marching up the hill with the energy of a much younger woman. Elle waited for Grace and Sophie, then they all trailed in Genie's wake, only catching her up when they reached the gate to the churchyard.

"You should have a look in there once we've seen the graves," said Genie, pointing to St Mary's church. "That church has seen a fair few Watson weddings and funerals over the years. But first, this way."

"Oh, my goodness," said Grace, stopping beside a gravestone. "Look, on here it says Rose Watson. That's got to be Annie's grandmother, surely?"

"Aye," said Genie, "and yours."

"And look, next to it are Jimmy and Clara Watson," said Elle, kneeling and stroking the marble headstone. "Isn't it lovely that they're buried together?"

"They were a true island love story, those two," said Genie. "It came as a relief to everyone that they died within a few days of each other."

"They were childhood sweethearts, weren't they?" asked Elle.

"Aye, but then they had many years apart before they found love with each other again."

"That's so sad. Such a waste." When Elle looked up, she realised Grace was staring at her, a sad look in her eyes. Elle turned her head away, refusing to acknowledge the meaning in Grace's gaze.

"Ye could see it as a waste," said Genie, "but they had decades together in the end. They lived long and happy lives, and from what I could tell, were as in love at the end as they'd ever been."

"You see," said Grace quietly, "it's never too late."

Elle stood up and went to find Sophie. "What have you found there?"

"I know these people aren't related to us, but from what Grace has told me, they were an important part of our family story."

Genie heard them and walked over to the graves. "Ah yes, Bill and Anna Robson. That's another love story that one, although after Anna's death, Bill married a Watson."

"He did?" asked Elle.

"Oh, aye, Jimmy's sister Rachel. They had a lad together, Ben."

"Oh yes," said Sophie, "I remember Grace said about that."

"All these people, all this family," said Grace, looking from one gravestone to another.

"Don't be sad," said Elle, walking over to Grace and wrapping an arm around her.

"I'm not sad, at least not about death itself. These headstones represent lives that I could have gone to my grave never knowing about."

"But you haven't, have you? You've found out before it's too late. You've found Annie before it's too late."

Grace sniffed and dabbed her eyes with a handkerchief.

"I'm so sorry, Grace," said Genie, "it was insensitive to bring you here."

"No," said Grace, "it wasn't insensitive. I can't think how to repay you, Genie. All these years I've felt so alone and today you've opened my eyes to a family I'm part of. These members of the family are no longer with us, but we have their stories, their example. And look at what it's brought me." Grace held out a hand for Sophie to take. "Finally, we're together again. The Watsons reunited at last."

"The Watsons reunited?" said Genie, her eyes sparkling. "That sounds like a toast to me. Come on, last stop the pub."

Chapter 53

1979

Dear Grace,

This is a quick note, as I had to share my excitement with someone, but Sam would have a fit if I mentioned it to him. We have a woman as our Prime Minister! Can you believe it? Sam and Bobby detest the poor woman, but I can't keep the smile off my face. I may disagree with some of her politics, but a woman in the highest office in the land? Surely that is something worth celebrating.

When I think back over the previous generations of women who worked their fingers to the bone, supporting their men and yet had no rights, it makes me feel ill. I'm grateful I was brought up among strong women who weren't afraid to speak their mind. I bet my Grandma Rose is doing a jig in her grave at the thought of a woman reaching the top. She'd have hated Maggie's politics though and would have enjoyed having a good old moan about those.

I've been thinking a lot about Grandma Rose lately. She'd hate to hear this, but something about Thatcher reminds me of Rose. Of course, they've lived very different lives, but I think it's the steeliness about them that leads to my comparisons. I get the impression Mrs Thatcher takes no nonsense from men, and Grandma Rose was the same. She was the first to call out Blaine McCloud for what he was and was never afraid to speak her mind. I sometimes wonder what her life would have been like had she been born in this day and age. Would she still have ended up with a man like Alex Watson? We'll never know, of course, but I like to think if she'd been born today, she would have had more options open to her, and the freedom to choose how her life turned out.

I've also been thinking about Mum and it's hard to believe she's been gone nine years now. Sometimes I'll glimpse Sophie and see Marnie staring back at me. I don't think I ever gave Mum enough credit for all she overcame in her life. There are things about Mum's past that I need to keep to myself but believe me when I say all the decisions she made were born out of the best intentions. She suffered much loss, particularly as a young woman, but it never seemed to dent her spirit.

Anyway, I promised a quick note so I shall leave this here. I hope all is well with Arthur and Elle. I'll write again soon with all our news,

All my love,

Your friend,

Annie

Chapter 54

April, 2018

Sophie leaned against the ancient stone wall, staring at the river below without truly seeing anything. She was lost in her thoughts, having discovered so much over the previous few days. It had been sad to wave Elle and Grace off earlier that morning, but Sophie was also glad of a few hours to herself before catching the train.

The purpose of the trip had been for Grace to learn more about her roots, and it had shocked Sophie just how much she'd learned about her own family in the process. She turned her back on the river, pulled out a tissue from her pocket and dabbed at her eyes. A passing jogger gave her a quizzical look and Sophie managed a small smile to show she was alright.

With a shock that stole her breath, Sophie realised what she was experiencing was grief. Grief for a mother who was still living, breathing, but no longer there. Sophie kicked her heel against the wall in frustration. Why hadn't she made more of an effort with Annie while she still had all her faculties? But then she remembered Grace's words, that whatever Annie kept to herself would have been to protect either Sophie, or someone else she loved.

Sophie jumped as the ringing of her phone broke through her thoughts. Her heart hammered as she saw Ben's number flash up. "What is it? Has something happened to Mum?"

"No, Gran is completely fine."

"Oh, thank God."

"Are you OK? You sound kind of weird."

Sophie laughed. "I suppose I am feeling a bit weird. It's been an intense few days. Sorry I haven't called you sooner, we were so busy, and I needed to gather my own thoughts before sharing them with anyone else."

"That's fine, I completely understand. We can wait till you're home to chat, if you like?"

"No, it's fine. I've still got two hours before I need to catch my train, so I'm killing time in Berwick."

"Is it a nice place?"

"Yes, it is. There are a lot of historic buildings, and I'm currently working my way around the Elizabethan walls."

"Goodness, that sounds exciting."

"I'm not sure exciting is the right word. Interesting, maybe, and great for seeing the town. Not that I've been paying much attention to my surroundings. We met one of Mum's old friends on the island. She told me all kinds of things about Mum and Dad."

"Good things, or bad things?"

"A bit of both. It's strange being here in Berwick. It's a long story and I'll tell you the full version when I'm home, but the highlights are that Mum got herself into a muddle while living on the island, ran away to Berwick, and my dad came up here to rescue her."

"Sounds pretty romantic."

"Yes, and typical Dad, saving the day. He was always my hero, but even more so now. He must have loved Mum so much to travel all that way for her after everything she'd done."

"Yeah, there's was a proper old-fashioned kind of love, wasn't it?"

"What do you mean?"

"Well, they stuck together through thick and thin. Few people do that these days."

"I'm sorry."

"What for?"

"For not being able to work things out with your dad."

"Mum, that was not your fault. Besides, you're only fifty. Who's to say you won't find a love like your mum and dad had? There's still plenty of time."

Sophie pictured the dating sites her single friends spent all their free time on, and shuddered. "Hmm, I'm happy as I am for the moment. And it's rather strange taking advice on my love life from my son."

"Fair enough. Have you had a chance to see Luke while you're up there?"

"No, I messaged him to say we'd be here, but he said as he's so new to the job, he couldn't get time off."

"Typical."

"Don't be mean, he's settling in, that's all."

"Yeah, maybe. Anyway, I'll leave you to your walking and I'll meet you at the station when you arrive back in Lowestoft."

"Thank you. We'll have a proper catch-up when I get home."

Sophie hung up the call and smiled at her phone. She wondered what her mum and dad would make of her discussing her love life with Ben. Times had changed, and Sophie was pleased she'd chosen to be an open book where her children were concerned, not that there were any skeletons lurking in her closet.

After another ten minutes of walking, Sophie stopped to admire the views of the river meeting the sea. In her mind's eye she saw her mum and dad walking hand in hand, and smiled to herself. Annie might have made mistakes, but things worked out in the end. A life well lived and all that. Sophie left the town walls behind in search of a stationery shop. She would buy herself a notebook and use the long train journey to record everything Genie had told them. And while she was at it, she'd buy a thank-you card for her. She owed her a lot, for in her own way, Genie had brought Annie back to life, to the old Annie before a cruel disease stole her away from them all.

By the time she boarded the train, Sophie felt a new sense of purpose. She would visit Annie the next day and talk about her trip to the island and all she had learned. Annie might not follow her words, but Sophie felt certain it would mean something to her, and that it would bring her some peace.

Sophie found her seat and made herself comfortable. The train inched forward, and she was on her way home. She might be bound for Lowestoft but given the strong connection she felt to the island, she knew that she would be back.

Chapter 55

April, 2018

As they hit another patch of slow-moving traffic, Elle let out a frustrated sigh.

"Getting angry won't make the journey pass any quicker."

"I know," snapped Elle.

"Hmph, there's no need to speak to me like that. It was your idea to travel up to the island, and you knew how long the journey home would be."

Elle took a deep breath. It wasn't Grace's fault she was overtired and overemotional. It wasn't Grace's fault that she was terrified about having to hide her pregnancy from Jago, and even worse, say goodbye to him. They'd stopped over in Birmingham the previous night, sharing a bedroom in a hotel just off the motorway. Elle had lain awake most of the time, worrying about her ever-growing bump, and trying to process all they had learned while on the island.

"This is about Jago, isn't it?"

"Of course it's not," said Elle, her fingers tapping against the steering wheel.

"You have to tell him about the baby. He has a right to know."

"I don't have to do anything."

"What are you afraid of, Elle? Are you really afraid of him staying, or is it actually that you're terrified of how you'll feel if you tell him, and he still emigrates?"

"Please, can we change the subject? I don't want to end a wonderful trip with an argument."

"Who said anything about an argument? We're talking, that's all."

"No, you're talking. I just want to get through this bloody traffic and make it home in one piece."

"You can't run away from this."

"Maybe not, but you're the last person I want to be taking advice from. You can't even bear to be called Mum, and don't get me started on your relationship history." As soon as the words were out of her mouth, Elle regretted them. Yes, she could blame hormones, discomfort, or lack of sleep, but there was no excuse for the pain she'd just inflicted on the person she loved most in the world.

Grace turned her face to the window, but Elle saw the tears running down her cheeks in the glass's reflection.

"Grace, I'm so sorry. I didn't mean that."

"No, it's fine, you're right."

"No, I'm not. I understand why you've always wanted me to call you Grace, and I always understood. I guess now that I'm pregnant though, now I'm going to be a mother, I can't imagine not wanting to be called one. But I haven't lived through what you have. I'm sorry."

"Just because I've made mistakes in my life doesn't mean you will." When Grace turned to Elle, her eyes were shining, her cheeks damp with tears.

"What happened with Dad and your first husband wasn't your fault. You picked the wrong men, that's all."

"No, it was partly my fault. Not the violence I received from John, but with your dad." Grace sighed and folded her hands in her lap. "Despite all the love I received from Helen and Richard, I think not knowing where I came from had more of an effect on me than I realised. I think... I think it left me wary, untrusting, unwilling to give myself fully to anyone in case they left me. Oh, the irony." Grace let out a joyless laugh.

"If only Annie had told you the truth, things may have turned out differently."

"True, but different isn't always better. Who's to say I wouldn't have hated Helen and destroyed that relationship? Or made even worse choices with men. Your father's actions were dreadful, but I don't believe he ever set out to hurt me. Underneath it all, he has a good heart. He's just weak, that's all. If I'd found out the truth, I might have ended up with another John, or I might have cut myself off from everyone and ended up completely alone. No, there's no point in what-ifs or regrets. Annie made her choice, and she did it to protect me, Helen, Marnie. I can't blame her for that."

"I really am sorry for what I said to you."

Grace reached over and patted Elle's knee. "I understand what you're facing is scary. But you are a very different woman from the one I was at your age. You've had a successful career, you know your own mind, and above everything, I know you're going to make the most wonderful mother."

Elle's own eyes filled with tears, and she brushed them away before they could blur her vision. "I'm scared."

"I know you are. But I'm here for you, whatever happens."

Elle rested her head on Grace's shoulder. "I think there's some truth in what you've said about being scared Jago will leave me, even if he knows about the baby. I couldn't bear it if that were to happen, and I couldn't bear it if he stayed for the baby's sake, rather than for me. It's better I let him go."

"I understand your reasoning, but I still think—"

"It's my decision."

"You're right, it is."

"What would you like your grandchild to call you? Grace?"

Grace smiled. "How about Granny?"

"Really?"

"Yes, and if you'd like to call me Mum, I wouldn't mind. Not after all I've learned this past week."

"Maybe, although it would feel weird after calling you Grace all these years."

"True."

"Then again, maybe if I were to test it out... mum, mother, mummy, mam, momma..."

"Perhaps let's stick to Grace?"

Elle laughed, pleased the tension had been broken. "It doesn't look like this traffic is going to improve soon, and the little one is pressing on my bladder. Do you mind if we pull into the next service station for a toilet break? You need to keep stretching your legs, anyway."

"Of course not. Let's get something to eat while we're there. You need to keep your energy up. You're eating for two, after all."

As if expressing their agreement, Elle felt the now familiar bubbling sensation deep in her stomach. "You know, in all the excitement, I forgot to tell you. I've been feeling the baby moving, or I hope that's what it is, and not just wind."

"Oh, love, how wonderful. And what could be more fitting, that while discovering our family's past, the next generation has been making their presence felt?"

"I know," said Elle. As she pulled off the motorway and into the latest in a long line of grotty service stations, Elle felt the comfort not just of the baby inside her, but of all the Watson women who'd gone before. They were an example she should follow. Whatever adversity fell into her path, she would overcome it, just as they had.

Chapter 56

1982

Dear Grace,

What a terrible time of it you're having. Who would have thought that sensible Arthur could do something like that? From the way you've described him, he's always sounded rather dull, and the least likely person to run off with his secretary. I'm struggling to understand how any man could leave their child the way he has. How are you managing? Is there anything I can do to help? I've enclosed a pinafore dress I've made for Elle. Sophie had one very similar at Elle's age and looked so adorable in it. I hope it will cheer Elle up a bit, as it must be so confusing for her now her daddy has up and left her.

How are you managing? Has Arthur accepted the need to support you and Elle? I gather he's legally bound to provide you with maintenance payments, so make sure you get everything you're entitled to. Thank goodness Aunt Helen left you the cottage when she died. It must be such a relief to have a roof over your heads, and what a wonderful place for little Elle to grow up.

Do you remember all the fun we had together during those war years? I still think back to those days when we'd play together, and watch the soldiers manning the beaches, but you were so little I imagine you have few memories from that time.

Anyway, I'm getting off topic. Sam has asked me to reassure you that if you need any help financially, you are to ask us with no embarrassment. We know what it is like to struggle, and since our fortunes have turned around with Sam's work on the rigs, we have enough saved to help you if you need it. I consider you family, Grace, and that's what family does for one another.

It was a relief to hear your neighbour Mrs Mills could help you with some childminding. Not only will work be useful financially, it will give you something of your own, and some adult conversation, which I remember being sadly lacking during those early years of motherhood.

I've started hosting the occasional Tupperware party after my friend Beryl persuaded me to try it. Sam has been getting a little frustrated by all the tubs and boxes appearing in our kitchen cupboards, but I don't hear him complaining when his sandwiches are still fresh after hours on the boat.

Speaking of Sam, his dad's death last month has hit him hard. Although he's always been a sensitive soul, in the past few years, I've rarely seen him cry. That has all changed with Bobby's passing, and although he tries to hide it under the shower, I've heard his tears through the bathroom door. They were always so close, with their mutual love of all things seafaring, and were more like friends than father and son. I've felt Bobby's passing deeply too, not just because I miss him (which I do, so very much), but because he was the last link I had to my dad, Tom.

But enough of my maudlin talk, that's the last thing you need at the moment. Isn't it good news that the blasted Falklands War has ended? I understand why the government felt the need to defend our territory, but after all we went through with the last war, I couldn't believe it was all happening again. The fact it's all over is definitely something worth celebrating.

In other news, Sophie has become obsessed with that singer Michael Jackson, and after much nagging persuaded Sam to buy her a tape player for her bedroom (she has Sam wrapped around her little finger!). It sounds like there's a herd of elephants in her bedroom these days, but apparently it is dancing. I've stopped bothering to ask her to turn the music down, and Sam gently reminded me how fond I was of a dance in my youth.

Anyway, I must go, but please take our offer of help seriously, and let me know if there's anything else I can do for you. I know it must be a terrible time for you, Grace, but just remember you've weathered worse, and you are as strong as any woman I know.

All my love,

Your friend,

Annie

Chapter 57

April, 2018

Walking back into the cottage was like stepping into a hug. Yes, it smelled a little musty and unloved, but after two weeks away, the familiarity of being back in their own space was welcome. As Elle watched Grace pottering around, she could tell Grace felt it too. The journey had been tough going for both of them, and the relief at being home showed itself on Grace's face in the smoothed lines, and in her movements as she seemed somehow lighter.

"Cup of tea?"

"Do we have any milk that's not rotten?"

Elle opened the fridge and frowned in confusion. "I don't understand this. The fridge is full."

"Full of rotten food? I thought we emptied it before we left?"

"No, not full of rotten food, full of fresh food, from the local farm shop, by the looks of it. Oh no, I hope this isn't Tasha's doing. She barely earns enough to feed herself, never mind us."

"This might explain it," said Grace, picking up an envelope from the worktop addressed to them both. She pulled out a postcard showing a picture of Padstow harbour, picked up her reading glasses and read, "Thought you could do with a few supplies after your long trip. Call me when you get back. I have some news. Jago. Isn't it kind of him? He's such a good boy."

"The message was rather cryptic though, don't you think? I'll call him now and find out what this news of his is."

Elle made the tea and took her cup upstairs to the living room. She carried it to the window and dialled Jago's number.

"Hi, you're back then. Did you find the food?"

"Yes, thanks, that was very thoughtful of you. You said you had news?"

"Yeah, I do, but first tell me about the trip. How was it?"

"It was good, fantastic, in fact. A bit of a surprise to end up in Northumberland, but I'm very pleased we went. Maybe we could meet up later and I can tell you about it properly?" Elle held her breath, praying he'd agree to meet. She'd decided he needed to know the truth and didn't want anything to give her an excuse to change her mind.

"Actually, meeting up is partly what I wanted you to call me about. Things have been moving rather quickly here while you've been away."

"Quickly? In what way?"

"The job I told you about in Sydney was keen for me to start as quickly as possible, but I'd told them it was unlikely I'd be able to leave here until the end of the season. But, when I broached the subject with the brewery managers, they said it would be straightforward to put a temporary manager in place. Anyway, to cut a long story short, they're bringing down a temporary manager from up country who should arrive any minute now."

"What do you mean?"

"I mean I'm leaving, Elle. Tomorrow."

"What?" The cup in Elle's hand shook, liquid spilling over its rim.

"I'm sorry, I know this is a bit of a shock, but I've only found out in the last few days, and I've been manic trying to get everything organised.

Plus, I didn't want to disturb your trip, as I knew how important it was to you."

"But what about meeting Ben? I thought you two had been emailing?" Elle squeezed her eyes shut. Ben? Of all the reasons she could come up with for him to stay, she picked a meeting with a stranger to discuss local history.

"I'm sure I can Skype Ben once I'm settled. So, I'm having a leaving party tonight at the pub. You'll come, won't you? I'd hate to leave without saying goodbye."

"Yes, I'll be there," said Elle, her words pushed out through a throat that felt coated in sandpaper.

"Great, see you around seven-ish."

Elle hung up the phone and staggered to an armchair, sitting down and grabbing a cushion. With the cushion clutched to her face, she screamed into it, letting her tears soak into its fabric. What had she done? She'd left it too late. She'd missed her chance. There was no way she could tell Jago now, not when his flights were booked and his job all lined up.

By the time Grace came up to find her, Elle had cried her tears dry and was cuddling the cushion to her, rocking back and forth in her chair.

"Goodness me, whatever has happened?" asked Grace, rushing to Elle as quickly as her fragile knee would allow.

"I've left it too late. Jago's leaving tomorrow. That's why he wanted me to ring him. He's invited me to his leaving party tonight. I'm sure you'd also be welcome. I... I..."

"Hush now," said Grace, perching on the arm of the chair and pulling Elle into her. "Everything will work out for the best. You can tell Jago about the baby tonight. Better late than never, as the saying goes."

"I can't tell him tonight, not now he's paid for his flight, and everything is arranged. Don't you see? I've made such a mess of everything."

"Wait here."

Elle heard Grace climbing the stairs to the attic and wondered what she was doing in her bedroom. Her questions were answered minutes later when Grace walked in, carrying the patchwork quilt in her arms. She laid it over Elle, tucking it in around her.

"Aunt Helen told me this quilt was a gift from my mother. We now know who that was. I may never understand why Marnie left me with Helen and Richard, but I know this quilt was made with love. It must have taken months, probably the duration of her pregnancy. I've always thought it's as close to a hug as I'd ever get from my mother, and you could use a hug of your own right now. Use this afternoon to rest, sleep, cry some more if you need to. Then, once that's done, we'll get you cleaned up and ready to face Jago. I know it will be hard, but you need to have a proper conversation with him."

"I'm not going to tell him about the baby now."

Grace ignored the statement. "You're tired. We've done a lot of travelling. Close your eyes and everything will feel better after a rest."

She pulled the curtains shut and left the room, closing the door with a quiet click. Elle thought she'd never sleep again with all the thoughts running through her mind, but the long journey must have caught up with her, for within minutes of Grace leaving, she was fast asleep.

Chapter 58

April, 2018

Grace smiled at the sight of Elle's unruly red curls pouring like lava over the chair's arm. She was tempted to leave her daughter to sleep, but knew she'd want to look her best when she saw Jago, whatever the outcome of their conversation.

"Elle? Elle, wake up, it's already six."

Elle grunted and shifted position. The folds of her T-shirt caught behind her back and Grace took a sharp intake of breath at the defined bump Elle usually kept so well hidden. She wanted to reach out and touch it but felt that would be an invasion of Elle's privacy. Instead, she walked over and opened the curtains, letting weak sunlight stream into the room. The light did the trick and Elle stirred in her chair.

"What time is it?" she asked, her voice groggy with sleep.

"Time to be getting up. It's already six."

"Six?" Elle sat bolt upright, checking her watch. "Why didn't you wake me sooner?"

"It's alright," said Grace, "you've got plenty of time. I tried to run you a bath, but the boiler's on the blink again. I've boiled a kettle with hot water and will help you wash your hair if you like."

"Thank you."

"Have you decided what to wear?"

"I'll probably just stay in this," said Elle, pointing to her jeans, T-shirt and cardigan.

"To a party? I don't think so."

"It doesn't feel like a celebration to me."

"Maybe not, but it's a party, nonetheless."

"None of my smart clothes fit me anymore, and those that do make my bump too obvious."

"What about that floaty black dress you wore at Christmas?"

"Yes, I suppose that will do."

"Come on." Grace held out a hand and pulled Elle up. The patchwork quilt fell to the floor, and she bent to pick it up, taking a moment to run her hand across the squares. "Go into the bathroom and put a towel over your shoulders. I'll bring up a bowl of warm water and you can lean over the bath while I wash your hair."

"I can manage by myself."

"Let me do this for you."

"OK."

Grace went down to the kitchen, filled a bowl full of warm water, and carried it back upstairs. Elle had stripped down to a vest top, her bump prominent beneath the stretchy fabric. "There'll be no hiding the little one soon," said Grace, nodding to Elle's stomach.

"I know. It seems to have grown twice as big just in the past couple of weeks."

"Right, kneel down and bend over the bath."

Elle did as she was told, and Grace scooped warm water in a jug and poured it over her scalp. She filled her palm with a dollop of shampoo and began massaging it into Elle's hair.

"That feels amazing," said Elle.

"Consider it payment for all the looking after me you've done lately. Right, eyes closed, I'm rinsing out the shampoo."

After adding a layer of conditioner and repeating her gentle massage, Grace towel-dried Elle's hair, wrapping a second towel across her shoulders.

"This reminds me of when you were a little girl. Bath time was always my favourite time of the day."

"Because it meant bedtime was just around the corner?"

"Partly," admitted Grace with a smile, "but more because, at bath time, it was just the two of us. It was such a struggle after your dad left, but you loved having your hair washed, and it was one thing I always felt I got right."

"You got so much more than that right, Mum."

Grace's breath caught. "You called me mum."

"You are my mum."

"Come here." Grace wrapped her arms around Elle. "I'm sorry if it feels I've been nagging a lot about Jago, but I know how hard it is to raise a child alone. Anyway, enough of all that. Come on, you've a party to get to."

An hour later, Elle hovered outside the pub. Someone opened the front door and Elle was hit with a blast of heat and noise. There was no doubting Jago's popularity if the number of well-wishers were anything to go by.

With a deep breath, Elle lifted her head up and walked into the bar. She spotted Jago on the far side of the room, surrounded by a group of men Elle recognised from their high school years. Reluctant to join a large, noisy group, she ordered herself a tonic water and went on the hunt for a spare table.

"You can join us here," said a voice as Elle walked through the pub.

She looked down to see an elderly lady and gentleman nursing their drinks at a table in the window. "Thank you. If you don't mind, that would be great."

"I'm Ralph and this is Elsie," said the man, extending a hand for Elle to shake.

"I'm Elle. Pleased to meet you."

"You're the girl who lives by the harbour?" asked Elsie.

"Yes, that's right, with my mother, Grace. Are you both here for Jago's leaving drinks, or were you looking for a quiet pint and stumbled on this rowdy crowd?"

Ralph chuckled. "I'd love to say we're out on a date, but I've been asking Elsie out for the past twenty years and I've near enough given up."

Elsie rolled her eyes. "Ignore Ralph. He's a silly so-and-so. We're here for Jago's leaving drinks, as friends, not as a couple."

"Oh right. And how do you know Jago?"

"We're neighbours," said Ralph.

"Yes," said Elsie, "but that doesn't describe all Jago does for us."

"What do you mean?"

"He cuts my lawn once a week," said Ralph, "and we're partial to a game of darts in my shed if he's at a loose end of an evening."

"And he drops my shopping round twice a week," said Elsie, "and feeds my cats when I go away. I don't know what we'll do without him."

"I didn't realise Jago had a second job away from the pub."

"It's not a second job, maid," said Elsie, looking rather offended. "He does it all out of kindness."

"Oh, sorry," said Elle, blushing.

"And we've been helping him with his recent history project," said Ralph, "so it goes both ways."

"History project?"

"Yes, he and a pal have been collecting information about the Lowestoft fishermen who used to come down here. Now, I'm no local, but before moving here, I lived in Milford Haven, so I know a fair amount about the history of fishing," said Ralph.

"And I was brought up in London," said Elsie, "but my mother was a Padstow girl, so I've been letting Jago take copies of her old photographs and letters. I think he's donated all his research to the museum now he's leaving."

"I had no idea he'd been doing all this," said Elle.

"It doesn't sound like you know our Jago all that well," said Ralph. "Are you sure you're in the right place?"

Before Elle could answer, Jago was at her elbow. He had a wide smile on his face, but Elle knew him well enough to know it didn't stretch to his eyes.

"Thanks so much for coming, Elle," he said.

"Of course I came."

"We've been filling her in on your history project," said Ralph.

"And all you've done for us over the years."

Jago blushed and took a sip of his pint. "I'm sure they've been exaggerating," he said, "and anyway, it's a two-way street. Ralph's kept me company on numerous evenings, and I don't know how I'll manage without Elsie's regular shortbread deliveries."

Ralph and Elsie beamed up at Jago, and Elle was struck by the realisation that Grace had been right. She hadn't bothered to get to know Jago as he was now. All she'd done was make assumptions based on a man she knew twenty years ago.

"Can we have a chat outside?" asked Elle. "It's boiling in here."

"Sure," said Jago. "Keep her seat warm, you two. We'll be back soon."

They stepped out into the cool evening air and Elle tried to form the words she needed. But before she could gather her thoughts, Jago stepped forward and took her hand.

"Elle, before I leave tomorrow, there are things I need to say to you."

"Can I go first? There's something really important..."

"Please, let me say this or I'll lose my nerve."

"OK."

"You know I love you, God, I've made that plain enough. But I've been unfair to you, Elle. It's obvious you don't feel the same about me, and in the past couple of weeks you've been away, I've realised you were right to push me away. We're not the same people we were back in the day, and I accepted the fact we were never meant to be together. I've got a new life ahead of me, and it's time for us both to move on. But I'd love it if we could stay friends?"

Elle tried to speak but no words would come, so instead she nodded.

"Great. Come here." Jago pulled her into a bear hug and kissed the top of her head. "Come on, let's get back to the party."

"Actually, I've got a headache starting. If you don't mind, I think I'll head home. Good luck with your travels, Jago. You'll be missed around here."

"Elle..."

Before Jago could say any more, Elle turned and ran away from the pub, not stopping until she reached the wall outside her cottage. She climbed up onto it and hugged her arms around herself. When she closed her eyes, images of Jago over the years played against her lids. She opened her eyes and climbed off the wall, trudging up the path to the cottage. All she wanted was to curl up under her patchwork quilt and sleep away her broken heart. But deep down, she knew sleep would not come, and her heart would be just as shattered come the morning as it was now.

Chapter 59

April, 2018

Elle lifted her head from her pillow and blew her nose. She reminded herself she was doing the right thing by letting Jago go. It would be selfish to expect him to stay on her account. Still, the pain of losing him sharpened inside her. She pulled herself to standing and stood sideways, looking at herself in the mirror.

The pregnancy had been easy to hide; no morning sickness, only a slight bump that was easily concealed beneath baggy T-shirts and jumpers. Should she have told Jago last night? He'd said he wanted to be friends, and friends could raise a baby together, couldn't they? Grace had kept quiet the previous evening when Elle explained what had happened, but Elle had seen the silent fury in her eyes. The thought of facing another disapproving look was too much to bear, so she buried down deeper in her bed. Jago would be on his way to the airport by now. She had to pick herself up and be strong for the child growing inside her.

A banging on the door downstairs made Elle jump. Whoever it was sounded angry, or desperate. She checked her watch and saw it was already ten. Grace would be out at her regular WI meeting. Had something happened to her while she was out of the house?

Elle sprinted downstairs, stunned to find a red-faced Jago standing on her doorstep.

"What the... What is it? You should be at the airport. Why are you here? Has something happened to Grace?"

"Grace is fine," said Grace, walking up the path behind Jago and into the kitchen. "I'm not sure the same can be said for Jago here." Grace refused to catch Elle's eye, walking to the sink and filling up the kettle.

"Grace? What's going on?"

"I could ask you the same thing," said Jago, banging a clenched fist against the door frame.

"Come in and sit down," said Grace. "Nothing will be achieved here while you're in such a state."

"I don't understand. I thought you were leaving this morning?" asked Elle as Jago perched himself on the edge of a chair.

"I was. Then I got a message from your mum."

"I'll leave you two to it," said Grace, making her way to the staircase.

"Oh no you don't," said Elle. "You stay right there and tell me what you've done."

Grace sighed. "All I've done is what you should have done long before now. For goodness' sake, Elle. The man had a right to know."

Elle felt the colour drain from her face, her legs turning to jelly. She grabbed a chair and sat down, throwing her head into her hands.

"Were you ever going to tell me?" asked Jago, his voice strained.

"I was," said Elle, looking up at him. "When you were settled in your new life."

"What the hell? You mean when I was too far away to interfere?"

"No, it wasn't like that."

Neither Jago nor Elle noticed Grace slip from the room.

"Then you're going to have to explain this to me, as from where I'm sitting, it looks like you were trying to cut me out of my child's life, out of your life."

"I didn't want to hold you back."

Jago stared at Elle, open-mouthed. When it became clear he wasn't going to speak, Elle continued.

"You're a free spirit, Jago. I know how much travelling means to you and I'd never want to deprive you of that. I thought if I told you, you'd stay and spend the rest of your life resenting me, or worse still, find it too much, and up and leave. I didn't want that kind of disruption for our child."

"And depriving a child of its father is better, is it? And what's all this crap about me being a free spirit? I was in my twenties, that's true, but, Elle, I'm a forty-year-old man."

"I don't see what age has to do with anything."

Jago ran his hands through his hair and let out a howl. "My God, Elle, you're really quite something. You treat me like I'm still in my twenties. All that talk of forgiveness is bullshit. You've never forgiven me for leaving you all those years ago. And then you dare, *dare* to talk about trust? You wrongly assumed you can't trust me, but now I'm certain I can't trust you. Not after keeping something like this from me." Jago stood up to leave and Elle placed a hand on his arm.

"I'm sorry," she said. "There have been so many times I almost told you, but it never seemed the right time. I wanted to tell you last night, but you seemed so set on starting over. What are you going to do now?"

"Go back to my parents' house."

"You're not going to Australia?"

"Of course I'm not going to bloody Australia. What do you take me for?"

"But it's your dream."

"Haven't you been listening to anything I've said? It was my dream twenty years ago! The only reason I was going back was to get away from you!"

"From me?"

"You're so stupid sometimes, you know. I love you, Elle. I've always loved you, but you've made it very clear we will never be together, and I've accepted that. But being around you, knowing you'll never feel the same way, is too hard. Now, though, things are different. I want to be there for my child. We can work out details another time, but I intend to be in my child's life whether or not you want me to."

This time, when Jago went to leave, Elle didn't stop him. His bluster was gone, and it was a deflated man who walked away from her cottage. Elle made two cups of tea and climbed the stairs to Grace's room.

"I can't believe you did that," said Elle, laying a cup down on Grace's bedside table.

Grace looked up from her book, peering over her reading glasses. "Someone had to," she said. "It wasn't right, keeping him in the dark."

"I thought I was doing it for his own good."

"You were doing it because you were scared. You thought he'd leave you, so wanted to get in there first. Don't forget, Elle, I know you better than anyone."

"Sophie said I was scared too."

"I knew there was a reason I liked her," said Grace. "Come here."

Elle climbed onto the bed beside Grace and let her mother pull her into her arms. Grace stroked her wayward curls as Elle relaxed into the warmth of the embrace.

"I've really messed things up."

"You have, but not so much they can't be mended."

"I'm not sure they can. Jago's furious."

"You've hurt him badly. He needs time."

"Time is something we don't have much of," said Elle, pulling her T-shirt tight to reveal the growing bump beneath. "I'm almost halfway through my pregnancy. By September we'll be parents. He's going to have to speak to me before then."

"Let me ask you something," said Grace, pulling away so she could look Elle in the eye. "Do you love him?"

"What a silly question," said Elle, turning away.

"Elle," said Grace, her voice stern. "Look at me." Elle turned to face her mother. "I'll ask you again, and I want the truth this time. Do you love Jago?"

"Fine, yes, I love him, I've always loved him. Happy now? But love isn't always enough."

"Maybe not," said Grace, "but it's a bloody good place to start."

Chapter 60

1990

Dear Grace,

It was wonderful to hear all your news, and it sounds as though Elle has settled in well at the high school in Wadebridge. I'm sure you have nothing to worry about where friends are concerned. She'll find some girls to pal up with at the new school. It sounds as though her and Jago are thick as thieves in their gang of two, but that will change now they're moving on to a bigger school, and even if it doesn't, I've learned over the years that a handful of very good friends are far better than a plethora of mediocre ones.

Are Elle and Jago in the same classes at high school? My Sophie always preferred friendships with boys rather than girls. Girls can be so catty when they hit their teenage years, whereas boys seem more straightforward, or at least that's what Sophie always said.

I'm a fine one to talk, for Sam was my best/only friend (apart from you, of course), right until I started working for Birds Eye. I never bothered much with the girls at school either, partly because they teased me mercilessly for the West Country accent I'd gained during my years with you, Helen and Richard. Sam never even seemed to notice my accent had changed, he just saw me as the Annie he had always known. I'm sure it's the same with Elle and Jago. There's something about a long friendship that can never quite be replicated in more recent attachments.

Speaking of Sophie, she came home last weekend with some momentous news. Not only is she engaged to a man named Will (they met at university), she is also expecting a baby. I'm afraid I struggled to hide my shock, which made her very cross. It's not that I'm not happy for her, just that I worry. She's talking about moving home to Lowestoft and buying a house here. I suppose I hoped she'd have longer to find out who she is and what she wants before settling down to all a family entails.

Sam says I shouldn't be such a worrywart, and that I should let her live her life as she sees fit. He's right, of course, but isn't it a mother's job to worry about their child, even when said child is in their twenties and expecting a child of her own? Sam reacted to their news just as you'd expect – calm, loving, delighted. All the things I should have been.

Will seems nice enough, but there's something flaky about him. Maybe it's just that they don't make men like they used to. I can't imagine Jimmy, Frank or Bobby floating around with airy-fairy ideas that they may find a job "in the creative sector", whatever that means. In our day, men went out to do an honest day's work, so did women, for that matter.

At least Sophie has now qualified as a teacher, so they will have one steady wage coming in. But you know what it's like for women these days, not only are they expected to be the breadwinner, they're also expected to do all the jobs they did before. It makes me wonder if men are becoming surplus to requirements. You've certainly managed fine without one all these years!

I mustn't moan. Sam says I need to give Will time to find his feet with me and find his way in the world. And we spent a pleasant weekend with them, it's true. We showed Will around the town, although we avoided the area that was once The Grit. It's unrecognisable from what it once was, Grace. There are barely any houses down there anymore. All have been demolished to make way for the new factories. I know I shouldn't complain, given all my years at the Birds Eye factory, but it's an entire way of life gone, just like that. There's currently a big controversy over Birds Eye's plans to build yet another new factory on the Denes. On the one hand, I can see the additional jobs it will bring to the town are welcome, but when I think back to the community that once lived down there, it really is heart-breaking. Youngsters these days have no idea what their town once was, how important it was. I suppose it's down to us older generation to enlighten them, but I find talking about the past hard and prefer to look forward rather than back.

Speaking of looking forward, me and Beryl have another trip planned and this one will be our most daring yet. Next month we're flying all the way to America to visit the Grand Canyon! I've tried to talk Sam into coming with us, but he's never been on a plane and says he never wants to. I think I've almost convinced him to come on a cruise with me next year (he can't object to being on a boat, surely!?), but we'll see if he's as keen when a final decision needs to be made.

I'd better get going, but I'll write again with more news about the wedding preparations and thank you ever so much for the photograph of Elle. She looks so smart in her uniform and all that curly red hair is rather magnificent! I'll write again soon, and if I don't write before my trip, I'll send you a postcard from America.

All my love,

Your friend,

Annie

Chapter 61

1995

Dear Grace,

I'm delighted to announce the birth of baby Benjamin, another grandson! Will and Sophie are already calling him Ben, and the name suits him. Oh, Grace, he's really the most darling little chap, and must have inherited his grandad's temperament, as he's such a calm baby and no trouble at all. I remember worrying about Sophie moving back to Lowestoft, but these days I'm so grateful she did, as it means both my grandchildren are just around the corner.

Luke is delighted to have a baby brother. He's five now and has taken to being a big brother like a duck to water. It turns out it was a sensible decision on Sophie's part to wait before having a second child. She's been able to settle into her career and has full maternity pay, something sadly lacking when she was pregnant with Luke.

Will is lovely with the boys but is no more reliable than when they first married and flits from job to job with no firm career plan. He's started calling himself a 'house husband', which is utterly ridiculous as it's Sophie who still does the lion's share of cooking and housework. Sam rubs along with Will well enough, but although he doesn't say it, I know he would have liked more for his precious daughter.

But I shouldn't complain, as without Will there would be no Luke or Ben, and truly, Grace, they are the light of my life. They have also helped bridge the gap between me and Sophie, and for the first time, I feel I have a role to play in her life. There are certain things only a mother can help with, and I've been delighted when she's come to me for advice about feeding, or other women's complaints that are so common after childbirth. I know I can never compete with Sam for her affections, but we've developed a closeness over these past few years that I never expected to have. It truly is a gift, and I have my gorgeous grandsons to thank for it.

Thank you for your latest letter, it was lovely to hear all your news. It sounds as though things are getting very serious between Elle and Jago. Do you think they'll end up getting married? I know you worry about Elle getting her heart broken, but from everything you've said Jago sounds like a nice young man and I'm sure he will continue to treat her well. I agree that a serious relationship isn't ideal with exams just around the corner, but she's a bright girl, so I'm sure will do well, regardless.

It sounds as though Padstow is going through a lot of changes with so many houses being sold for second homes. You're right about it changing the character of an area, and it must be a real worry for all the young people wanting to settle in the town they came from. I suppose at least all the tourists bring money into the local economy.

I'm afraid Lowestoft is no longer the prosperous town it once was. It used to be such a popular destination for holidaymakers, but these days people prefer to hop on a plane to Spain and lounge by a pool rather than shelter from the wind in a Lowestoft beach hut. I suppose it means more space for us locals, but still, it's a sad sight to see a near-empty beach at the height of summer.

Anyway, I don't want to end this letter on a dreary note given our recent celebrations. I'll send you photos of baby Ben as soon as I've had them developed. I've been knitting furiously since his arrival and I have a pair of blue mittens to get back to, but I'll write again soon,

All my love,

Your friend,

Annie

Chapter 62

1998

Dear Grace,

My heart is breaking having to write this letter to you. Earlier this week, my darling Sam passed away. I know it's soon to be writing, but I need you, Grace. I need to talk to someone who understands how I felt about my wonderful husband. When Sophie came round yesterday, she said she was surprised I'm so upset. How could she say such a thing? Was it not obvious how much I loved Sam? What if he never knew my true feelings?

Sophie's husband, Will, was here when she said it and took her off for a walk to calm her down. He came back alone, having taken Sophie home and put her to bed. Thank goodness she has him for support. He told me she didn't mean what she said, and that Sam knew how much I loved him, and I pray that's true.

I can't bear to think of how I nearly lost him all those years ago. It takes a certain type of man to forgive what I did up on that island, but that was Sam for you. He was the loveliest, kindest man I've ever known, and it feels so unfair that such a bright light could be extinguished at only sixty-four years old.

Did I tell you he was planning to retire next year? We'd spoken about going on adventures together now Sophie's all settled with her own family.

We were even talking about coming down to Padstow to see you. All those plans, all those years we should have had.

What will I do without him, Grace? Everyone thinks I'm this independent woman who goes gallivanting off with my friends here, there and everywhere, but I could only do that because I had Sam to come home to. He was my anchor, my rock. Without him, I don't know who I am anymore.

My friend Beryl has been by my side since it happened and keeps telling me to focus on the happy memories shared and everything I still have. But that's easier said than done. He'll never get to see his beloved grandsons grow into men, and that breaks my heart. I love both those boys, but Sophie's youngest, Ben, reminds me so much of Sam. He has his auburn hair and calm manner. I think Sam always hoped he'd get him working on the boat one day.

As for Sophie, she's in bits. I wish it was me who had gone first, for she and Sam could have comforted each other and they would both have been alright. But rather than coming together in grief, Sam's death seems to have pulled me and Sophie further apart. She's so angry, and much of that anger seems directed at me. But I tried, Grace, I really tried so very hard to be the best wife and mother I could be.

Will tells me she just needs time to grieve alone, and that things will improve between us before long. I've never had much time for Will, as you know, but he has really stepped up these past few days. He brought the boys round to see me. Poor Luke didn't know what to do with himself and spent most of the time kicking a ball about in the garden, but little Ben came in and went straight for a hug. He didn't leave my side for the duration of the visit and had even drawn a picture of me and his grandpa to cheer me up. They're such different little boys, but each is lovely in their own way.

I suppose life from now on will be about my grandchildren and daughter (once she's ready to speak to me again). But they have their own little family unit, so for much of the time I'll be alone. I haven't felt this alone since I was eighteen and fumbling my way around the country making mistake after mistake. I didn't much like that version of Annie, so I hope now I am older (and hopefully wiser) I will deal with this newly enforced solitude with more dignity than in my past.

Anyway, my lovely Grace, I had better go. I have a funeral to organise. Sam always said he wanted to have his ashes scattered at sea and I can't think of a more fitting send-off for a man who loved his boat almost as much as me. I will do my best to take Beryl's advice and be thankful for the life I had with my Sam. As a wise person once said (Tennyson?), it is better to have loved and lost than never to have loved at all.

All my love,

Your friend,

Annie

Chapter 63

June, 2018

"Sophie, there's a call for you. Can you go to reception, please?" Miss Constantine stood in the doorway, looking with trepidation at the children sitting on the carpet.

"Do you know what it's about?" asked Sophie.

"It's your son."

"OK. Beth, do you mind?"

"You go," said the teaching assistant, taking Sophie's seat at the front of the class.

Sophie ran through the corridor, not caring who saw her. Ben would never call the office phone unless it was urgent.

"Here," said Brenda, holding the phone to Sophie as she arrived at the office.

Brenda left the room and closed the door behind her.

"Ben? What's wrong?"

"It's Gran. We think she had another stroke in the night."

"Oh no. Is she at the hospital?"

"No. The doctor's been out to see her. He thinks it's best she stays where she is. She's comfortable, and there's nothing more that can be done."

"You mean?"

"I'm so sorry, Mum. I think you'd better get here quickly."

"I'm on my way."

Sophie ran back along the corridor, grabbing her coat and bag. She poked her head around Miss Constantine's door. "I'm sorry, it's my mum. I have to go." Without waiting for a reply, Sophie sprinted off towards the front entrance.

When Sophie arrived at the nursing home, Ben was waiting outside.

"How is she?"

"Not good. Well done for getting here so quickly."

Sophie followed Ben through the corridors of the nursing home. When they reached Annie's room, Ben stopped, turned, and pulled Sophie into a hug. Without a word, he opened the door, took her hand, and walked with her to Annie's bedside.

Annie looked peaceful beneath the sheets, as though in a deep sleep. The only sign something was wrong was her breathing. It was shallow and sporadic.

"Mum," said Sophie, taking Annie's hand in her own. "It's me, Sophie. Ben's here too."

She didn't respond, but Sophie felt a slight tightening of Annie's fingers around her own.

"She knows we're here," said Ben.

"Has anything brought this on?"

"No, I don't think so. I think the end has been close for some time now. If anything, I'd say she was hanging on long enough to find her sister. You know they've been video calling each other lately?"

"Mum and Grace?"

"Yes, Grace has been calling every couple of days."

"Did Mum understand what was going on?"

"Not at first, but she got used to it. Grace did most of the talking, and Mum just listened. I tried to give them privacy, but I caught enough to realise Grace was reading letters."

"The letters Mum wrote to her over the years," said Sophie, almost to herself. "How was Mum after these calls?"

"Peaceful. More peaceful than I've known her in a long time."

Sophie turned to Annie and leaned closer. "Is that right, Mum? You've been talking to Grace? We found her, didn't we? We found Grace. We've talked about you a lot and shared your stories." Annie's eyelids fluttered and Sophie leaned even closer. "I told her all about your travels, Mum. I showed her photos of you and Dad. I told her how happy you were. And Grace told me things I never knew, about your dad, Tom, about your time on the island. We both know the real you now, and we both love you with all our hearts." The corner of Annie's lip twitched.

"I think she's trying to smile," said Ben.

The doctor came into the room and nodded to Sophie and Ben, his face solemn.

"How's she looking?" asked Ben.

"Her pulse is weak and slowing. I don't think it'll be long now."

Sophie and Ben kept vigil at Annie's bedside for several hours. The doctor made frequent visits. All knew there would be no rallying, no change in fortune. It was only a matter of time.

Ben left to make a cup of tea, and when he came back, Sophie accepted the offered mug and put an idea to him. "You say Grace and Mum have been video calling lately? I wonder if they'd like to do that one last time?"

"You mean now?"

Sophie nodded.

"OK, I'll give Grace a ring and check she's at home, then I'll grab the iPad."

Five minutes later Ben reappeared carrying the device, Grace's face filling the screen.

"Hi, Grace," said Sophie. "We thought it was only right that you are here with us." Sophie propped the screen beside Annie's pillow.

"Hello, Annie. That lovely grandson of yours tells me you're very tired. We're all here with you now, and you're free to go and find your darling Sam again." Grace's voice caught in her throat and Sophie took over.

"Mum, I want you to know how much I love you, how much I've always loved you. Me and Dad were peas in a pod and that meant I sometimes found him easier to understand and easier to be with, but it didn't mean I loved you any less. I've always admired your courage and determination and have often wished I were more like you. I know you never doubted Dad's love for you, but I think you may have sometimes doubted mine. But I want you to know I love you, Mum. I love you so much. Go and be with Dad now, knowing you'll be missed by all of us."

Ben brushed tears from his eyes, leaned in to give Annie a kiss and whispered, "I love you, Gran."

There was no dramatic shift between life and death. Instead, with her family gathered around her, Annie gave one tentative, final breath, and slipped off to find her Sam.

Chapter 64

June, 2018

The van pulled up at Bodmin Parkway station and Grace snapped out of the daydream she'd been lost in for a good twenty minutes. "Thank you, Jago. It was very kind of you to give me a lift."

"It's no problem at all. How long until your train arrives?"

Grace checked her watch. "Another forty minutes."

"Fancy a coffee?"

"Are you sure you've time?"

"I've always got time for you, Grace," said Jago with a smile. He parked the van, helped Grace climb out, then grabbed her suitcase from the back.

They settled themselves in the small station café and Jago ordered two coffees.

"Thank you," said Grace, when he handed her a cup. "It really is very kind of you to wait with me."

"It's a difficult time for you. You've lost your sister and friend. The least I can do is wait with you for your train."

"At least I was with her at the end," said Grace, "and I found her again. That's all that really matters. Thank you for all you did helping me find my sister, Jago."

He flushed and took a sip of his coffee.

"How are things going with that daughter of mine?"

Jago choked on his coffee. "I'm not sure what you're asking."

"Well, I suppose I'm asking if you've both stopped being so stubborn and had a proper conversation about everything."

"No, not really. We're rubbing along at work together OK, but that's about it."

"At least you got your old job back."

"Yes, that's something."

"You need to sit down and have a proper talk about things. In a few months' time, you'll be parents, and you won't have the time or energy for important discussions."

"Advice noted," said Jago.

Grace sighed and stirred a teaspoon around her mug. "It's so frustrating, you know."

"What is?"

"I've not been all that lucky in love, Jago, and have spent most of my life alone. You and Elle love each other, you always have from what I've seen, and yet you're letting the chance to be together slip through your fingers. It's ridiculous, if you ask me, you need your heads banging together." Jago smiled, but Grace noticed the way he shifted in his seat, and felt a pang of guilt for making him uncomfortable when all he'd done was show her kindness. "I'm sorry. I didn't mean to interrogate you. Let's finish up these coffees, then if you could help me carry my suitcase to the platform, I'd be very grateful."

"Of course. And, Grace, I promise to think about what you've said."

"Good."

*

It was a relief to have navigated her way across London unscathed, and as Grace sat on the slow train bound for Lowestoft, she thought how difficult the journey must have been for Marnie with a young

Annie in tow. And how had she felt on the return journey, having left two daughters behind and knowing she was returning to an area under threat of enemy attack? A closeness to the mother she'd never truly known enveloped Grace. She'd had plenty of time to think through Marnie's choices and felt no residual bitterness. Nor did she resent Annie for keeping the secret from her. Reading back over their decades of correspondence had reignited the closeness she'd always felt to the friend she now knew to be her sister.

With thoughts of family swirling around her mind, Grace closed her eyes, only coming to as the train creaked its way into Lowestoft station. A young man on the seat opposite helped carry her suitcase off the train and Grace stepped onto the platform, looking around her.

"Over here," called Sophie.

Grace wheeled her case over to where Sophie was waiting and pulled her into a hug. "How are you?"

Sophie shrugged. "To be honest, I'm not really sure. I'm upset, yes, but it felt like we lost Mum a long time ago so there are also feelings of relief in the mix. I'm pleased her ordeal is now over and she's at peace. How about you? How are you feeling about everything? It was so good of you to come."

"Of course I came. And I understand what you mean about mixed feelings. I feel the same. I know this will probably sound strange, but I've realised lately that Annie was my best friend. She was there for me all of my life. We went over fifty years without meeting in person, and yet she knew me better than anyone, even better than Aunt Helen. Of course, I've had plenty of other friends over the years, but none I'd have dared be so honest with."

"Mum kept your letters. They were among the old photographs I found. I haven't read them. I'll give them back to you before we go."

"Thank you. What are the arrangements for tomorrow?"

"We're going to do things a bit differently and start at the crematorium. It will just be immediate family there, then we'll go to Christ Church for a service to celebrate Mum's life, then there will be a wake in the church hall."

"That sounds like a wonderful way to honour Annie."

"Yes, and if you're up for it, we've booked a boat trip at the end of the week to scatter Mum's ashes at sea. That's what we did for Dad, and I'd like to think of them being together."

"I have a feeling that's exactly what Annie would have wanted, and I'd be delighted to join you, if it's alright?"

"Of course it's alright. You were Mum's sister. You have as much right as anyone. Now, how about we head home and have a proper catch-up over a cup of tea? Ben's really looking forward to seeing you again."

"And I him. A cup of tea sounds perfect. Lead the way."

Chapter 65

June, 2018

Sophie woke feeling exhausted. The funeral had gone as well as it could, but the effort of holding it together in front of all the people who paid their respects had taken all the energy she had. Luke and Ben had stepped up as waiters during the wake, making sure the mostly elderly gathering was well fed and watered. Grace had done a sterling job chatting endlessly to curious neighbours and friends keen to find out her connection to the family. Between them, they had decided that there was no need for subterfuge. Any hint of a scandal had died with its participants, and Annie was now free from the burden of secrets she had kept. So, Grace freely declared herself Annie's sister, answering questions with patience and efficiency.

The entire event had felt surreal, and Sophie knew that she'd been saving her goodbyes for today. She climbed out of bed and opened her curtains. The sun shone bright in the sky, having had very little rest as it barely set at this time of year. The beach was a creamy yellow, the sea unusually blue. Two figures were sitting on a bench looking out to sea. They were easily recognisable, Grace with her long white curls, and Luke with his hair cut so short he looked as though he'd joined the army.

It pleased Sophie to see him taking such an interest in his family, particularly Grace. Although Sophie hated to admit it, he'd changed a lot for the better since living with Will and Rosie. The work he was doing for Rosie had given him a sense of purpose, and since his return, Sophie had noticed him holding his head higher. His relationship had broken up within weeks of moving, and Sophie suspected he'd met someone new, not that he'd said anything. But she recognised the twinkle in his eye, a tell-tale sign he was falling in love.

"Morning," said Ben, poking his head around the door. "I've brought you a cuppa."

"You're an angel."

"How are you feeling about today?"

"In a weird way, I'm looking forward to it."

"I know what you mean," said Ben, sitting down on the edge of the bed. "The funeral was for everyone else. Today is for Gran."

"Exactly. Hey, Luke and Grace seem to get on well."

"Yeah, weird, isn't it?"

"You sound jealous," said Sophie, laughing.

Ben grinned. "I guess I am a bit. Not about Luke getting on well with Grace, but about his newfound interest in our family history. That has been our thing, and I'm not sure how I feel about him muscling in."

"Don't worry, he'll lose interest once he's back in Edinburgh, and I have a sneaking suspicion he'll have other things on his mind when he goes back."

"Ah, so you've noticed it too?"

"A new woman? Has he said anything to you?"

"No, but he always gets this weird, soppy look when he's just met someone, and I caught him listening to Ed Sheeran the other day."

"God help us."

"He seems well, though, not as annoying as usual. Anyway, drink your tea. We need to be down by the harbour in an hour."

*

Despite the day being beautifully calm, as the boat travelled further out to sea the wind whipped at Sophie's hair, and she wished she'd worn a hat. Her dad must have been very hardy to be out at sea day in day out in all weathers throughout the year. Plumes of white foam sprayed up into the boat, and Ben and Luke whooped and cheered, encouraging the skipper to push the boat to its limits.

"We're here to scatter Gran's ashes," yelled Sophie, "we're not here for a joy ride."

"Sorry, Mum," said Ben, "we got a little carried away."

Ben and Luke sat back down and huddled in the corner of the boat like two naughty schoolboys. A rush of love swept through Sophie as she watched them, thinking how much joy they had brought not just her, but also to her parents, who had both adored their grandsons.

The boat slowed once they were about a mile from the coast. "Here alright?" called the skipper.

"Yes, this is great." From their position in the boat, they could see Lowestoft harbour, miles of sand stretching out from either side of it. "It's perfect."

Grace reached across and squeezed Sophie's hand. "Are you alright?"

Sophie nodded. She reached into a bag and pulled out the box containing Annie's ashes. "How should we do this? I haven't really thought about it."

"Why don't we each take a handful and say a few words?" said Ben.

"That sounds lovely," said Grace.

"Boys, do you want to go first?"

Sophie handed the box to Luke, who tilted it and let a handful of ash fall into the air and down to the water. "Bye, Gran. Thank you for all those years you let me play football in your garden and never told me off for ruining your flowers, even though I knew you were secretly livid.

Your cakes were the best, and I loved it when you used to read me stories when I was little. I'll miss you."

Ben took the box from Luke and shook some ash from it. "Goodbye, Gran. Thank you for always believing in me and encouraging me to follow my heart and dreams. You were my Gran, but also my friend. I know you were poorly when you came to live with us, but I loved having you around all the time. Thank you for remembering me right up until the end. I'll miss you every day, but I'm glad you get to be with Granddad now."

Ben passed the box to Grace, and she dipped in her hand, letting ash run through her fingers for a moment before taking another handful and throwing it over the gunwale. "Goodbye, my lovely sister. May you find your Sam, and all the happiness you deserve in the afterlife. Thank you for never giving up on me, for always watching on from a distance, and for being my big sister even when I didn't know it. All my love for always, Annie, go well, sweet girl."

Sophie was the last to take the box. Through vision blurred by tears, she tipped the remaining ash out in the air, watching it catch the breeze before floating down to the waves below. "Goodbye, Mum. I hope you know how much you were loved. I'll miss you and Dad always, but I'm happy you're together at last..." Before Sophie could say anymore, tears overwhelmed her, and Grace, Ben and Luke gathered her up into their arms. The four of them stood joined in grief, as the boat bobbed gently on the water. Their tears mingled, and as they finally pulled away they dried their eyes and smiled at each other, united not only by their loss, but by all they had gained. They were family, and would always be there for each other, no matter what.

When the boat returned to the harbour, the skipper helped them climb back onto dry land and said his goodbyes. Ben and Luke strolled on ahead, and Sophie hung back with Grace.

"Before we go back to the house," said Grace, "there's something I'd like to give you." She reached into her bag and pulled out a pile of envelopes, secured together by a piece of ribbon. "These are the letters Annie wrote to me. I'd like you to have them."

"I can't take those. They belong to you. They're private."

"It's right that you have them, Sophie. You've learned so much about Annie over the past few months, but these letters are her in her own words. You may not be up to reading them yet, but they'll keep your mum with you. Poor Annie had been so ill lately, but these letters are a good reminder of the woman she was before that dreadful disease took hold. Please, take them. I think she'd want you to have them."

"Are you sure?" asked Sophie.

Grace nodded and pressed the letters into Sophie's hands. She clasped them tight, then held them to her heart. She might have just said goodbye to Annie, but with the gift of the letters, part of Annie would live on, and she'd be able to get to know her mum all over again.

Chapter 66

July, 2018

Elle stood at the door to the bungalow, her heart hammering and palms sweaty. For three months, the only contact she'd had with Jago had been polite conversations at work, or businesslike meetings where they drew up proposed schedules for childcare. Nothing about the situation made Elle happy, and neither, it seemed, was Jago. He'd been like a bear with a sore head the past few months, and it wasn't just Elle who'd noticed. There'd been several complaints from customers about his attitude at work, and members of staff were grumbling about looking for other jobs.

Jago answered the door, looking dishevelled. His chin was covered in stubble, his hair stood up on end, and he was wearing an old pair of jogging bottoms and a T-shirt that had seen better days.

"Oh, it's you. Did we have a meeting arranged?"

"No. I wanted to talk to you."

"Is everything OK with the baby?"

"Yes."

"Then I don't see what there is to talk about. We've made all the necessary arrangements. There's nothing left to discuss."

"Please," said Elle. "Can I just come in for five minutes? Hear me out, then if you still want to kick me out, fine, I'll go."

Jago sighed and stepped aside so Elle could enter the bungalow.

"Tea? Coffee?"

"Tea, please. Are your parents still away on their cruise?"

"No, they got back from that a few weeks ago. They're on a wine-tasting trip to Italy at the moment."

"Lucky them," said Elle. While Jago made a pot of tea, Elle looked around the bungalow. It didn't seem like Jago was taking care of himself, or his parents' home. The usually tidy, bland interior was littered with beer cans and take-away containers. Dirty clothes lay strewn on most surfaces and a pile of post clogged up the hallway by the front door.

"So," said Jago, laying a cup of tea on the kitchen counter. "Why are you here?"

"First, I have some news. I've got a job."

"Oh, so you're here to hand in your resignation. I see. Where is this new job?"

"With my old company in Bristol."

Jago slammed his mug down. "You're moving back to Bristol? My God, Elle, just when I thought you couldn't sink any lower."

Elle took a deep breath and counted to ten. "Thanks for having so much faith in me. No, I'm not moving to Bristol. I can do the job from home. All that time I've spent searching for jobs, and in the end, it was them who approached me."

"Congratulations," said Jago. "Do they know about the baby?"

"Yes, and they're fine with it. Grace is fighting fit these days and is keen to help with childcare. I've said I'll work right up till my due date, then go back after three months of maternity leave."

"Isn't that soon?"

"I don't think so. Not as I'll be working from home."

"Well, good for you. I'm happy for you, honestly. Now, if you don't mind, I should really get in the shower."

"Hang on," said Elle. "There's something else I need to say."

"What?"

Elle sighed. "I know this won't make any difference to our situation, I know you'll never trust me, I know all that, but I have to say it. I love you, Jago. I've loved you since I was seventeen and as hard as I've tried to move on, I can't. It's why all my relationships have broken down. No one compared to you."

"My God," said Jago, leaning against the worktop and putting his head in his hands. "Why tell me this now?"

"Because we're about to become parents. Because I've missed you so much these past few months. Because I hate myself for almost driving you away. Because I can't bear the thought of you finding someone else. Because I want our child to have a proper family."

"Wow," said Jago, smiling for the first time since Elle arrived. "That's a lot of reasons. I would have been happy with one." His smile widened and Elle's mirrored his own.

"So... what do you make of my announcement?"

"Hmm, let me see." Jago walked to Elle and took her in his arms. "Are you sure about this? It's not just your hormones talking, is it?"

Elle laughed. "Jago, I've loved you since long before I got pregnant. Maybe I needed a few racing hormones for me to realise it."

"Thank you, hormones," said Jago. He pulled Elle closer. Their lips met, and it was as though the past twenty years melted away and they were back to being teenagers again.

"Jago," said Elle between kisses.

"Hmm..."

"You stink."

Jago pulled away from Elle, looking hurt, and she laughed. He sniffed his T-shirt. "OK, so maybe you have a point."

"I'll expect better standards moving forward," she said, grinning.

"Well, now I'm not nursing a broken heart, I guess I have no excuse not to wash or wear clean clothes."

"Hey, before you get in the shower, I wanted to ask you something."

"Uh oh," said Jago. "Just when things were going so well."

"It's not bad, at least I don't think it's bad."

"Go on."

"I wondered how you'd feel about moving in with me?"

"Really?"

"Really."

"Don't you think that's soon? I mean, we only got together..." Jago checked his watch, "five minutes ago."

"Maybe, but we've known each other for a lifetime. I don't think there's anything we don't know about each other, and let's face it, I've seen you at your worst."

"Fair enough," said Jago, laughing. "I guess I could help with odd jobs around the house, look after the baby while you're working."

"About the cottage," said Elle. "Now I know I'll have a decent salary coming in, we've re-mortgaged the cottage in my name. I've had a builder round to cost the work out and he should be making a start right about now."

"Wow, you don't hang around," said Jago.

"Time's marching on," said Elle, stroking her swollen stomach. "I don't fancy coming home from the hospital to a toilet that only works intermittently."

"Fair enough. When do you want me to move in?"

"In a couple of weeks? I've asked the builders to concentrate on our bedroom and the bathroom first, the rest we can do gradually."

"Our bedroom? You must have been pretty sure I'd say yes."

"I know you too well," said Elle. "Right, I'd better get going. Goodness knows what state the house will be in when I get back."

"Sure thing, but I want you ready and waiting at seven o'clock tonight."

"What for?"

"Our first date. I'm not the kind of man to move in with a woman before the first date." Elle laughed as Jago drew her back into his arms. Her stomach sat between them like a fat cushion. *My own little family*, she thought, smiling.

Chapter 67

July, 2018

"Sophie, can I have a word?"

Sophie forced a smile onto her face as she looked up at her boss. She was trying to get her classroom organised so she could leave and make it to the station in time. Grace was coming for another visit, and Sophie wanted to be there the moment she stepped off the train. An interruption from the simpering Miss Constantine was the last thing she needed.

"Take a seat," said Sophie, pulling out a tiny chair beside her. She fought back a giggle as the head teacher perched awkwardly on the child-size seat. "What can I do for you?"

"Well... this is awkward...given the timing... I know your mother died recently and the last thing I want to do is upset you further."

"OK, now you're worrying me."

Miss Constantine let out a nervous giggle, refusing to meet Sophie's eye. "I've been at a meeting with leaders of the Academy Trust who are taking over the school, and I'm afraid it's not good news."

"In what way?"

"Finances are very stretched."

"Aren't they always?"

"The trust needs to find efficiency savings from somewhere. Currently, their biggest outgoings are on staffing costs."

"Do they expect the children to teach themselves?"

Miss Constantine gave another nervous chuckle. "Of course not. As you're aware, staff salaries vary depending on years of service."

"Are you trying to tell me I'm too expensive and need to take a pay cut?"

"No, no, of course not. Although you are our most expensive member of staff after senior management."

"Because I've given the longest service of anyone to the school."

"Very true, and your contribution hasn't gone unnoticed."

"So...?"

"So, the decision has been made to move the teachers around to different year groups next term. We're going to be putting a newly qualified teacher into the reception class."

"And what does that mean for me? You know I'm an early years specialist."

"I do, and I wish we could keep you where you are, really, I do. Moving might not be such a bad thing though; it can be wonderful for career development."

"Where do you propose I move to?"

"Year Six."

"Year Six? Are you insane?"

Miss Constantine coughed. "Obviously, we understand you may not feel this year group suits your skill set."

"And if I don't? What then?"

"Then you're well within your rights to hand in your resignation. I'm aware this is all rather last minute, so on this occasion we'd forgo the usual notice period."

Sophie stood up, towering over Miss Constantine in her tiny chair. "Let me get this straight. Despite all I've given to the school, you want to fire me because I'm too expensive. Only, you can't do that, can you? Hmm, I wonder what you can do instead. Oh, I know, offer me a job in a class I'm completely ill-equipped to deal with and hope I hand in my notice and give you what you want."

"Sophie, please stop raising your voice at me."

"Raising my voice? Huh! You know what you can do? *Go to hell*!"

Sophie grabbed her bag and ran out of the school building. The drive home passed in a blur. Sophie didn't bother to take her school bags out of the car when she pulled up outside. Instead, she let herself into the house and sank down to the floor as soon as the door closed behind her.

"Mum?"

"Oh, Ben, I wasn't expecting you home yet."

"I was on an early shift today. How about you? You're not usually home for a good couple of hours yet, and I thought you were going to meet Grace at the station."

"Could you get Grace for me?"

"Sure, as long as you tell me what's going on."

"They're trying to force me out," said Sophie, pulling a tissue from her pocket and scrubbing her eyes.

"What do you mean?"

"Apparently, I'm too expensive. The school needs to make cuts."

"They can't do that."

"No, not technically. What they can do, though, is offer me a new position they know I don't want and hope I leave."

"Oh, Mum," said Ben, sinking to the floor beside her and wrapping an arm around her shoulders. "What are you going to do?"

"Part of me wants to march in there on Monday and accept the job in Year Six just to spite them. But that would leave me miserable in a job I'd hate, and working for people who want me out. I'd be hurting myself as much as them."

"And the alternative is?"

"Look for another job. But the thought of starting again..."

"Could you take some time out?"

"I can't afford to."

"It's a shame Gran didn't have millions to leave us in her will."

Sophie smiled. "That reminds me, Mum's solicitor has asked to meet me next week. Apparently, there are some documents she asked him to give me after she died. But there won't be any hidden riches, any money Mum had went on her care long ago. It was worth it though, I think. The nursing home was the right place for her, and I think her last few years were as happy as they could be."

"It's weird without her there," said Ben. "I keep going into her room for a chat, but there's an old chap called Arnold in there now. He's a perfectly nice fellow, but it's Gran I want to see when I open that door."

"Those last years sometimes felt like torture. In a way, we lost her years ago. I didn't expect to feel so sad, if I'm honest. I haven't been able to pull myself together since the funeral. At least Grace's visit will take my mind off everything."

"Come here," said Ben, pulling Sophie tighter.

"You're a good boy," said Sophie.

"That's what Gran used to say."

Mother and son laughed through their tears. "Unfortunately, we can't sit here all night. Grace arrives in an hour's time. Are you sure you don't mind going to meet her?"

"Of course not."

"Thank you. Right, we'd better get the house sorted and a bed made up in the spare room. I didn't have time before work this morning."

"I'll grab the sheets."

*

"We're back."

"Grace," called Sophie, running down the stairs to greet her aunt. "It's great to see you again. How was the journey?"

"Very good," said Grace, letting Sophie take her bag. "I'm sorry to descend on you again so soon, but with Elle's due date approaching, I thought I'd better squeeze in another visit while I still can. I suspect my child-minding services may be called upon once the baby arrives."

Sophie laughed. "I'm sure they will. How is Elle?"

Grace rolled her eyes. "Like she's seventeen again. I'm beginning to wish I hadn't encouraged her to give Jago another chance. I keep finding the pair of them smooching on the sofa in the living room."

"I wouldn't worry," said Sophie. "That will all stop once the baby arrives. It's lovely they're back together, though."

"Yes, it is. It only took them twenty years."

"Better late than never."

"Precisely."

"Listen, Grace, I've had a bit of a rotten day and don't feel like cooking. I thought I'd treat us to dinner at a local hotel by the beach, if that's alright with you?"

"That sounds wonderful," said Grace.

"Would you like a bit of time to settle in before we eat?"

"Oh no, I'm famished."

"Me too," said Ben.

"Looks like we're going now then," said Sophie, grabbing her jacket. "Lead the way."

It would have been quicker to walk along the road, but Grace was keen to see the beach again, so they took a longer route to the hotel.

"I can see why Annie never left," said Grace, looking out over pristine yellow sand.

"She did a fair amount of travelling," said Ben, "but I guess she concluded this was the best place to be."

"And you, Sophie? Have you ever thought of leaving?"

Sophie glanced at Ben. "Maybe one day." In the hours since her conversation with Miss Constantine, an idea had been forming in Sophie's mind, but she wasn't ready to share it yet. What she needed was a few glasses of wine in the company of her aunt to distract her from all thoughts of school.

"Right, here we are," said Sophie, pointing at a smart-looking hotel.

"This looks rather posh," said Grace, frowning. "Are you sure I'm not underdressed?"

"No, you're fine. And I think we deserve a treat. When you were here last month, it was such a sad time, so I think we should make this visit a celebration of all we've gained over the past few months, rather than all we've lost."

"What a lovely idea," said Grace. "First round's on me."

Chapter 68

July, 2018

"You shouldn't be doing that," said Jago, rushing to take Elle's hand as she climbed down from a ladder.

"Don't be such an old woman," said Elle. "I was only changing a bulb. I know the rest of the house is a shambles, but we need at least one finished room before this baby arrives."

"You could've fallen."

"I was careful."

Jago sighed. "I need this baby to hurry up. I'm a nervous wreck. My hair will have turned white soon."

Elle laughed. "There are another three weeks to go yet." She put her arms around Jago's neck and gently pressed her lips to his. "You know the worry will only increase once the baby's here?" she said.

"Don't say that. I don't know if I can cope with the stress. I'm going to turn into one of those awful overprotective fathers."

"You're going to be an amazing dad," said Elle, kissing him again.

A cough caused them to pull away from each other. One of the builders stood in the doorway, flushing at having disturbed a private moment.

"What is it, Trev?" asked Jago.

"Nothing to worry about, only we found something while sanding the floorboards."

"Woodworm?"

"God, no," said Trev. "There was a loose floorboard, and when we pulled it up, we found this." He held out a yellowing envelope.

Elle took the envelope from Trev and turned it round in her hands. "It's addressed to Helen. Grace should be the one to open it."

"She's not back till tomorrow," said Jago.

"I'll leave you to it," said Trev. "We're knocking off for the day, so I'll see you tomorrow."

"Bye," said Jago.

"There's a Lowestoft postmark," said Elle.

"Open it," said Jago. "You need to be prepared in case it's something that might upset Grace."

Elle raised an eyebrow. "More like you're too impatient to wait," she laughed.

"Guilty as charged," said Jago.

They sat down against the wall and opened the envelope. Elle's breath caught as she read.

Dear Helen,

I can't believe so many weeks have passed since I saw you. When I looked at my calendar this morning, I realised it's a month to the day since I got on that train and left you all behind. I think of you and Richard every day and miss you all very much. I hope Annie is behaving herself for you and Grace is allowing you to get at least some sleep.

It was the right decision to come back here as Roy and Sally need my support more than I realised. Grief hangs over this house like a dark cloud, but my in-laws are remarkably resilient and are determined to continue living as best they can, despite the shadow surrounding them. Being back in this house has made me miss Tom ever so much, but I'm trying to follow Roy and Sally's example and keep my chin up. Goodness knows I'm not the only widow around here, and at least my Tom didn't live to see the destruction of another war.

I have found work at the department store in town where I was once assistant manager. I have a far more junior position than I used to, but I'm enjoying the freedom a weekly pay packet brings.

Things are tense in the town as Hitler continues to wage his senseless war, and The Grit has suffered badly at the hands of the enemy, but life goes on.

I wanted you to know that although I'm still certain leaving was the right decision, I think of Grace often. As she grows older, she may ask about her birth parents. As agreed, I'd rather she didn't know the truth, but please reassure her she was deeply loved, and that I would never have left her had circumstances been different. Be sure to give her the patchwork quilt I made when she's old enough to sleep in her own bed. As gifts from mother to daughter go, it's not a lot, but it was made with love, and I pray she'll feel that love as she wraps herself up in it on cold winter nights.

When it comes to my choice of her new parents, I have no regrets. You have the child you always wanted, and my daughter has the parents she deserved. I know you will raise her in a home filled with love and give her the life I never could.

Please pass on my regards to Jack and tell him I wish him well. Grace will know him as her uncle, a position to which I'm sure he will devote himself fully. I'll always be grateful for his support in the choice I had to make. Everything I did was for my daughter, for both of my daughters.

Thank you for the care you gave me while I was there, for taking on the responsibility of looking after Annie, and for the love I am certain you continue to share with my youngest daughter. I feel terribly sad when I think we shall not meet again, but I know it is for the best.

I will never forget all you have done for me.

All my love,

Marnie

"Wow," said Jago as Elle finished reading. "Come here." He pulled her into his chest, wrapping an arm around her shoulders. Elle let a tear creep down her cheek.

"What an awful decision for a mother to make."

"Will you show the letter to Grace?"

She nodded. "Yes, it shows how much her mother loved her, even if she had to give her away. I think it will be a big comfort to her."

"I think you're right."

"Oh, no."

Elle and Jago looked down as a pool of water crept across the newly varnished floorboards. "Is that...?" he asked.

Elle nodded.

"What do I do?" Jago jumped up, scrubbing his hands through his hair. She tried to answer, but an intense wave of pain stole her words. "Elle? What should I do?"

"Get the van."

"Don't we need to wait a bit?"

"Jago, I've been having pains all..." Elle paused as another wave of pain swept through her "... day."

"What? Why didn't you tell me?"

"I thought they were Braxton Hicks. I didn't want to worry you."

"Well, I'm pretty bloody worried now," said Jago, pacing the room.

"Jago," whispered Elle, her face scrunched in pain. "Get the van."

"The van's at Mum and Dad's. Shall I ask Trev to drive us to the hospital?"

"I'm not risking having a baby in the back of a builder's van. Hang on," said Elle as another wave of pain hit. "Get... get... ow! Catch up with Trev and get him to drive you to your van. Go!"

Jago sprinted from the room and Elle doubled over. Reaching for her phone, she called the only person she knew who could stay calm in the situation.

"Hi, Elle. How are you?"

"I've been better, Tash. I don't suppose you're anywhere nearby?"

"Yeah, I'm just up the road. Why? What's wrong?"

"I'm in labour."

"Shit."

"Yeah. Look, Jago's gone to get his van, but I'm not sure I've got that much time. I don't suppose you could..."

"I'm on my way."

Five minutes later, Tasha was by Elle's side. "You know I'm not a midwife, right?" she said, throwing off her coat as she entered the room. "I'm not even a trained nurse."

"You're here. That's all that matters. Can you help me up to my bedroom?"

"I can try." Tasha put her arms around Elle's waist and helped her off the floor. She leaned against the wall, letting out a cry as another wave of pain hit. "You need to breathe," said Tasha. "Like this." She showed a breathing technique to Elle, who copied it.

"Seems like you know what to do," said Elle, through clenched teeth.

"I don't want to worry you, Elle, but I learned everything I know from the TV. *Call the Midwife*'s my favourite programme."

"Great," said Elle, leaning all her weight on Tasha as they stumbled towards the door.

Climbing the few stairs to Elle's bedroom took an age. On every other step, Elle stopped, bending over in agony. When they reached the bedroom, she collapsed onto the bed, crying out in pain.

"I know this is embarrassing, but I need to take your jeans off and have a look down below," said Tasha.

"I don't care," said Elle, "do whatever you need."

Tasha made a call on her mobile and balanced the phone beneath her chin as she pulled off Elle's jeans.

"Hi, yes, I've got a woman here in labour. I don't think there's time to get her to the hospital. Yeah... yeah... hang on a sec." Tasha put the phone down on the bed and bent down to look at Elle. "I can see the head. Right, yes, OK, will do. I'm putting you on speakerphone."

"What's happening?" asked Elle.

"It looks like this baby's desperate to make its way into the world. There's no time to get you to the hospital. I've got a midwife on the phone who's going to talk us through everything, and they're sending an ambulance."

"I'm back," came a shout from downstairs.

"Jago, we're up here," Tasha shouted back.

Jago arrived in the room, paling as he took in the sight of Elle on the bed. "Oh my God, this can't be happening. You should be in hospital having a water birth."

"The closest she's getting to a birthing pool is the bath downstairs, but I don't think she'll make it in time."

"Do you know what you're doing?" Jago asked Tasha.

"No, but the nice lady on the phone does," said Tasha, nodding her head to where the phone lay on the bed.

Chapter 69

July, 2018

Sophie yawned loudly and took a deep glug of coffee.

"Bit of a sore head today?" asked Ben.

"If you can't have a few drinks the day you get fired, when can you?"

Ben shook his head. "Dear oh dear. I blame Grace, she's rather feisty when she gets on the wine, and I almost fell off my chair when she ordered a round of shots!"

"I don't remember that bit."

"It was right after you told Grace about being fired and how your boss can shove her Year Six job offer up her bum."

Sophie groaned. "Please tell me I didn't embarrass myself in front of her?"

"No, you didn't. You were crying a fair bit, but that's understandable, especially with Gran's death being so recent. The bum comment was as bad as it got."

"Phew. Is Grace up yet?"

Ben laughed. "Mum, it's the afternoon. Of course she's up."

"Oh no, I can't believe I slept so long. I'm a truly awful host. And what was I thinking, getting so drunk at my age? I'm a respectable teacher, not some boozy teenager!"

"Don't worry, Grace knows these were exceptional circumstances. I went out with her this morning. We went for a tour of the old fishing boat in the harbour, then for a fry-up at the café on the front."

"Where is she now?"

"Walking along the seafront. She can't get enough of it, keeps saying how different it is to what she's used to."

"Thank you for looking after her."

"She doesn't strike me as a woman who needs much looking after," said Ben, pouring himself a coffee from the pot. "You, though... are you alright? I mean, between losing Gran and all that's going on with work, it's OK if you're not OK."

"I'm sad, but I am honestly OK. I couldn't sleep last night and kept thinking about the future, about work."

"Please tell me you're not actually going to tell them to stick their job where the sun doesn't shine? It's fine if you want to quit, but Gran always said it's important to leave well."

"Good advice," said Sophie, smiling at her son. "I did briefly consider getting myself signed off sick, but I couldn't do that to the kids. I had a look at various job sites yesterday while you were out fetching Grace. Given the time of year, there wasn't much about as most positions will have already been filled, but there was one that caught my eye."

"Is it local?"

Sophie shook her head. "Not exactly. It's in Singapore."

"Wow," said Ben, scrubbing his hair with his hand. "That's not what I was expecting. Are you thinking of applying?"

"I applied last night."

Ben slumped down into a chair opposite Sophie. "You applied while drunk? What on earth did you write on your application? And don't you think you should have given it some more thought?"

"I might not get it," said Sophie, "in fact, given the state I was in when I applied, I probably won't. The only thing going in my favour is they sound in desperate need of a teacher, and they want someone with experience. There can't be that many out-of-work experienced teachers looking for jobs at this time of year. I know it's all a bit sudden, but I wanted to give it a shot before I changed my mind. All that talk of Mum's travel at the funeral got me thinking. And then there's the fact that everyone is moving on with their lives while I stand still. Your dad's got his new life with his new wife, Luke's doing well in Scotland, and you're doing so well at the nursing home."

"Will we have to sell the house if you get it?"

"No. I thought maybe you could get some flatmates in to help pay the mortgage. The job's not forever, it's only a year contract initially. I'd like to have a home to come back to if things don't work out."

"Part of me hopes you won't get it," said Ben. "Who will look after me if you're not here?"

"You seem to do rather well at looking after yourself these days."

"I'd miss you."

"I'd miss you too. But it wouldn't be forever. Just a little adventure before I get too old and haggard for such things. Now, why don't I get dressed and we both find Grace? If I end up getting the job, I want to have spent as much time with family as I can before I leave."

Sophie dressed quickly and afterwards, despite her hangover, was presentable enough to leave the house within half an hour. She met Ben in the hallway, and they stepped outside. Just as she closed the door, she heard her phone ringing from behind it.

"Leave it," said Ben.

"But what if it's Grace? There's no point us going traipsing along the sea front looking for her if she's gone somewhere else."

"Fine," said Ben, unlocking the front door.

Sophie rushed inside and grabbed her phone. "Hello? Oh, hi, Jago. Is everything OK? What? ... Oh my God. Yes, we're on our way to meet Grace now. Yes, yes, I'll tell her. I expect she'll want to jump straight in the car. Is that OK? Great. I'll speak to you later."

"What was that about?" asked Ben, as Sophie pocketed her phone.

"We need to find Grace right now. Elle's gone into labour."

"What? Isn't that too early?"

"Only by a few weeks. Come on."

Sophie and Ben half walked, half ran along the seafront. As they drew closer to a series of brightly painted beach huts, Ben pointed across the beach. "Isn't that her?"

"Yes," said Sophie. "Come on." Grace looked like something from a film, gazing out to sea, her long white curls flowing behind her as the wind caught them. Sophie and Ben stumbled over tufts of grass, crunching puddles of stones, cursing as the terrain hampered their progress.

"Grace," called Ben.

She turned and waved, a wide smile on her face. By the time Sophie and Ben reached her, they were red-faced and panting.

"Whatever's the matter?" asked Grace. "You look like you've run a marathon."

"It's Elle," said Sophie. "Jago called. She's gone into labour."

"I have to be with her," cried Grace, pushing past Ben as pebbles scattered beneath her feet. "Can you help me book a train?" she called over her shoulder.

"We can do better than that," said Sophie, jogging to catch up. "I'll drive you there myself. It will be much quicker."

"I'm coming too," said Ben. "You can't drive all that way on your own, Mum. Not after the amount you drank last night, you won't be able to stay awake. I'll take the first shift, give you time to down a few cups of coffee."

"Are you sure? What about work?"

"I'm not due back in until Wednesday, and if it looks like we need to stay in Cornwall longer, I've accrued a few days' holiday. It will be fine," said Ben.

"Great," said Sophie, taking Grace's arm and helping her towards the sandy area of the beach.

Once back at the house, they bundled clothes into bags, climbed into the car, and began the long journey west.

Chapter 70

July, 2018

Jago leaned over and placed a series of kisses on Elle's damp hair. "You're incredible," he said, brushing away tears.

"No more incredible than all the other women who've been doing the same thing for millennia."

"You're incredible to me," said Jago. "And as for you..." With his finger, he caressed the tiny hand of the baby in Elle's arms.

"Don't start crying again," said Elle. "You'll set me off."

Jago laughed. "If a man can't cry at the birth of his first daughter, when can he?"

"First daughter?" asked Elle. "Mate, you saw what I just went through. You've got another think coming if you think I'm ever doing that again."

"Fair enough," said Jago, stroking his daughter's cheek. "My only daughter. Is that better?"

Elle smiled at him.

"Here," said Tasha, laying two mugs down beside the bed. "There's plenty of sugar in these to keep your strength up."

"Thank you, Tash. I don't know what we'd have done without you."

"I couldn't have done it without the midwife on the other end of the phone."

"The paramedics said you'd done a great job, and they know what they're talking about."

In the end, the paramedics had arrived half an hour after the birth. They'd cleaned Elle up, given her a clean bill of health and suggested she go into hospital for a thorough check-up. She'd refused, insisting home was the best place for her.

"Grace is on her way," said Jago.

"But she's not back till Tuesday?"

"Sophie and Ben are driving her down. They should be here in a few hours. I called them when I went to get the car. Don't worry though, you're not going to have a houseful, Sophie and Ben are staying elsewhere."

Elle let out a loud yawn.

"I think mother and baby both need to sleep," said Tasha.

"Yeah, and you need to get home," said Jago.

"You're right, I probably should get going, as long as you're OK, Elle?"

Elle nodded, yawning again. "Thanks so much, Tasha. I don't know how I'll ever repay you."

"By giving me open access to as many newborn cuddles as I like," said Tasha, grinning.

"Deal," said Elle.

"I'll see Tasha out and leave you in peace," said Jago. "Just shout if you need me. I'll come and check on you soon."

"I'm fine," said Elle, "just exhausted."

"See you in a bit," said Jago, kissing Elle again before leaving the room. After saying goodbye to Tasha, he walked to the fridge and grabbed a beer. "Cheers," he said to himself, taking a glug. "To new life."

*

Jago woke with the start as the back door opened. For a moment, he wondered where he was. Looking around him, he saw an upturned empty bottle of beer beside him.

"Anyone would think he'd been pushing out a baby for hours," laughed Grace, walking over to Jago and wrapping an arm around his shoulder. "Congratulations, my love. This makes you officially part of the family."

Jago rubbed sleep from his eyes. "Sorry," he said. "I think all the excitement caught up with me. I must have dropped off."

"How is she?"

"Good. I left her and the baby sleeping upstairs. How did you get here so fast?"

Grace laughed and pointed to a tall man filling the doorway behind her. "Ben drove like the clappers all the way here."

"Thanks, mate," said Jago, crossing the room to shake Ben's hand. "I'm Jago. Nice to meet you, although I feel like we've already met after geeking out about local history over so many emails."

"Likewise," said Ben. "And congratulations."

"Good to see you again, Sophie," said Jago, hugging her as she followed Ben inside.

"I hope it's alright us being here. We won't stay long. I remember what it was like when I had my own kids. The last thing I wanted was a houseful."

"Why don't I head up and see if my girls are awake?"

"Good idea," said Grace, "and Jago? *My girls* has a wonderful ring to it."

Jago grinned from ear to ear. He took the stairs two at a time, pausing outside the door and listening.

"Is that you, Jago?" asked Elle.

"Hi," said Jago. "I wasn't sure if you were awake."

"This one needed feeding," said Elle, gazing down at the baby on her chest. "Can you believe we're parents? It's mad, isn't it?"

"Mad in the most wonderful of ways," said Jago, sitting down beside her. "I don't know if you're up to it, but Grace, Ben and Sophie are downstairs. I can hold them off till tomorrow if you'd rather be on your own resting."

"No," said Elle, "send them up. Just give me five minutes to straighten myself out. I'd rather not have my boobs on display, even if they are all family."

"Will do. Do you want me to give Grace the letter we found?"

"No, not yet. Let's wait until all the excitement is over and she has a quiet moment to process it."

"Good plan," said Jago, kissing her again before going to fetch the others.

Elle grinned as her room filled with smiling faces. Sophie had come prepared and handed round glasses of fizz. Grace rushed to the bed, smothering her daughter and granddaughter in kisses.

"I'm so, so proud of you," said Grace. "I just wish I'd been here to help."

"Don't worry, Tasha was amazing. We owe that woman big time."

"That we do. Now, can I have a cuddle with my granddaughter?"

Elle handed the baby over and Grace cradled her in the crook of her arm, her face filling with love.

"She's beautiful," said Sophie. Her eyes were glassy with tears, and even Ben let out the occasional sniff.

"Have you thought of a name yet?" Ben asked.

Elle looked across at Jago and smiled. "We have," she said. "Everyone, I'd like you to meet Marnie."

"Marnie Grace," added Jago, putting an arm around Grace as her tears fell.

"Marnie Grace Annabel Rose," said Elle, smiling at Sophie. "I know it's a bit of a mouthful, but it felt right."

"It's beautiful," said Sophie, dabbing her eyes with a tissue. "She's beautiful."

"How about a photo?" said Ben, pulling out his phone. "Let's start with Mum, Dad and baby."

Once the photo was taken, Jago stood up. "I think we need an all-female one now. Come on, Grace, Sophie, bunch in beside Elle."

"You know," said Grace, sitting down beside Elle. "This bed has been here for donkey's years. The mattress has changed, of course, but this will be the same bed Marnie was in when she had me. I wish Annie could be here with us."

"Me too," said Sophie, squeezing Grace's hand.

"To new life," said Ben, holding up his glass of champagne.

"To new life," they all agreed, raising their glasses in the air.

"And to the Watson family," said Elle, "those who are here with us now, and those who've gone before."

Chapter 71

2008

Dear Sophie,

If you're reading this, I'll be dead and freed from the responsibility of keeping other people's secrets. But before I get into that, I want you to know how much I love you, and how proud I am of the woman you've become. I'm not sure I ever told you either of those things enough when I was alive.

Now, on to a very important matter. I have a sister, and her name is Grace. I made a choice many years ago to keep my mother's secret after deciding it was in everyone's best interest to do so. I don't know if that decision was a wise one, but in the end, it wasn't my secret to tell. Enclosed are two separate envelopes. One contains as detailed a description as I can give about how my mother came to have a second child, and why this child was given away (to very kind people, I might add.) The second envelope contains a letter I would like to be passed to Grace in the event of my death.

I have kept in contact with Grace all these years, whilst also keeping her at arm's length. I wanted nothing more than to meet her in person and hold her in my arms, but I knew that if that were to happen, I wouldn't be able to stop the truth from spilling out, and I couldn't risk it. But we wrote to each other for over fifty years, and you'll find my letters from her in the large brown envelope marked 'letters'.

I have just posted the last letter I will write to Grace. Although we haven't spoken the words aloud, both you and I know my mind is going, and I don't know how much longer I'll have. The last thing I want is to be writing the words of a garbled old fool to my beloved sister. It's better to cut all contact now, before things reach that point.

So, why am I telling you all this? I want you to find her, Sophie. Find my sister Grace and tell her I loved her from a distance all my life. Also, tell her that our mother loved her too, and that is why she gave her up. Ask her to forgive me, and my mother Marnie, and all of us who kept the truth hidden. We did what we thought was best. If she is still alive, please give her one final letter, which I hope will explain things to her.

All my love,

Mum

Chapter 72

2008

Dear Grace,

The first thing I ask is that you forgive the abrupt end to a correspondence that has made me so happy over the years. My mind is going, dementia, I think they call it. I've not had a formal diagnosis yet, but it's only a matter of time. Sophie tries to hide it, but I see the worry on her face when I can't recall a name or have lost my keys for the hundredth time. I want you to remember me as I am, not pity me as I descend into a new way of being, which, frankly, terrifies me. Hopefully, by the time I'm completely gone, I won't be aware of what's happening to me, but now, in these early stages, the fog and blind spots in my mind are terrifying. Last week Sophie came to my door, and I had no idea who she was, other than a nagging feeling of familiarity. I pretended all was well, and by the time she'd made me a cup of tea I'd remembered her name, and by the time I'd drunk the tea, remembered she was my daughter.

Sophie has offered me a place in her home, and I've agreed to give up my house and move in with her. At some point, we will need to have a conversation about what happens when my condition becomes unmanageable. I have booked an appointment at the doctors for next week, and Sophie will come with me.

Anyway, enough about me. This letter is for you, Grace. I need to tell you the truth before I forget, and the secret dies with me.

You are my sister, Grace. My mother, Marnie, was your mother. Your father was the man you knew all your life as Uncle Jack, Helen's brother. I found out when I was eighteen and I can't tell you how angry I was that the secret had been kept from the both of us. I thought long and hard about telling you at the time and I hope you don't hate me for keeping it from you all these years.

I kept the secret to protect you, and to protect your relationship with Helen. You were so happy, Grace, and I didn't want to be the cause of destroying that happiness.

In the last few years of my mother's life, she opened up to me about her childhood on a small island, about how she ended up in Lowestoft, about the death of my father shortly after we arrived in Padstow before the war, and, about you, Grace. I have recorded her stories with as much detail as I could, and they stretch to several volumes and hundreds of pages. These are with my solicitor, ready for you to collect should you wish. If you would rather not know about our mother, and the stories she told, please allow Sophie the chance to read them. They are rather lengthy, the 'Watson Family Saga', I suppose you could call them. They document a changing world, and there are lessons we can learn from those who've gone before us.

The main thing you need to know, Grace, is both your parents loved you. Helen wrote to Mum regularly with news of you, and Mum treasured those letters. I often caught a hint of sadness in her eyes and knew it was because she was thinking of you. Every day she wore a locket containing a lock of your hair, and often I would catch her twirling it between her fingers, lost in thought.

Your sister loved you too, Grace. I have loved you from afar since the day I found out you are my sister, and I have tried my best to be as close to a sister to you as I could through my letters. Sometimes I have given bad advice, or not listened carefully enough to what you were trying to tell me, but overall, I hope I have done a good job of supporting you over the years.

I don't know what the future holds for me, Grace, and fear you may fade from my memory. If this happens, please forgive me, and know that I have always loved you.

All my love,

Your sister,

Annie

Acknowledgements

Years ago, one Christmas, when I began writing about my own experience of island life, I could never have imagined those ramblings turning into *Silver Darlings*, or that *Silver Darlings* would have expanded to become the *Watson Family Saga*.

The Watson family have been my companions for over three years now, and I am very sad to be saying goodbye to them. I hope you have enjoyed your time with them, celebrating their triumphs, mourning their losses, and shaking your head at their foolish mistakes.

Through this fictional family, I have been able to explore areas of history I would otherwise never have known about. I have a new appreciation for Lowestoft and its remarkable history, and a much better understanding of how our coastal communities in the UK are linked. There isn't room to include all the books I've used for research (I'll put a list on my website) but for anyone wanting to explore the history further, *The Grit* by Dean Parkin and Jack Rose is a very good place to start.

This series would not have been possible without help from the following people.

My parents – for deciding it was a good idea to move their young family to a Northumbrian island. It was an experience full of highs and lows, but was an adventure I wouldn't have wanted to miss. It broadened my mind and lived experience, and without those years of island life, this series would never have existed.

Ian and Bridget Fosten – for supporting this series from the start, accompanying me to museums, sharing local knowledge, providing me with research books, and hosting me while I explored the local area. Thank you both for your continued support.

Jo Egleton – for patiently reading through endless drafts and offering wise editing advice as the Watson family moved through the generations. You do so much behind the scenes to support my writing and it is very much appreciated.

Julia Gibbs – for taking my grammatically challenged manuscripts and polishing them until they were reader-worthy. I really appreciate your patience, expertise, and encouragement and look forward to working with you on future projects.

Jamilla Takac – for designing a series of covers that work beautifully together and capture the essence of these stories. I'm sorry for suggesting the borders that have proved rather tricky, but they look great so I'm grateful for you sticking with them!

Pete, Joe and Tom – for being endlessly supportive of my writing and putting up with me being holed up at my desk for days on end. I couldn't do it without you.

Sally Middleton – for sharing memories of life in Lowestoft as a little girl and telling me stories about her fisherman grandad.

Heather – for meeting me and talking about Lowestoft in days gone by and bringing the past to life.

All the people I've met at the various museums I've visited, who've shared their knowledge with patience and enthusiasm.

And finally, you, the reader. There would be no series without readers who wanted to follow the Watsons through their trials and tribulations. Thank you to everyone who has stuck with this series, has left reviews, or offered words of encouragement. I really appreciate every one of you.

About the Author

Author and musician LK (Laura) Wilde was born in Norwich, but spent her teenage years living on a Northumbrian island. She left the island to study Music, and after a few years of wandering settled in Cornwall, where she raises her two crazy, delightful boys.

To keep in touch with Laura and receive a 'bonus bundle' of material including the novel *The Island Girls*, join her monthly Readers' Club newsletter at-

www.lkwilde.com

Or find her on social media- @lkwildeauthor

Finally, if you enjoyed this book, please consider leaving a review or rating on Amazon. Reviews are so important to indie authors as they're the best way to help more people discover the book!

Also By LK Wilde

People say you get one life, but I've lived three.

I was born Ellen Hardy in 1900, dragged up in Queen Caroline's Yard, Norwich. There was nothing royal about our yard, and Mum was no queen.

At six years old Mum sold me. I became Nellie Westrop, roaming the country in a showman's wagon, learning the art of the fair.

And I've been the infamous Queenie of Norwich, moving up in the world by any means, legal or not.

I've been heart broken, abandoned, bought and sold, but I've never, ever given up. After all, it's not where you start that's important, but where you end up.

Based on a true story, *Queenie of Norwich* is the compelling tale of one remarkable girl's journey to womanhood. Spanning the first half of the 20th century, Queenie's story is one of heartbreak and triumph, love and loss and the power of family. It is a story of redemption, and how, with grit and determination, anything is possible.

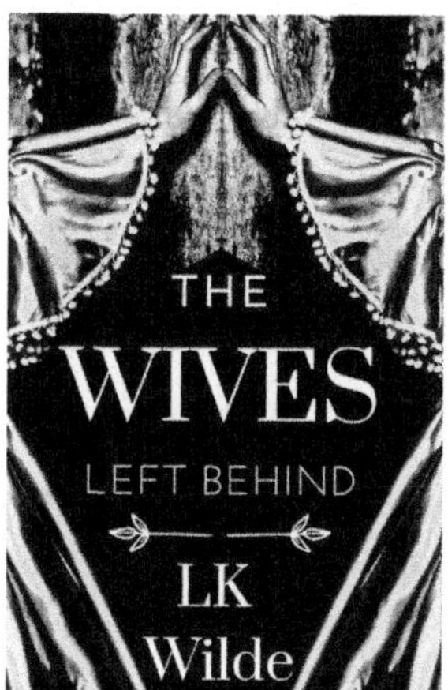

1840, Cornwall. The victim, the accused, and the wives left behind. Welcome to the trial of the century...

Based on a true story.

When merchant Nevell Norway is murdered, suspicion soon falls on the Lightfoot brothers. The trial of the century begins, and two women's lives change forever.

Sarah Norway must fight for the future of her children. Battling against her inner demons, can Sarah unlock the strength she needs to move on without Nevell?
Maria Lightfoot's future looks bleak, but she's a fighter. Determined to rebuild her life, an unexpected friendship offers a glimmer of hope...
With their lives in turmoil, can Maria and Sarah overcome the fate of their husbands? Or will they forever remain the wives left behind?

Book 1 in the Cornish feel-good *The House of Many Lives* series
Kate is stuck in a rut, She works a dead end job, lives in a grotty bedsit and still pines for the man who broke her heart.
When Kate inherits a house in a small Cornish town, she jumps at the chance of a fresh start. A surprise letter from her grandmother persuades Kate to open her home and her heart to strangers.
But with friends harbouring secrets, demanding house guests, and her past catching up with her- can Kate really move on? And will her broken heart finally find a home?